Red Dawn Rising

A NOVEL

SUE DUFFY

Kregel
Publications

Red Dawn Rising: A Novel
© 2013 by Sue Duffy

Published by Kregel Publications, a division of Kregel, Inc.,
P.O. Box 2607, Grand Rapids, MI 49501.

Scripture taken from the *Holy Bible*, New International Version®,
NIV®. Copyright © 1973, 1978, 1984 by Biblica, Inc.™ Used
by permission of Zondervan. All rights reserved worldwide.
www.zondervan.com

ISBN: 978-0-8254-4266-7

Printed in the United States of America
13 14 15 16 17 / 5 4 3 2 1

To my family

Acknowledgments

$\mathcal{T}$his second book of the Red Returning trilogy draws from the same rich resources of the first book, which include the technical knowledge and life experiences of Mike Duffy, J. D. Railey, Scott Railey, U.S. Coast Guard boatswain's mates Brian and Krystyna Duffy, Kim Beasenburg, Laura and Ryan Player, Marc T. Canner, Florance Anderson, and Sandi Hendrickson Esch.

To that mix I add Edward Lee Pitts, Washington, DC, bureau chief for *World* magazine, whose capital-insider perspective helped shape certain plot points.

As always, Kregel editor Dawn Anderson lent an insightful and practiced eye to the manuscript. The whole Kregel team has been an enormous support to me. And my agent, Les Stobbe, remains my faithful friend and advocate.

My deepest gratitude to you all.

Chapter 1

*T*he Moscow night had frozen in place. But at three in the morning, a lone figure hurried along the back streets and alleys of a worn and grizzled neighborhood, leaving tracks in fresh yet impure snow. It was the safest hour for Evgeny Kozlov to surface from his warren. Once a warrior spy for Soviet intelligence, he had fallen to his own conscience and the conviction that everything he'd believed in was a lie. Now, the liars hunted him.

Where an alley emptied onto a main boulevard, Evgeny stopped and peered cautiously through the brittle light of a streetlamp. He would have to cross the street to reach the bookstore where, in a back room with shades drawn, the only person he could trust waited for him. He resisted the urge to sprint headlong to safety. Instead, he pulled the hood of his coat lower over his face and emerged slowly from the alley onto the sidewalk, nearly colliding with an old woman long past sobriety. Ragged and absent-eyed, she hardly looked his way as she shuffled around him, hunched and rattling in her breath. He watched after her a moment and wondered how many others like her might perish this forbidding night, within reach of the gilded Kremlin, home of the government charged with tending even the least of its people.

He veered into the street, ambling in the fashion of the old woman, his heavy boots slurring against the pavement, the backpack that never left his side slung over one shoulder. To anyone watching, his boozy charade would make no impression. They wouldn't see the gun he gripped firmly inside his coat pocket.

When he reached the front of the bookstore, he was about to turn into the alley running toward the shop's back door when a face stopped him. In the display window lit by the streetlamp was a rack of CDs. He knew better than to linger in the exposing light, but he couldn't move. The face on one of those CD covers wouldn't let him. She was a striking young woman in a shimmering green gown seated at a concert grand piano, her long amber hair cascading over one shoulder. The title read *Liesl Bower Plays the Russian Masters*.

He stared into the eyes that couldn't see him. Eyes that had, on three occasions, flashed with terror for what he might do to her. Now, gazing at her fixed, radiant smile, Evgeny brooded. *Liesl, forgive me. I did not know the ones I served then. But now I do.*

He remembered his last words to her. He'd slipped into her dressing room at Avery Fisher Hall just moments before a performance and warned her about those he would serve no more. "Never stop watching them," he'd told her. Regrettably, though, he had.

After a quick scan of the street, he darted into the alley. At the back of the shop, he tapped lightly on the door and waited. When it opened, the spidery hand of Viktor Petrov reached to pull him inside. "Hurry! They are near!"

"They found me?"

"Yes. You cannot return to the apartment."

Evgeny searched the older man's face, the hollows beneath his fierce eyes, the sagging jowls that belied the ramrod strength that had sustained his double life. The old-guard member of the KGB secret police had transitioned easily into that agency's post-Soviet successor, the Federal Security Service. Viktor Petrov had served the new Russian Federation with exemplary dedication—while secretly plotting with other revolutionaries to overthrow it.

But no longer. He and Evgeny had penetrated the heroic, all-for-the-people veneer of Vadim Fedorovsky's anarchist movement to discover its corroded underside. Fedorovsky and his mounting legion of Kremlin and military recruits had so dazzled themselves with the promise of a powerful new Russian empire that they had cultivated a callous disregard for the everyday plight of their own people.

"But how?" Evgeny rasped as he slipped inside the store, his joints protesting the cold. "No one ever finds me." He raked his fingers through his dark, thinning hair. His fifties had pressed hard against him, and he'd felt himself begin to wither.

"My friend, you are not as invisible as you once were," Viktor said. "Somehow, you left a trail. And now you must flee. But first, there are things you must know." He motioned for Evgeny to follow him to a small room in the back of the bookstore where they'd met several times before. Viktor had once saved the store's owner from arrest and certain imprisonment for his part in a riotous demonstration against the sitting president. The owner had given Viktor a key and unrestricted access.

Without turning on a light, Viktor set a small flashlight on a shelf and aimed its beam toward the wall, allowing only a dim glow in which to see each other. "Sit," Viktor instructed. "We do not have long."

Evgeny pulled a straight-backed chair beneath him and waited. Viktor eyed him gravely. "It is far worse than we thought. I have just struck the richest vein of intelligence yet. Hear this. For all his authority, Fedorovsky is only a puppet and always has been, even before he went to prison." When Evgeny's brow arched, Viktor held up a hand to halt interruption. "Just listen. There is someone else who commands Fedorovsky and his coconspirator Pavel Andreyev. Someone who is the mastermind of it all. He is called the Architect by the few who know he even exists, a man removed from Russia but whose roots are deep in her intelligence network. He has immense wealth and power beyond our own president."

Viktor paused long enough for Evgeny to respond, "Do *you* know this man?"

"No."

"Where is he?" Already, Evgeny's mind calculated the inevitable mission of stopping him.

"It is believed he operates from the sea, headquartered on one vessel or another within his fleet. He could be anywhere in the world."

"Fleet?"

"This is a man of uncommon means. He—" Viktor quickly raised a quieting hand and looked toward the open door to the room. "Listen," he whispered.

Evgeny leaned far enough to peer through the doorway, but he saw and heard nothing. Then a beam of light pierced the front window and arced through the store. He jerked back out of sight and glanced at the flashlight above him. Dousing it would only signal that someone was in the room.

Already hidden, Viktor remained still, but Evgeny could hear him wheeze. When the light retreated and didn't return, Evgeny leaned forward in his chair and whispered, "A policeman making rounds." It was both a statement and a hope. Surely his skills hadn't failed him so miserably that he'd led others of his own trade to this place and to his trusted compatriot.

A cautious interval passed before either spoke again. Then, "There is something else," Viktor said, his shoulders sagging. "Your uncle and cousins."

Evgeny stopped breathing. But he already knew, in the way that assassins such as he knew death and those who forced it on others.

"They are all dead," Viktor announced bitterly.

"When?" Evgeny struggled to ask.

"Last night, as they slept."

Through the years, others had met the same fate at Evgeny's own hand. How dare he mourn now. But how could he not? These innocent peasants had died for no other reason than their tenuous kinship with him. A solitary spy, Evgeny had long since severed the distant and fragile ties to family, to spare himself and them any harmful entanglements.

Fedorovsky had ordered their execution even from prison, Evgeny was certain. His late mother's brother and his two sons, the last of his family, had scraped a bare living from the soil with no hope of improving their lot. Evgeny was certain they had never heard of Fedorovsky, never knew of the man's raging quest to overtake their country. They wouldn't have cared anyway. Their country could fail them no worse under his reign than at the hands of all the despots past.

"I am very sorry," Viktor offered.

But Evgeny had already shifted from the hateful news to something within his control. Vengeance. "I must go," he told Viktor as he rose from the chair.

"Where?"

"Someplace where Fedorovsky's people will not look for me." Evgeny hoisted his backpack to his shoulders. "His house."

Chapter 2

The next night, Evgeny's SUV slowed at the entrance to Vadim Fedorovsky's country home, about eighty miles from Moscow. He was grateful to find no fresh blanket of snow as in the city, no untouched canvas for him to imprint with telltale proof of his visit. With headlights extinguished and guided by a waning moon, he shifted to four-wheel drive and turned into the rutted slush of the lane, certain his tracks would be largely indistinguishable from those already laid, some recently, judging from the clear tread marks. The patrols, no doubt.

He bounced along the lane toward the handsome old dacha, its rock walls and dark timbers visible through a skeletal troop of aspens. Its owner had been confined to a prison cell for just over a year. Evgeny feared prison wouldn't hold Fedorovsky for long, though.

Evgeny had been here once before, when he was still a loyal soldier of the anarchy spawned along the back corridors of the Kremlin under the breeding hand of veteran intelligence officers Vadim Fedorovsky and Pavel Andreyev. The home had been the movement's outpost, a safe house whose secrets were kept in files Evgeny had only glimpsed during that one prior visit to these woods. Surely they had been removed by those who'd arrested Fedorovsky for the attempted assassination of the president and other crimes against the state. But Evgeny would conduct his own search.

Despite the fine sleet plinking against his windshield, he stopped the vehicle and lowered his window to listen. The night was still. He raised the window and moved on toward the house.

Because Fedorovsky's loyals believed Viktor Petrov was still one of them, Evgeny's old friend had gained limited access to a bank of communications between operatives within the secret movement, enough to determine their watch on the incarcerated leader's Moscow apartment and his dacha.

Evgeny hoped the information Viktor had gathered was correct. Patrols checked the house twice a week but according to no discernible schedule. He knew the risk of being here, but there had to be something inside to lead Evgeny to this phantom Architect, the one who killed, not championed, the people—Evgeny's people, his pitiable fringe of family and all the others who'd toiled under oppression.

When he finally rolled to a stop behind the house, Evgeny pulled the gun from his pocket and pat-checked the bulk of ammunition still inside. Then he strapped on the critical backpack with its tools, falsified passports and identification, currencies, backup weapons, and trace-secure phones. When he got out, he didn't close the door, didn't move, only listened and watched. Then making his way slowly through the trees, he reached the back door of the house.

He stopped abruptly. Where was his plan of escape? Viktor was right. His wits had dulled during the last year of dormancy. He turned toward the distant logging trail Fedorovsky had once pointed out to him, then headed back to his vehicle.

Fifteen minutes later, he had moved the SUV a short way down the trail and into an overhang of wild brush, camouflaging it further with branches stripped from young trees. He doubted such a move was necessary, especially on such a brutally cold night when even Fedorovsky's most devoted security guards would surely prefer to turn over beneath their down comforters and go back to sleep.

He returned through the ice-crusted field and glanced up at the slope rising behind the house. About fifteen yards up a rocky path was a storm shelter Fedorovsky had built into the bank. He sneered. *Imagine, the executioner of innocent peasants afraid of the weather.*

It took little time for the veteran spy to disengage the security and locking systems on the house. When he slipped inside, he was glad to see the drapes drawn and to feel even a minimal discharge of musty heat. He switched to a flashlight capped with red tape to filter the light. The crimson glow was enough to lead him through the house, though he knew already where he would begin his search.

For what, he didn't know.

On his way through the opulently furnished dining and living rooms, he allowed only passing notice of the late Mrs. Fedorovsky's penchant for ruby glassware, embroidered table scarves, and expensive samovars ringed by porcelain tea cups fit for royalty. But the grand piano beside one window made him pause and remember.

Fedorovsky had been a music professor at the Moscow Conservatory, beloved by students and faculty alike, none of whom knew of his simultaneous, subterranean career as a KGB spy and Kremlin power broker. For many years, Fedorovsky had worked in tandem with his American counterpart, Harvard music professor Schell Devoe.

Evgeny flashed back to the afternoon when, at Fedorovsky's orders, he pumped three bullets into Devoe after the CIA had turned him to work for them—an execution witnessed by Liesl Bower. He closed his eyes and saw her face, heard her scream. He would never forget. Now, he gazed at the graceful lines of the instrument that sounded with such beauty and purity. How had Fedorovsky compromised such a thing with the instruments of death?

Quickly dismissing the troubling muse, he shifted toward the study off the living room and moved to a heavily carved walnut desk. He found its two file drawers empty, as he'd feared, then looked around the room. Only a couple of lounge chairs and a bookcase crammed with little more than pulp fiction filled the cozy room. Just then, Evgeny remembered the bedroom at the end of the upstairs hall. Fedorovsky had converted it to a workshop for his and his wife's jigsaw puzzles, a favorite winter pastime. But it also held two more file cabinets, one with a collection of photographs. In that room, Fedorovsky had given Evgeny photos of Liesl Bower, after ordering him to capture and later dispose of her—an assignment Evgeny was grateful he had failed. It was the code Liesl had found hidden in her music, left there by her professor, Schell Devoe, that led to Fedorovsky's and Andreyev's arrests.

Taking the steps two at a time, Evgeny entered the workroom and headed straight for the cabinets. Empty. He closed the drawers and wandered back down the hall, pausing at the top of the stairs. His gaze fell on the piano below, and something sent him bounding down the steps. When he reached the fine ebony instrument, he laid the flashlight down, lifted the heavy curved lid, and affixed the support. Retrieving the light, he searched the stringed cavity beneath. Nothing. He squatted before the low music cabinet alongside. Nothing on top or inside it. The arresting officers had swept the house clean of evidence.

Evgeny slumped to a sitting position. He looked up at the window holding back the night and pondered his next move. Would he have to wait for whatever shreds of information Viktor might stumble upon next? Waiting didn't come naturally to Evgeny, but neither did charging blindly down dead ends. The need to charge somewhere, though, was overwhelming. They had killed his family. They had lied to those like him who'd sacrificed themselves for the good of the cause, the redemption of Mother Russia. They had promised to raise her up from ashes and restore her honor, her reach, her benevolence toward her people. But they had disguised their one true motive—power and riches for themselves. And now Evgeny knew it had all come down from one man. *Who is he?*

Evgeny rolled back his head and sighed, his eyes resting on the nearest leg of the piano. He ran a hand along its rise to the underside of the instrument. And there it was.

He grabbed the flashlight and rolled beneath the piano. Taped into an upward crevice between two wooden supports was a white, legal-sized envelope. Evgeny stared at it. What peculiar prompting had led him to such a hiding place?

But as he reached for the envelope, he heard sounds. First the whine of an engine, then the slogging of tires along the ice-packed lane. Not a second to waste.

He grabbed the envelope and scrambled to his feet, taking one instant to peer around the drape. A truck was bearing down on the house. Evgeny flew to the back door, knowing there was no time to reinstate the alarm and locks. He had only moments to close the door and race for the tree line behind the house. To the storm shelter. How ironic that Fedorovsky's fears might save his enemy.

Not daring to turn on even the red-filtered flashlight, Evgeny searched through only a dappling of moonlight for the entrance to the shelter, which surely was overgrown by now. He slipped on ice and fell hard against a rock, but righted himself instantly and kept hunting until something glinted through a drape of vines just ahead. A metal door. And again, the sense that something had prompted him to hide his vehicle, to look beneath the piano, to find a covered door in the dark.

He parted the lattice of vines and branches and felt for the latch, which gave instantly in his hand. With no thought of what might lurk inside, he threw open the door, stepped onto the uneven floor boards of the tiny space, pulled as much of the leafy screen back over the door as he could, and closed himself in.

Two truck doors opened and closed. Evgeny guessed the guards would scan the grounds before going inside. Five minutes tops, he estimated, before they discovered the break-in.

But it was only three.

One man yelled. Another answered, and running footsteps ensued. The unsecured back door slammed, and Evgeny imagined their tense search inside. But they would find nothing left behind by an intruder, and nothing obvious removed. They would alert a superior, then begin their search of the nearby woods. If they were good, they would find his tracks through the open field, but maybe not up the rocky hillside.

How long could he remain in the shelter meant only for passing storms? No storm in Evgeny's life had ever passed quickly.

Moments later, he heard two voices trail from the house into the field leading to the logging trail and his SUV. The loss of one escape route now led to a new one.

He eased open the door of the shelter and looked down the hill. The guards' truck stood in a beacon of moonlight, as if it were a summons for

Evgeny to run, and run now! Looking toward the field, now washed in the same lunar light, he saw the men disappear into the trees along the trail. Evgeny mostly slid down the hill and raced to the truck, flinging open its door and finding, against the odds, the keys still in the ignition. The sweat of his scalp tingled beneath his hood. *Such good fortune doesn't come to me. Why now?*

The truck roared to life and spun furiously away from the house, lights blazing the way. It didn't matter that they saw him now. In moments, they would no longer, as if he'd never been there. He slipped a hand inside his coat and felt the envelope safe in an inside pocket. No time to explore its contents now. They'd be looking for this vehicle. He had to make a switch soon.

A half hour later, he sped along the highway back to Moscow at the wheel of a small car he'd acquired in his usual way, this one parked behind a village tavern not far from the dacha. Soon, he pulled into a small town and behind a cluster of shops that wouldn't open for a few hours. When he cut the engine, he finally pulled the envelope from his coat. Inside were a single sheet of folded paper and one unredeemed airline ticket to New York. Evgeny set the ticket aside and examined the short letter, written in a feminine hand. It was dated September 2011, just a few weeks before Fedorovsky's arrest.

Vadim, we anxiously await your upcoming visit. Enclosed is your first-class ticket. You will be pleased with our progress here in what the Americans call "the city that never sleeps." Our own sleepers are in place throughout the country, awaiting the Architect's signal. But first, we will give a preview demonstration of our skills, something to convince the American president of how foolish it would be to interfere with us. You shall return to us in 2013 for the start of it all. That January promises to be quite spectacular. And America will never look the same.

Evgeny gaped into the dark. "January 2013 is now!" He clenched his jaw and read on.

You must leave Pavel behind this time. The Architect is concerned about his stability. We will discuss that further when you arrive. Our best to you.

Evgeny slapped the letter onto the seat beside him. He knew the translation. There were Russian sleeper agents in the United States, most certainly saboteurs about to unleash their long-calculated destruction. That would mean inevitable retaliation on Russia by U.S. forces. His Russia brought to its knees by its own arrogant madmen.

Who was this Architect?

The letter held no signature. But Evgeny would find the writer, find them all. He was through running. He would leave immediately for New York—and begin the chase.

Chapter 3

Cass Rodino passed the lonely vigil watching the first snowflakes dash themselves against the windshield. What did it matter that no two were the same when they all plunged anonymously toward the same fate?

A shiver of dread pulsed through her as she stared past the lamentable mush at the imposing doorway beyond. She shouldn't be here. Not hunched down in the rusted little Honda she'd borrowed, certain that no one in this neighborhood would recognize it. Not lurking in a delivery zone near the posh apartment building where her mother and stepfather lived. Not spying on him during another of his mysterious forays into the New York night.

The call had come soon after she arrived home from the theater that Tuesday evening. "He's leaving in thirty minutes. Hurry!" Her mother's voice stretched into the treble of fear. Cass remembered how that voice had once resonated with strength and resolve during the long, arduous marriage to Cass's father. Even at his sudden death, her mother never lost her composure. But now, the voice had grown reedy, halting.

A gust off the Hudson River funneled its way down the street and slapped at the aging little car as if to alert its lone occupant. The man now emerging from the glassy door ahead stepped quickly to the curb and hailed a cab. Hans Kluen was bundled in a black trench coat belted around his thick waist, a red scarf wrapped high on his neck, and his bald head oddly bare on a night when the windchill flirted with single digits. Cass turned the key without pumping the gas pedal. No revving motor to draw his attention. She waited until her stepfather dropped into the back seat of the cab before turning on her lights.

Pulling behind the cab, she wondered if her mother was prepared for news of an affair. Surely that was it, though they'd been married barely three years. What was wrong with men who called themselves husbands but lived by no vows? Even worse, what led a man to marry a vulnerable, trusting young woman when he already had a wife? Cass stared at the cab's taillights, one of them broken, and remembered the night she followed her new husband for many miles out of the city, all the way to a fine Westchester house where, she discovered, he lived a part-time life as husband to someone else and father to their two children.

She hated the hot tears that now sprang unbidden. It had been four years since the debacle of her fraudulent marriage. She'd been twenty-three then, married for just six months. Everyone had said she'd heal quickly. Everyone was wrong.

Not everyone knew that the marriage was the lesser blow to her young life, that it had only sliced into an earlier, deeper wound.

Distracted by memories, Cass had let the taxi get too far ahead in a sea of identical cars. She spotted the one-eyed rear of the cab a block ahead, turning left and heading north. To what? He'd told her mother it was business. Always business.

She followed the cab up First Street past the United Nations building, then left into a tree-lined residential area. It stopped in front of a small apartment building of dark stucco with a patch of well-tended shrubbery in front. Cass slipped the little car into a no-parking zone a safe distance away, switched off the lights, and watched. Hans Kluen stepped from the cab and did something that convinced Cass this was no ordinary meeting. He slowly surveyed the street in a thorough one-eighty before hurrying inside the building. Cass had already slinked as deep into her seat as she could and pulled the hood of her jacket even lower over her shiny blond head. She was quite certain she hadn't been detected.

She looked up at the windows of the handsome building, some shuttered or draped, some open. A few minutes after Hans entered the building, Cass saw a man step to a third-floor window overlooking the street. As he began to close the drapes, she saw a woman and a man pass behind him. The man wore a black trench coat with a red scarf at his neck. Cass couldn't see who else might be in the room, if anyone. She made note of the position of the window, knowing she would have to return.

For nearly an hour, she watched and waited, her mind turning over possible scenarios for this gathering. The light snow turned to sleet, and the heat she'd pumped hard into the car en route dissipated. She didn't know how much longer she could keep up her surveillance. The temperature continued to plunge, and she'd told Jordan Winslow, her friend and neighbor, that she'd return with his car by nine.

After flicking on the wipers just once to clear the windshield, she was about to open her thermos of coffee for another sip when a cab pulled up in front of the building. Cass slid down in her seat and peered through the steering wheel. Hans stepped from the front door, scanned the street, and then left in the cab, having taken no apparent notice of the Honda.

There was no need to follow him again. She looked back at the third-floor window, the light from inside still burning. And she knew what she had to do.

Chapter 4

*I*t was half past nine when Cass pulled into the parking garage next to her SoHo apartment building, just two of the properties her late, industrialist father had willed to her. She locked the car and hurried to meet Jordan, who lived in the loft apartment next to hers. He was waiting for her at the coffee shop down the block.

She pushed open the door, glanced quickly around the cozy room enclosed by brick walls and a low, stamped-tin ceiling, and caught Jordan's wave from a back table. He was with a couple of their friends, who now turned to greet her.

"This is no time of night for a defenseless young woman to be out," said Reg Brockman, a former classmate of Cass's and Jordan's. He glanced at the others and winked.

"Oh yeah. As defenseless as a Navy SEAL," said his wife, Myrna, before sipping black brew from her mug.

"Actually, I think New York muggers should be warned about the heat-packing little vigilante walking the streets disguised as the Sunbeam bread girl," Jordan said. "Park your firearm right here." Jordan patted the spot next to him. "I'll get you a coffee." As he rose from his chair, Cass caught his arm and pulled.

"Sorry to cut this little dialogue short," she said with only a flicker of a smile. "But I need to talk to you, Jordan. And by the way, let's put the concealed-weapon thing to rest. It's just a tiny revolver."

"And she *just* plugs the center of the bull's-eye every time with magnum bullets from that itty-bitty gun," Jordan noted to the others. "Furthermore, do you know how hard it is to get a concealed-weapons permit in this town if you're not someone like Donald Trump or Nicholas Rodino's daughter?"

Cass wasn't in the mood for this. "Enough," she said, pulling again on his sleeve and steering him into the hallway to the restrooms. He was six feet to her five foot three, yet he'd been following her lead ever since their college days at NYU. But now he turned and firmly planted himself before her. "What happened?" he asked, downshifting his tone to open concern.

She ran her fingers through the tangle of loose, blond-streaked curls that fell just below her ears. "I followed him to an apartment near the UN, where I saw him through the window with a woman and a man. I don't know if there was anyone else. They closed the drapes, and Hans left about an hour later." She shoved her hands into her pockets. "I'm going back there, and I want you to come with me."

He raised his dark, bushy eyebrows. "Why go back?"

Cass stared at a crack in the wide-planked wooden floor. A sliver of lemon rind had wedged its way deep inside.

"He was somewhere he didn't belong. And he was nervous about being there."

"How do you know that?"

"When he got out of the cab, he looked around like he was worried someone might see him."

Jordan cocked his head. "Well, I guess so if he's having an affair."

"I don't know what he's having, but I'm going to find out."

Jordan sighed. "Think you and your mom might be reading too much into this? Maybe he's just selling Amway on the side."

Cass stiffened and eyed him with disdain. "Okay. I'll just go alone."

She turned to leave, but he caught her hand. "Fine. Fine. We'll go, but just what are we supposed to do?"

She pressed her lips together. "I need to see who lives in that apartment. Find out anything I can. I don't know how yet, but I will by tomorrow night. That's when we're going."

He rolled his eyes. "This will be good. The Broadway set designer and the hapless shoe merchant taken hostage by Amway salesmen."

Jordan Winslow's gift of levity had helped pull Cass from depression after her faux marriage failed. She studied his wide-set brown eyes and the honesty she'd always found in them. "We'll leave at seven," she said. "See you then. I'm going home."

He snapped a salute and turned to rejoin their friends.

"Oh, by the way," she said, "I thought you needed the car by nine. You were going somewhere?"

"*Am* going."

"Where?" She had no right to ask, but couldn't help it.

"Late date."

She nodded slightly, something in the pit of her stomach turning over.

Chapter 5

Cass tapped the entrance code to her building and swung open the heavy glass-and-wrought-iron door. Its heft had always conveyed the semblance of security, its scrolling design the notion of art as armor. Wasn't that why she'd immersed herself in her own art? For the way its deliberate illusions shielded her from reality?

The heels of her boots sounded a staccato trail across the polished wood floor of the entrance hall. On the elevator to the fourth floor, she closed her eyes and wondered if her stepfather was home yet, if her mother had successfully feigned disinterest in yet another of his after-dinner sojourns. Cass had reported her findings to her mother the moment Hans Kluen left the UN apartment. They were useless findings that had revealed nothing about what went on behind the closed drapes.

Now home, Cass unlocked the second deadbolt in her royal purple door and stepped into a realm of her own design, not unlike the fantasies she helped construct on the boards of Broadway. She had worked on the sets of *Phantom of the Opera*, *Lion King*, and now *Wicked*. Her loft's twenty-foot walls encased a quirky mix of those worlds.

A smaller, lighter-weight replica of the chandelier that the phantom sent crashing onto the heads of a nineteenth-century Paris audience hung from one of the exposed pipes running lengthwise just below the ceiling. A faux-stone staircase rose to a mezzanine level where a stuffed Lion King—and Cass Rodino—slept each night beneath tiny stars dangling over a Serengeti-like bedroom. In a world of make-believe, she just might survive. She crossed to the kitchen, where a corner grouping of green laminate cabinets hung above black-and-white tile countertops. "Emerald City meets New York subway," Jordan had quipped after her recent renovations to the kitchen. She flipped a light switch. A suspended tree branch strung with lights illuminated the countertop of the island below. She smiled up at her latest creation, remembering Jordan's first reaction to it. "You're out of control," he'd declared.

You might be right, my friend. Her one friend. That's all she allowed herself at a time, realizing the risk of smothering that one person. She glanced at the oak desk across the room, at the framed photo on top. From behind the glass, the girl's eyes followed Cass wherever she moved in the room. Why couldn't she just put the picture away?

Cass set down the cup she'd just taken from a cupboard and walked to the desk. She picked up the photo and traced a finger lightly over the face of a laughing young woman with thick, chestnut hair, her arm draped around Cass's shoulders. She and her best friend, Rachel Norman, newly graduated from high school, rolled diplomas in their hands and the dewy promise of new beginnings on their faces. They had just shared that pinnacle moment in their young lives when Cass's mother took the picture. Surely they weren't the same two girls who took the boat into the bay that night barely two years later.

Lingering over the photo as long as she dared, Cass put it back on the desk, turning it slightly away from her. In the kitchen she reheated a cup of cold morning coffee, and then, turning off all the lights, folded herself into the red cracked-leather wingback chair she'd brought from the Southampton house. She propped her feet on the sill of a tall window and brought the hot cup to her lips, gazing over the urban nightscape.

It had stopped sleeting, and the air was clear, as if swept clean by the tiny, scouring crystals. The lights of her SoHo neighborhood twinkled against the ornate buildings. This was New York's cast-iron district, historic for its artful architectural treatments. This building that she owned was clad top to bottom in a lacy, cast-iron overlay wrought by artisans of the 1800s. From her perch, Cass surveyed the building across the street, its own ironwork as distinct from hers as fingerprints. In the dark of her apartment, she could see out, but no one could see in. So much like herself. Why would anyone want to see inside her anyway? Nothing there worth the effort.

Her eyes were beginning to glaze when the doorbell rang, jerking her from the gloom. She turned her head to the sound. Jordan was on a date. Who else could it be? A tenant whose plumbing had just sprung a leak? She had a very capable management team to handle those sorts of things. The bell rang again, and she sighed irritably, turned on a couple of lamps, and went to the peephole in the heavy wood door. She saw a fish-eye image of a man making goofy faces at her.

She unlatched two chains, turned two deadbolts, and opened the door just a crack. "Thought you had a date," she said dryly.

"Well, I can stand out here and explain why I don't so the rest of the neighbors will know," Jordan replied. "Or consider this, I could come *in* and talk."

In the instant before she opened the door all the way, she wondered at the thing she'd felt in the pit of her stomach when Jordan had told her about the date. Of course he had dates. What eligible, nice-looking guy wouldn't? And why should that bother her?

"I brought you a coffee—decaf so you won't lie awake in your counterfeit jungle up there"—he motioned toward the bedroom as he walked in—"counting fake stars and wondering about old Jordan's date."

"I don't care about your dates," she answered with too much petulance. She knew it and instantly regretted it.

He handed the coffee to her without comment.

"Thank you," she said, then turned and walked to one of two plump white sofas facing each other over a hammered-copper coffee table. "Have a seat," she said, slumping onto a sofa and tucking one leg under her.

"You're welcome," he said crisply, taking a seat on the same sofa. "I don't know what this little pout is about, but you need to lose it and talk to me. What's wrong?"

Cass turned hooded eyes on him and wanted to weep. But what good would that do? She unbuckled her leg from beneath her and stood up, glancing swiftly at the framed photograph on the desk. *There's so much you don't know, Jordan.*

She looked down into his upturned face, at the kind eyes with lashes too long and thick to waste on a guy. She resisted an overwhelming urge to drop into his arms and hold him. But he wasn't interested in being anything more than a loyal friend. She was fairly sure of that.

Willing herself to rebound quickly, she turned away, raised her arms over her head, and stretched her petite, tightly muscled frame. She turned to look at him. "Nothing wrong. Just a mother going berserk over yet another wayward husband. What is wrong with you men?" Immediately, she regretted that remark too. What was wrong with *her*?

Jordan flinched as if struck.

"Oh, Jordan, I didn't mean you," she said, taking a step closer to him. "Not you." She held his searching eyes a moment too long. She couldn't stop herself from reaching to touch his cheek, brushing it softly with her fingertips. Suddenly self-conscious over this vulnerable display of affection, she stepped to the window and looked out, her back to him. "I'm just mourning what looks like the passing of yet another marriage at the hands of a delinquent husband."

When Jordan didn't respond, she looked back at him, surprised by the strange look on his face, by the hand he dropped quickly from his cheek. Had his face colored slightly?

He stood and joined her at the window. "You don't know that Hans has a mistress, Cass," he finally replied. "Let's give him the benefit of the doubt before you toss him into the fiery pit with the rest of us males." He winked. She winced. And they moved on.

"Now here's what we're going to do," he told her flatly. "Tomorrow night, you're going to stay in the car while I go to the door of this place."

"But—"

"No buts. I don't want you going to some strange door and getting dragged in by the hair."

She couldn't help but smile. It was amazing how thoroughly he could lift her mood.

"I'll just make up a reason for being there," he said.

"And what's that supposed to tell you?"

"Not sure. But if there's something funny going on, I don't want him, or them, or any extraneous hers getting a look at you. I mean who could resist all that curly blond hair and pouty mouth?"

She was about to speak when he raised a hand. "I'll go it alone, and you keep the engine running. A plan?"

How did you land in my world? she mused, with full recall of her freshman biology class at NYU and the big beefy guy assigned as her lab partner. Jordan had a girlfriend at the time, and Cass had a sometimes boyfriend. A year later, though, she suddenly withdrew from school and Jordan's brotherly friendship. No explanation given. She severed all ties to the outside world, refusing his calls until he called no more. It would be four years before they happened upon each other again.

"That's a plan?" she asked doubtfully.

"Well, what would you do? Tell whoever comes to the door that you'd like a word with the woman your stepfather is sleeping with?"

"Not bad," she said, nodding agreement. "I can do that." She glanced at the huge round train-terminal clock on the wall. It was almost midnight. "Time for you to go, isn't it?" She punched him lightly in the stomach. "Your well-heeled customers will be lined up on the sidewalk wondering why the Winslow in Winslow Designer Shoes hasn't opened up yet."

"Ah yes. All the needy feet." He scratched his head and yawned slightly. "You do remember, however, that being the last of the Winslows, and the first to hand off the reins to a store manager, I can come and go as I please. A lousy work ethic, I'm afraid. But when it comes to selling shoes, I ascribe to the Peggy Lee anthem. 'Is that all there is?'"

Cass considered him thoughtfully. "For you? No. And someday you'll find the rest of it."

She patted him playfully on the back, urging him toward the door, then stopped and looked up at him, mustering her courage. "So, what happened to your date?"

"Canceled it."

"You did or she did?"

A mischievous grin slid across his face. "Well, you know, you just can't rely on an eighty-year-old woman to wait up all night for her grandson to come unclog the kitchen sink. I'll take care of it tomorrow."

Cass tried to mask the trickle of relief running over her.

After he left, reminding her to latch and bolt all the hardware on her door, she slipped into a plain flannel nightgown, turned off the lights, and climbed to the stars. Suspended from the ceiling at the ends of barely detectable wires, a sprawling constellation of tiny lights hovered over her each night as if they might watch out for her, protect her. She had assigned those powers to them—an illusion, their thin currents of energy wholly impotent. Mere decoration. She knew this. But what else was there?

She slid under the covers and pulled them nearly over her head, trying to eclipse the rest of the world. But nothing would shut out that one place, that one searing face.

Chapter 6

The next night, Jordan knocked at Cass's door promptly at seven. Soon, the Honda pulled from the parking garage and headed northeast. The January sky flung bits of ice again.

"Comfy?" Jordan asked, pulling the collar up on his jacket and issuing a whole-body shiver.

Cass curled inward against her down coat, her mittened hands balled up in her pockets. Preoccupied with her mother's state of upheaval, she didn't answer.

"They've been married how long now?" he asked, undeterred.

She looked sideways at him, strangely comforted that he, unlike most, could glimpse her thoughts. "Three years."

Jordan didn't take his eyes off the snarled, early-evening traffic. It was more boisterous than usual tonight, or was Cass more sensitive to its intrusion?

"And how did they meet?"

Cass had heard only one story about that, her mother's. "They dated during high school in the Bronx. Then my grandfather moved the family to Manhattan when he got a seat on the New York Stock Exchange, and my mom left all her Bronx friends behind, including Hans. Soon after that, she met my dad. My grandfather brought him home for dinner one night. He was about six years older than she and already wealthy. His family in Greece sent him here to run this end of their shipping empire." Jordan glanced her way. "You don't look Greek."

"Neither does Mom." In her mind, Cass flipped through portfolio images of her glamorous mother asserting herself on the covers of haute couture magazines through the late sixties and seventies. The stunning, strong-jawed face; the alabaster complexion; the naturally platinum hair pulled taut against the rouged, dominating cheekbones. It was her look from the teens on, and the New York ad agencies had paid handsomely for it. Even after delivering her only child, with certainly no need to augment her husband's bulging wealth, Jillian Rodino continued her modeling career.

"So you look like your mom?" Jordan asked.

Why had she never taken Jordan to meet her mother? "In some ways," she answered.

Though much shorter than her willowy mother, Cass had inherited the blond hair and startling blue eyes. But unlike her mother's cosmetically embellished features, Cass's were nearly bare. She had come close to sterilizing herself to the simplest essence. Scant makeup. No image-enhancing clothes. Only a strong, defensive body to mask what lay beneath.

"So how did this high school sweetheart reappear?"

"Hans came to my dad's funeral. Seems he'd been pining for Mom all those years. He was divorced. They sort of picked up where they left off, I guess. They were married a year later. Mom was so happy. I'd never seen her like that with my dad. Then something changed. She wouldn't talk about it. Just that Hans was under a lot of stress at work. I think I told you before, he's an investment banker for a Wall Street firm."

Jordan was quiet awhile, then shifted away from the troubling conversation. "Well, how was the *Wicked* set today?" he asked brightly.

He was driving his usual slow, careful pace. But Cass was anxious to reach their destination and not in a conversational mood. Still, she was grateful for his company. "Oh, someone tripped and flattened a row of black corn after the performance last night. I spent all morning rewiring it before the matinee. Then a scale fell loose on the time dragon, and guess who they sent scrambling up to the ceiling to repair it?"

"The fittest of the fit, I presume." He grinned at her, but she pretended not to notice.

"That's your turn up ahead," she announced. "Better move into the left lane." She was too distracted to talk about what she loved most, the stage and keeping it filled with imitation storefronts, medieval balconies, haunted forests, and flying dragons. She'd been building such things since she was a kid left to her own devices on a lonely stretch of Southampton beach, where her parents had kept an oceanfront home for weekends and summers.

Jordan soon pulled within a block of the apartment and parked beneath a streetlight. He turned to Cass and made her look him in the eye. "Now, you promised. You'll stay here and wait for me. Right?"

Cass nodded. "I will, but I still don't know how you're going to do this."

"That's two of us," he said, then got out and locked the doors.

Only one lamp burned in the living room of Ivan Volynski's apartment. He opened the heavy drapes to gaze into the street below. Patting his firm, flat stomach, he felt the tingle of the fine cognac he swirled in his glass, just a small after-dinner indulgence. He prided himself on how little he consumed in food and drink, two of the few things he denied himself.

A light sleet had begun to fall, tracking delicately against the pane. Outside, few people were on the street, now cast in the gauzy blaze of electric light filtered through the freezing rain.

"Hans worries me," came the voice from behind him. Sonya Tretsky lowered herself heavily into the French provincial chair, her plump hips wedging between the slim, gilded arms with hardly enough padded cushion on top to support her own fleshier arms. "Regardless of the all-is-well picture he painted for us last night, I was doubtful enough to do some checking today. I am told he is not monitoring his people as he should."

"Who told you that?" Ivan asked without turning from the window.

"Other overseers. There are only four of us running the whole network.

We cannot afford mismanagement. So I routinely check on how the other three overseers are handling their people."

"And what exactly did they tell you this time?" He lifted his glass to his lips, feeling the silky swish of his sleeve as he raised and lowered his strong arm. His seventy years were disguised by a youthful body.

"The dam engineer has not heard from Hans in months. And now the man wonders if that target has been abandoned. After all these years, he fears he has been compromised and should flee his post."

Ivan set down his glass and finally turned to face her. He brushed a hand over his neatly clipped gray hair, then crossed his arms and studied Sonya for a moment. She was handsome, but not feminine. Her large, soft green eyes had a radiating effect, as if something hypnotic stirred behind them. She'd been the force to reckon with in his Kremlin office many years ago. Now in her fifties, she was his most loyal soldier, committed to the cause, bristling with expectancy of how high it would take her into the resurrected Soviet Socialist Republic of Russia. Take all of them. And the time was near.

He smiled at his longtime compatriot. "I am glad you made such inquiries." He paused to think. "Let me take care of it. Perhaps Hans needs to draw closer to the action, to feel more personally invested in it. He is still a valuable member of our network."

She looked doubtful. "Are you confident he is in full charge of the inauguration?"

"I am. Everything is in place to my satisfaction."

"January 20 is less than a week away," she persisted. "You can understand the security net I have watched fall over the Capitol and Mall. You are certain Hans's Secret Service agent is completely under our control?"

"Everything is in motion, Sonya. Do not worry."

She rose steadily from her chair and reached for her handbag on the floor. "I leave for Washington in the morning. I have much to—"

The doorbell rang. Sonya looked sharply at Ivan.

He strode casually to the door and lifted the cover over the peephole. A young man he'd never seen before stood on the other side. Ivan watched him look nervously around the hallway before turning back to the door. "Who is there?" Ivan asked bluntly.

"Uh, I'm looking for a friend and not sure if I have the right floor. Could you help me?"

Ivan paused. "What is your friend's name?"

"Last name's Hamilton, I think."

Ivan knew none of his neighbors. This was one of six residences he kept throughout the world. He was about to dismiss this lost person when a sudden instinct halted him. Something wasn't right.

Against Sonya's low-issued warnings coming from behind him, Ivan suddenly flung open the door and confronted the visitor head-on. The young man was clearly startled. "You *think* you know this so-called friend's name?" Ivan's old KGB interrogative edge surfaced. He noted the awkward stance of this man who stood a head taller and probably twenty pounds heavier. "You are not even sure whom you are looking for?"

The young man stammered a reply. "I'm, uh . . . uh . . . sorry, sir. I didn't mean to disturb you." But before he turned to go, he seemed to make a deliberate attempt to look past Ivan into the apartment. "My apologies, ma'am." Then he excused himself and walked toward the elevator, never looking back.

Even before Ivan closed the door, he motioned with his hand behind him, a clear directive for Sonya to follow the man into the street.

She threw on her coat, grabbed her bag again, and the moment the young man disappeared into the elevator, Sonya stepped quickly down the stairs. The man had already exited the building when she emerged from the stairwell. She pushed open the front door and, from behind one of the tall potted cedar trees flanking the entrance to the building, she watched him almost sprint toward a small car parked at the end of the block. He didn't leave immediately, and Sonya was about to head that way, but the car finally pulled from the curb and approached. As it drew almost even with her position, she stepped boldly from behind the cedar to peer into its front seat, noting what she believed to be a female in the passenger seat, her face partially concealed by the hood of her coat and a misty film on the window.

As the car passed, Sonya memorized the license plate number, then recorded it on a pad from her bag. She looked back at the retreating car and smirked. "I've got you!"

Chapter 7

That was no mistress," Jordan reported when he dropped into the driver's seat beside Cass, who fidgeted with anticipation of his news. "Fifties. Dowdy. Got that Friar Tuck haircut going. Built sort of, uh, broadly. Didn't smile a whole lot, either. Neither did the man. He was an older, feisty kind of guy, maybe sixties."

"So what happened?" she asked expectantly, pushing a lock of hair back under her hood.

Jordan described the brief encounter as he cranked the engine and turned in his seat, waiting for an opening in the traffic.

"Were they rude?" Cass asked.

"No, but suspicious. It's New York. Who isn't?" He pulled from the curb and merged with the traffic, heading toward the apartment building he'd just left. "Guy had an accent," he added. "Sort of Russian sounding. Woman didn't speak, just glared at . . . oh, I think that's her by the door!"

Cass turned slightly to see the woman, but the side window was too fogged for a good look.

"She is really giving us the once over," Jordan said as they passed by. He glanced in his rearview mirror. "And still looking. What's that all about?"

Cass was at a loss to understand. She recalled her mother's frightened face the morning she'd asked Cass to trail her stepfather. The cover-shot face had lost its poise and sagged into despair. But how could Cass help when all she knew was a world of make-believe?

Jordan lightly patted her knee. "You know what this is? It's just Hans paying a house call on one of his investment clients. Don't they do that with the high rollers?"

Cass looked appreciatively at his effort to allay her fears. "Maybe." It was possible, she considered, and much preferable to infidelity. Cass had witnessed enough of that growing up in the household of an imperial alpha male who set no boundaries to his lusts for money, power, and other women. By her teenage years, Cass had lost hope that her mother would ever extract herself from such devastation, she alone clinging to her vows.

"I don't believe there's anything to this, Cass, so let's drop it into a tall cappuccino and get rid of it. Ready?" They were approaching their neighborhood.

But Cass could only see her mother's desperate eyes, pleading for her daughter's help.

"Jordan, I need to see my mom. It's time you met her and Hans anyway, now that you're an accomplice. Will you go with me?"

He slowed the car and considered it. After a moment, he nodded. "I'd like that. Where to?"

It wasn't far from SoHo to the Tribeca apartment of Jillian and Hans Kluen, who were now expecting them. Jordan had insisted that Cass alert them to their—particularly his—coming. "I don't want to take anybody else by surprise tonight," he'd said.

After wedging the Honda into the only curb space they could find, Jordan and Cass walked the two blocks to a converted textile warehouse. Jordan looked up at the ochre-hued building that rose about five floors. Like other industrial buildings in the Tribeca district, this one had been repurposed and renovated for residential space, some of the priciest in New York.

Jordan opened a gleaming oak door inset with elaborately etched glass, and they entered a lobby floored in black marble. In the center of the space was a slender, stainless-steel sculpture of something abstract and wholly unidentifiable to Jordan, he admitted to Cass.

"It's a woman with a child in her womb," she told him.

"Oh, well, thank you. Foolish of me not to see that such a cold, stark piece of steel represents motherhood."

Cass grinned at him and urged him toward the elevator. "Now behave yourself," she chided.

The elevator deposited them into a long hallway also in shining black marble, floors and walls. Cass led him to the Kluen apartment and rang a doorbell that resounded in a three-note chime. The door opened immediately and a courtly gentleman wrapped in a soft gray cardigan opened his arms to her. "Cass, sweetheart, we're so happy to see you . . . and your friend, uh . . ."

"Jordan Winslow," she supplied while stiffly accepting her stepfather's embrace.

Then the man's hand reached for Jordan's and gripped it quite fraternally. "I'm Hans Kluen, Jordan. So pleased to meet you. And this"— he turned, extending his arm and motioning behind him—"is my wife, Jillian."

Cass's mother glided toward the door, her mint green caftan sweeping across a frothy white carpet, her eyes momentarily flaring conspiratorially at Cass. She extended a delicate hand toward Jordan, her forefinger mounted with a dazzling emerald cocktail ring. "I've been wanting to meet you, young man," she said in a neutral tone.

Jordan slid a questioning glance at Cass.

"She means she wants to make sure that the man who lives next door to me probably doesn't keep sharp axes and formaldehyde in his apartment."

"Cass!" her mother protested.

"It's okay, Mrs. Kluen," Jordan said. "I don't use axes anymore."

Both Kluens fell mute, their unblinking eyes fixed on Jordan.

"Oh, brother," Cass moaned and took off toward the kitchen. "Mom, have you got anything to snack on?" she called over her shoulder. But that wasn't her intent in leaving the room. She glanced back long enough to catch Jordan's eye and issue a signal for him to stay put.

When her mother followed her into the kitchen, Cass ushered her quickly into the pantry and delivered her report. "There was no one but an older man and a not-so-attractive older woman there, Mom. It's got to be the same man I saw at the window last night. Nothing going on there. I guarantee it."

Jillian looked away, her freshly powdered brow wrinkling into even folds. "But why—"

"Jordan believes he's just visiting clients like he said." Cass second-guessed her mother's question. "It makes sense, Mom."

"At that hour? Why not during the business day?"

Cass shrugged. "Maybe that's the only time he can meet with some of them. Anyway, please don't work yourself up over nothing. Hans told you it was business, and I believe it is."

The thin, emerald-clad hand wavered near her mouth, painted delicately in frosty pink. Jillian Kluen never failed to mystify her daughter. In the hour of dread over the fate of her marriage, there was still lipstick and powder. And that familiar pretense so practiced and critical to survival. Cass wanted to mourn for this woman who'd given life to her child, then somehow misplaced her own. When did that happen?

"Jilly, why don't you bring an hors d'oeuvre tray for us, dear?" Hans called from the living room.

"I'll be right there," Jillian answered, her voice lilting on the final syllable. Cass knew the singsong habit her mother sometimes affected to mask her distress.

"Mom, let this go," she implored. "Hans adores you and always has. Anybody can see that. Why can't you?"

The pink lips quivered, releasing a tremulous sigh. "I know he does." She smoothed the flowing skirt of the caftan. "I guess after . . . after all the years with your father, it's just hard to believe in adoration." She extended a cupped hand and held it to her daughter's chin. "Except the kind I feel for my Cassandra." She smiled sweetly, then dropped her hand, though her clear blue eyes lingered on Cass just a moment longer. The air shifted, the mood brightened. Now scurrying to retrieve an assortment of small dishes from the refrigerator, Jillian chirped over her shoulder, "Jordan is an eyeful, don't you think?"

Cass scrunched her face. "As in large?" She settled onto a bar stool and playfully popped an olive into her mouth.

"As in you make a handsome couple." Grabbing a paring knife, Jillian began to slice a small round of brie, her eyes darting inquisitively at her daughter.

"We're not a couple, Mom. Just friends." Cass picked up another olive.

"Well, isn't he the NYU guy you used to gush over before you dropped out and—" Jillian suddenly clipped her words and put down the knife. She looked anxiously at Cass, who slowly returned the olive to the tray and didn't look up. "Oh, honey, I didn't mean to—"

"I know you didn't. It's okay." Cass stood up and grabbed one of the trays. "I'll take this out."

The men sat in matching club chairs, a glass of wine and a can of soda on a small table between them. Cass imagined Hans—an avid collector and consumer of fine wines—all but grieving over her friend's allergy to alcohol.

"I was just telling Jordan that my mother used to shop in his store when his grandfather was still there." He sipped his wine as if toasting a fond memory. "We'd take the train from the Bronx into the city on a Saturday morning and head straight to Winslow's. As a little boy, I didn't understand the fascination women had with shoes."

"You still don't, dear," Jillian offered lightly as she breezed into the room with a silver-handled serving tray, setting it on a zebra-print ottoman.

Cass looked down at her own scuffed sneakers. No fascination there.

"But of course," Jillian reasoned, "it had to be all those German winters sloshing around in thin-soled shoes while those awful Russian soldiers—"

"Yes, we all know what the Russians did after the war, Jilly," Hans interrupted curtly.

Cass was startled by the sharp retort. She'd never heard Hans speak to her mother that way. But he hastily changed his tone. "Now, where were you both off to on such a bitter night?"

Cass's heart leapt, and she dared not look Jordan's way. Methodically placing a gooey mound of brie on a cracker, she focused only on her task. "Visiting friends, that's all." She leaned back in her chair and forced the morsel into her dry mouth.

Jordan cleared his throat. "Mr. Kluen, tell me more about your firm."

What's he doing? Cass fretted.

"Oh, we peddle the usual financial products. Stocks and bonds, annuities, commodity futures, those sorts of things."

"Do all your clients come to you?"

Hans hesitated.

"I mean, do you ever make house calls to your fat-cat clients?" Jordan bludgeoned affably.

Oh, no. Cass didn't like where this was headed.

But Hans answered politely. Cass had no reason to think he wouldn't. In the four years she'd known him, he'd never shown her anything but kindness and courtesy. To her mother also. That's why his behavior just now had raised a flag.

Shifting his gaze between his wife and Jordan, Hans answered, "I'm afraid there are the occasional nights when I must tend to . . . a skittish investor or perhaps a valued client in town for just the evening. The fat cat, as you say." He chuckled and took a too-long swig of his wine. Dabbing the corners of his mouth with a linen napkin, he added, "Jilly hates for me to leave her at night. But it's not often." Cass watched something toxic simmer between the two and regretted having any part in it.

Jordan promptly defused the tense moment he'd created. Cass watched him turn to take in the room's sweeping view of the Hudson River. He stood and walked toward the broad window, stopping to study a collection of framed photographs on a table behind the sofa. "Mrs. Kluen," he said, raising one of the pictures for closer inspection, "this has to be your mother. You look so much like her."

Jillian rose, her caftan rustling as she walked toward him. "You're right. But she's long gone now." She took the photograph and smiled down at it. Then she picked up another and passed it to Jordan. "Twelve-year-old Cass," she informed him, "sawing wood in the back yard of our beach house. She built the most incredible playhouse all by herself." Jillian turned and beamed at her daughter, who allowed a self-conscious grin and wished to be somewhere else just then. But they were the inescapable cast of her personal drama. The proud, delusional mother. The tragically flawed daughter. And the clueless stepfather whose innocent life she'd so shamelessly meddled in. What Broadway producer would resist such a scenario?

As if receiving her subliminal prompt, Jordan finally turned from a quick scan of the view and asked, "Think we'd better be going?"

"Oh, so soon?" Jillian moaned.

"How about dinner next weekend?" Hans offered brightly. "Our treat." He smiled graciously at them. "We've discovered a new French bistro I think you'd like."

"Thanks, Hans," said Cass. "But we're going with some friends to Washington and staying over until Monday. We've got tickets for the inauguration."

It was almost imperceptible, but Cass didn't miss the shadow that flickered across her stepfather's face.

Chapter 8

Cass spent the following afternoon repairing a staircase to nowhere at the Gershwin Theatre. She welcomed the mindless task that allowed her thoughts to stray. As she sawed and nailed, distressing new boards to appear old and rickety, she caught a mental glimpse of herself in her workshop behind the beach house. It was a prefab structure her father begrudgingly purchased for her twelfth birthday, the only thing she'd asked for.

"What's wrong with you?" he'd scolded. "Why can't you be like other girls and play dress-up instead of acting like a boy? Get out of those overalls and go find some girlfriends."

But inside the metal workshop, she'd started building her own world, free of her parents' fractious marriage and her father's relentless disapproval of most everything she did. Her mother had created her own escape—Broadway. She never missed a show and nearly always took her young daughter with her. Together, they'd sit in the dark of one theater or another and slip around the jagged edge of reality into merciful illusion. By the stage lights, Cass would watch her mother's face glow as it rarely did at home. It was the same face Cass was used to seeing on glossy pages and on the occasional billboard, though its luster was paper thin and pasted on. It was her mother's job to coax a convincing glow from cosmetic bottles and jars, from plastic posing. But the face next to Cass in the theater radiated from unspoiled depths.

It was the stage sets that most captivated young Cass's imagination. She would sketch them during a performance, trying to figure out how they were built. Later, in her sprawling bedroom atop the three-story beach house, Cass drafted intricate plans for building her own sets. She began with a playhouse that took even her father by surprise, a cottage design with lots of gables, much like the grown-up, cedar-shake house behind it.

"Hey, Cass!" Arnie, her boss, broke into her thoughts. "It's gonna look real funny when the curtain goes up tonight and you're still nailing on those steps. Get a move on!"

"If I rush this job, Arnie, you know what's going to be even funnier? The wicked witch falling through these steps and landing on her pointy hat."

"Yeah, yeah. Just hurry up."

Pushing childhood memories aside, Cass refocused on the job at hand. She was about to open a can of quick-dry black paint when her phone rang.

Hans? She answered with a thin hello.

"Cass, would you be able to meet me sometime this afternoon? Maybe for coffee. There's something I need to discuss with you."

He'd never made such a request before. Could he possibly know she'd tailed him? There'd been no hint of it last night. Maybe something was wrong with her mother. Jillian was all she had. Of course she'd meet him.

Later, Cass entered an elegant little diner off Broadway. Hans waved to her from a tufted-leather booth near the back. He stood as she approached and took her jacket, hanging it with fastidious care on a nearby hook, then sat opposite her. A bitter unease rose inside her, and she tried to shake it off, affecting a casual air.

"This is a treat," she said. Then more hesitantly, "Or I hope it is." She studied his face and wondered when that pallor of fatigue had crept into it.

"What may I order for you?" he asked distractedly.

"Just coffee, thank you." She suddenly remembered the decaf Jordan had brought two nights ago. *So you won't lie awake in your counterfeit jungle up there*, he'd said. Something about that oddly soothed her at this awkward moment.

But the comfort didn't last. After ordering for them both, Hans turned reproachful eyes on her. "Cass, have you been following me?"

And there it was. No preamble. Her heart lunged against her chest and her mouth opened wordlessly. But there was no need to play the wrongly accused. She looked down at the white porcelain charger before her, its high gloss reflecting the outline of her face but not the fright in it. She looked back at Hans. He waited patiently, as if already certain of her guilt. *Just get it over with.* "Mom thought you were . . . uh . . . meeting another woman."

Now it was Hans who looked down, then squeezed his eyes shut. Cass waited for a response. What she got surprised her. When he looked up, his eyes were moist and red. He shook his head slowly. "I would never do that." He locked hard on her. "Don't ever doubt how much I love your mother." He looked away, then sharply back at her. "But evidently, she does."

Then what were you doing? Maybe it's none of my business, but Mom is. "So all those trips out at night were just business?" she challenged.

He sat back in his seat, blinking away the moisture in his eyes. "Clients, that's all." His tone turned guarded, triggering Cass's next question.

"How'd you know I followed you?"

He looked steadily at her. "Your friend Jordan is a clumsy sleuth. He, uh, frightened a couple I've been working with a long time. They managed to get his license plate number and run it through channels. When they called to tell me who he was . . . well, of course, you'd just brought the young man to my door last night. How quickly it all came together." Now he was angry.

But there was something he'd left out. "Hans, why would these people call *you* about Jordan?"

He looked blankly at her.

"I mean, if they thought he was just somebody casing their apartment, why wouldn't they call the police? Why would they think there was any connection between Jordan and you?"

Hans fidgeted with his tie before answering. "Well . . . I . . . can only assume that I must have told them about my stepdaughter at some point."

Cass stared at him incredulously. "And where I live?" she said too loudly. "Are you saying these clients of yours not only traced Jordan's license plate but somehow discovered that he lives next door to Hans Kluen's stepdaughter?" Cass was suddenly reeling with the implication. "Who are these people?" she demanded.

"Keep your voice down, Cass," he said gruffly, glancing quickly about the room.

But she fired the next question as if he'd said nothing. "How many other clients have you given my address to?"

Cass watched as he clearly struggled for an answer. "You're overreacting, and I wish you would calm down, please." He leaned forward and harnessed his own voice. "They are nothing more than business clients who got jittery over Jordan's intrusion last night. They are foreign, unsure of our ways, and he spooked them. That's all. I really don't know how they . . . discovered that Jordan was your neighbor."

He looked more earnestly at her. "I didn't mean to upset you, Cass, truly I didn't. But I need to warn you about following me or anybody else. You and your friend aren't very good at it. And if you don't know who you're messing with, you could get into trouble."

Cass latched on to that. "Just who did Jordan and I mess with, Hans? Who are you messing with? Are you in trouble?"

Hans grabbed his coat. "I think we should go."

"No. You asked to talk with me, now talk. Tell me what's going on here." She felt out of control but couldn't rein herself in. She was behaving badly, she knew, but an unidentified fear had risen in her, and she couldn't ignore it.

Defying her demands, he rose and retrieved her jacket, then extended his hand to help her from the booth. She refused his help, then got up and took her jacket from him. Leading the way out of the restaurant, she stopped on the sidewalk, swung around, and glared at him. He ignored her open hostility and steered her across the street to a small park. The late-afternoon sky was overcast, but nothing wet had fallen.

He settled onto a wood-slatted bench while Cass remained standing. "Please sit down," he urged. "Let's not quarrel."

After a fuming moment, she sat and turned abruptly toward him. "This isn't about domestic tranquility, Hans. Or patching up some silly argument. You just lit a fire, and it's not going to burn out anytime soon. I don't know if you're having an affair or just seeing clients or what. But my mother won't survive any more betrayal of any kind. If you love her, you watch what you're doing and who you're doing it with." Her head pounded, but she kept going. "And now I want to know one thing: Are Jordan and I at risk?"

Hans blanched. "What do you mean?"

"You said we *could get into trouble.* What kind of trouble?" She felt her eyes burn into him.

He answered firmly. "You don't go playing private eye and tailing people to strange apartments, knocking on strange doors. You don't know who might come to that door or what they might be in the middle of." His eyes flared back at her. "Don't you ever do it again."

Cass felt as if she'd been punched in the stomach. She couldn't speak.

"You mean a lot to me, Cass," he said after a blistering silence. "Don't be careless with your safety."

He looked into the overhead branches of a barren tree, but Cass didn't take her eyes off him. Something lurked beneath his words, just as sure as if the thing had jumped out and grabbed at her.

Without another word, she got up and fled from it.

Chapter 9

Cass had just returned to the theater when her phone rang. She stared at Hans's name on the screen and promptly aborted the call. After the voice-mail notification chimed, she wondered what more he'd felt compelled to tell her. To accuse her of. He'd been right, of course. She shouldn't have followed him, shouldn't have taken it that one step further and sent Jordan to the door of a stranger's apartment. It had all seemed so harmless, though, a simple one-two assignment just to realign her mother's fractured nerves.

But Hans's words came back to her, and she remembered the way his eyes had held hers when he said them. *If you don't know who you're messing with . . .*

Cass looked around the stage at the rest of the crew tending the punch list for that night's performance. This was her world, removed from the real one, just like her playhouse, still perched high above the ocean breakers. Just a short walk across the back lawn from the house where angry voices had filled the alcoves and stairways. Had she just done something to close that distance?

The phone in her pants pocket chimed a reminder, insisting that she listen to its latest message. She resisted for another hour, feeling the phone's weight pull against her. Finally, she listened. "Cass, after upsetting you the way I did this afternoon, I probably have no right to ask a favor of you. But I must. It would be best if you didn't mention our conversation to your mother. Now that you've told me of her suspicions, I will put her mind at ease, I promise. And hopefully, I won't need to continue meeting with clients after hours." A pause. "Not much longer." Another pause. "Now, please consider watching the inauguration with us here in New York, not in that Washington madhouse. We'll talk to you more about that soon. And, Cass, don't ever doubt how important you are to your mother and to me. Goodbye."

Before Cass could pocket the phone, it rang. She checked the caller ID and answered. "Hi, Mom," she said quietly, looking carefully about her. No need to attract a coworker's attention.

"Honey, I have the most wonderful idea. Why don't you and your friends come to our apartment for an inauguration party? You don't want to stand for hours in that freezing rain. That's what they predict for Washington, you know."

Hans was right about that talk, Cass thought. This is soon. "Thanks, Mom. I appreciate your concern, but we've already made arrangements. We'll be fine."

"But where will you stay? You and Jordan and, uh—"

"Married friends of ours, Mom. What are you getting at? Do you think Jordan and I are bunking in together?"

"Oh no, sweetheart. I didn't mean to imply anything. I just . . . would love to have you all here with us. Warm and well fed." She laughed nervously. "I'll put on a presidential brunch worthy of Travis Noland's second big day. And don't forget, Hans and I attended the president's first inauguration and still remember how painful the cold was. We both came back sick."

Cass regretted being so edgy and irritable. "I appreciate the invitation. And sorry I jumped at you like that. Just a hectic day so far." *Hectic* wasn't the right word.

"So you'll come?"

"No, Mom. I just want to see it for myself."

"But Hans will be so disappointed."

That stopped Cass. She glanced at her watch, less than two hours since her abrupt departure from her stepfather. Cass was certain he'd put her mother up to this. It wasn't just a casual invitation. *He wants me to stay in New York. Why?* Then Cass remembered the odd look on his face when she first announced she was going to the inauguration. It didn't make sense.

"Mom, when did Hans ask you to call me?" Cass felt no guilt over the loaded question.

Jillian Kluen sputtered. "Well, uh . . . why do you . . . he didn't . . . well, he did ask me a little while ago. But we both thought it was a good idea. My goodness, Cass, don't make such a big deal out of this."

"Mom, you're the one insisting I cancel my plans. Why?" But her mother was innocent. Cass knew that. "Never mind, Mom. Tell Hans I'm sorry, but I'm going to Washington. I'll see you when I get back."

"Well, please wear that full-length down coat I gave you. And take some of those hand warmers for your gloves. And maybe some—"

"Mom, I'll be fine. I really do have to go. I love you." She ended the call and sat down on the floor, still cradling the phone in her hands. Beside her rose a stand of synthetic black cornstalks backlit by a fiery red sunset that almost quivered in anticipation of the Oz witch's arrival. From above, a technician adjusted the trajectory of the spotlights for maximum impact of the visual lie. Had Cass lived so long in a mirage that she could no longer distinguish what was real and what wasn't? Who lied and who didn't?

Before Arnie could catch her dazed and distant, she forced herself to her feet to check the fittings on the great bubble ride of Glinda, the good witch. By the time Cass left the Gershwin Theatre, tense and knotted, she was eager for a long, brisk walk home and a workout at the gym, which she usually managed about four times a week. But the downpour she encountered on the other side of the stage door made her race for the subway instead.

"You've got a perfectly fine car, Cass. Please use it and stay off that filthy subway." Her mother's frequent refrain merely amused her. Who was Cassandra Rodino that she shouldn't swing a hammer in her chosen career or travel with the masses? Shouldn't inhale the same subterranean molecules as her coworkers? Did the Manhattan real estate her father left her and her mother—which included a couple of parking garages—exempt or entitle her in some way? She didn't think so.

Cass slung her gym bag over her shoulder and hopped aboard a southbound train to the SoHo neighborhood that had long ago flung its luminous membrane around her and snuggled her to its forbearing self. She had moved from her parents' Upper East Side apartment after dropping out of NYU her sophomore year, desperate for another life entirely, for a full retreat from the thing that had so disfigured her sense of self. It was along the byways around propriety and protocol that she'd found others like her, the damaged ones who'd redefined themselves within no one else's parameters.

From SoHo to Greenwich Village, Cass had gathered a new family about her—the poets who resonated from barstools in smoky bistros; the playwrights who clung to all-night cafés, tapping out their souls in dialogue no one might ever hear; the artists who filled studios and galleries with the images that cavorted inside them, set free in the shapes and colors of abandon. At the long, crude farmer's table in her apartment, she had delighted in nurturing those even needier than herself. She had fed out-of-work actors and stage hands, mimes and musicians. And one polygamous airline pilot.

Cass had met Everett Biggs in a karate class four years ago. He was almost ten years older than she. One night, he hung around after class long enough to engage her in conversation. He'd been intrigued by her theatrical habitat, and she, in turn, had welcomed his tales of world travel. The ensuing courtship had been swift and blinding, Cass would later admit. It took only three months for him to produce an engagement ring. A month later, they stood before a chaplain in Hudson River Park and proclaimed their undying love for each other, though Cass had no idea the chaplain was as fraudulent as the groom. The nuptials were witnessed by a few of Cass's bohemian and Broadway friends, dressed in the artful wilds of unrestrained fashion, and the recently widowed Jillian Rodino in a Dior suit with matching pumps and handbag.

Everett had moved into Cass's loft with little more than some pricey clothes, pilot uniforms, toiletries, a laptop, and an old StairMaster. Just months later, he fled her wrath and threats to file charges, which she never did. Some rancid little voice had surfaced within and convinced her that even such egregious betrayal was deserved.

Slogging from the subway through a torrent of rain, Cass decided against the gym that evening and headed straight home. The thought of curling onto one of her overstuffed sofas with hot clove tea and a book was far more appealing. But the likelihood of that peaceful respite ended when she reached her door and found Jordan emerging quickly through his. "Go in and lock the door," he ordered. "And don't open it for anyone. I'll be back." She was still staring after him when he entered the elevator down the hall.

Is this a joke? But she did as he said, then went to her living-room window and looked down into the street. In a moment, she watched him exit the front of the building, pull the hood of his slicker over his head, and take off down the sidewalk, now filling with after-work pedestrians and their bobbing umbrellas. When he turned the corner, she shrank back from the window and looked about the loft. Everything was in place, as clean and neatly arranged as it always was. No matter how disarrayed the rest of her life might be, her home was always in order, even the jungle upstairs.

She headed there now to shed her wet clothes and slip on warm sweats and socks, pausing every few moments to listen for Jordan. What had happened? She wondered if there'd been trouble with one of her tenants. Her tenants. She'd never grown comfortable with the notion of being anyone's landlord. It must have amused Nicholas Rodino to leave such responsibility to his runaway daughter, but she was surprised he'd left anything at all to her. She certainly hadn't asked him for anything, nothing but his affection and approval, neither one ever extended.

In the kitchen, she put a kettle of water on the stove, then assembled loose tea, cloves, and fresh lemon while keeping an ear tuned to the door. She dropped a few melon slices and crackers onto a small plate and settled uneasily on the sofa facing the window. The rain hadn't let up, and she wondered what could possibly have sent Jordan headlong into it.

She doctored her fully steeped tea and had just returned to the sofa when three quick raps sounded at the door. Seeing Jordan through the peephole, she unlocked the door and flung it open. He was a soggy bear of a man filling the doorway in a bright yellow slicker that made him look like a school bus emerging from a car wash.

"Didn't you see her?" he panted, lumbering through the doorway, dripping rainwater. "You almost ran into her." He quickly closed and locked the door securely behind him.

"Who?" Cass asked, reaching for his slicker.

"The woman from the UN apartment, the one who stared at us from the door." He shrugged out of the coat and gave it to Cass, who made no move to hang it up, her eyes fixed on Jordan as he swept a hand over his dangling wet hair. "I spotted her from my window, or I thought it was her. She was standing under the bakery awning across the street, looking up at the building, right at my window. If that really was her, how'd she know where I live?" Cass heard more irritation than alarm in his voice. "And why hunt me down? What's up with those people? How do they know I wasn't really looking for a friend's apartment?" He finally took the slicker from Cass's hand and headed for the bathroom. "This needs to hang over the tub."

"Are you sure it was the same woman?" Cass called after him. "You only saw her for an instant, you said."

"No, I'm not sure, especially through the rain. That's why I took off after her. You'd just walked past her and crossed the street; then she left. I wanted to get close enough to be sure."

"And then what?"

Jordan returned from the bathroom with a thick white towel around his neck, his hair squeeze dried and uncombed. "Well, I was going to slip up behind her and inject her with a homing pellet and . . . what do you mean, then what? What did you think I was going to do?" He mopped his face. "She was already gone, anyway."

Cass didn't respond. She was sorting through Hans's words, searching for something. *You don't know who might come to that door or what they might be in the middle of.* She closed her eyes. This was ridiculous! She refused to allow mistaken identity or her stepfather's unfortunate choice of words to disrupt her peace. She'd worked too hard to achieve even a semblance of it.

Still, it was foolish to ignore what she knew was true. Hans had told her. Those people had run Jordan's license plate number. They did know where he lived. Where she lived.

So what? They're just a couple of paranoid oddballs. She headed for the kitchen. "Jordan, we're going to have some hot tea and forget all about this silliness. Okay?" She felt his eyes on her as she lifted the kettle from the stove and poured more water inside. "Now, let's talk about the trip to Washington."

Chapter 10

A cab pulled up at the Juilliard School at Lincoln Center, and Liesl Bower stepped from the back seat, her hair tucked beneath a powder-blue woolen cap, a matching scarf coiled inside the lapels of a black pea coat. She tucked her head against the invasive cold and headed toward the front entrance of the venerable school. Throughout most of her celebrated career, she'd come to New York every few months to teach piano workshops and give a private concert for Juilliard's generous patrons. She'd always enjoyed her visits to the city until fifteen months ago when it tried to swallow her, when evil struck on a night street and chased her into a terrifying vortex.

Now, pummeled as much by the icy blows of winter as by the haunting memories, Liesl was anxious to return home to Charleston. *Next Tuesday*, she told herself, already warming to the promise of gossamer breezes off the harbor. And a wedding.

Pulling her coat tighter around her, she imagined Cade's embrace. He would soon be hers, joined in matrimony before God, before those who watched from the pews of St. Philip's Church. Next Saturday!

Her step lighter, she walked briskly toward the door. On this Saturday morning, she'd reserved a private studio for practice. President Travis Noland's second inauguration was just two days away. She was honored that he'd asked her to perform but nervous about playing outdoors in such finger-numbing temperatures. Today she would rehearse in the half-gloves she'd used only once before in her career, in the middle of Red Square with other students from the Moscow Conservatory. She loathed the constraining gloves then, and more so now. But she had promised the president, one of her most avid fans. She would fly to Washington that afternoon.

Just inside the door, she was stopped by one of her workshop students.

"Hi, Miss Bower. Thank you again for helping me with the Chopin."

"You're welcome, Steve. Just mind your fingering and don't neglect the scales."

The young man nodded, then stared at her for an awkward moment. "Uh, do you mind if I ask you a personal question?"

There had been a time when such a request would have caught her breath, but no longer. At thirty-eight, she'd finally found her peace. "No, I don't mind at all."

"The fall before last, you appeared at Avery Fisher Hall, and you did something very unusual."

Liesl knew where this was leading. She leaned her head slightly to one side, trying to smile.

"Before you began to play, you stood very still in front of the piano and stared at the audience for the longest time. I was there. Lots of us students were. And pardon me for saying so, but we thought something was very wrong with you." He waited for her response.

"And did you afterward?"

"Oh, no ma'am. Not after what you told all those people. That you believed the music you were going to play was about conflict between nations. But that God was the ruler over all the nations. Man, that was powerful stuff to lay on an international audience like that. And then you told them that God said, 'Blessed are the peacemakers.' Remember?"

Of course she remembered. "That meant something to you?"

He looked deep into her eyes. "That's what I wanted to tell you." Color rose on his face, and he looked away for just a moment, then back at Liesl. "You see, I grew up in Israel. We're not Jewish, but my parents loved the Jewish people and wanted to help them."

Liesl was now locked on the young man with the wavy dark locks. "In what way?" she asked.

"Well, my parents spoke Arabic and Hebrew and thought that in some small way they could help relations between the Palestinians and Jews. Imagine that." He looked toward the floor, his face somber.

"Had they done that sort of thing before?" Liesl asked, imagining the challenge.

"Oh, sure. They were both mediators for the court system in Chicago. They thought that if they could help Americans resolve conflict, they could do it elsewhere. So they kind of worked their way into the graces of both sides in Jerusalem and tried to help them understand each other." He looked squarely into her eyes. "They were peacemakers."

Before she found words to express her admiration, he added, "They were killed in the street outside our home, by a man who didn't want peace with the other side. Only vengeance." He patted her arm and smiled faintly. "So you keep on telling anyone who'll listen, Miss Bower. Peace is better." And he walked away.

She watched the young man until she couldn't see him anymore. She was too stunned now to think about practicing the Aaron Copland overture she would play at the inauguration, another special request of the president, who admired the robust frontier spirit of the American composer's work. Practice would have to wait. Her young student couldn't have known the flame he'd just stoked, the unrest it had caused, especially in the wake of gentler reflections on home.

Casting about for someplace to simmer down her soul, she walked back outside, feeling every swipe of unmerciful cold, and headed for a nearby coffee shop. She was crossing the street toward a sidewalk more traveled than usual for a sleet-prone Saturday morning, when a face in a doorway stopped her midstride. Even the hood of his jacket couldn't hide the pale, flat cheeks and riveting eyes.

No!

The light had turned and cars now honked as they slid toward the intersection where Liesl remained fixed to the pavement. She jerked around, held a restraining hand against a threatening cabbie, and sprinted to safety. Her eyes searching for the face, she nearly tripped on the curbing, but righted herself in time to see the face turn abruptly and the back of the man's hood blend with others headed away from her.

It's him! She drew a trembling hand to her mouth as her eyes strained to find him in the flux of pedestrians ahead. The hood. The gray backpack. Finally, she put a voice to her alarm. "Evgeny!" she wailed, drawing anxious looks from others. "Wait!"

But why? Why wasn't she fleeing in the opposite direction, like she had the night Evgeny Kozlov and his kidnappers had come after her? Instead, she now ran after *him*. One block, two, then three. No sign of him. She spun in every direction, scanned every face. He was gone.

Had he really been there? Had the story she'd just heard, the reminder of that night at Avery Fisher Hall, triggered a hallucination? After all, it was Evgeny who'd stolen into her dressing room moments before she was to perform that night. The man who'd once tried to kidnap her had come to offer strange comfort. "No one hunts you anymore," he'd said. "It is me they hunt." Before leaving, though, he'd issued her a warning. "Never stop watching them."

That was Evgeny. Watching me. Why? In the middle of a crowded Manhattan sidewalk full of Saturday shoppers, she lifted her face skyward and closed her eyes. *Lord, why?*

Evgeny slid from behind the dressing-room curtain of a discount clothier and paused before reentering the sidewalk traffic. *How did I let that happen?* he fumed. *She should never have spotted me.* He stepped guardedly out of the store and squinted against a blustery wind. No sign of Liesl Bower. He would find her again, though, should he need to. Nothing had signaled that need, yet. And more urgent matters waited.

Still, he was glad for the risk he'd taken. Glad to see her again, moving freely about and not cowering from the likes of him.

He hailed a cab and headed to his backstreet Harlem hotel. Soon, Viktor would call with whatever news he'd confiscated from the movement's communications bank. They were sketchy at best, but the only leads Evgeny had for finding and disabling the Architect.

Moments after he locked the hotel door behind him, one of the phones in his backpack rang. The secure line from Viktor.

"Yes," Evgeny answered.

"I only have a few seconds," Viktor began. "I tapped into an e-mail this morning. The letter you found in the piano, the woman's letter to Fedorovsky, is true. The Architect is about to strike the United States."

Chapter 11

January 21 slid into Washington on frozen feet. The inaugural ceremonies proceeded in spite of the weather. An elaborate, multitiered platform built over the Capitol steps housed many of the nation's political elite, overseeing the throngs who'd braved the punishing cold to witness President Noland's public oath of office. Because January 20, the constitutionally mandated end of a presidential term, fell on Sunday this year, Noland—like Eisenhower and Reagan before him—chose to honor the Lord's Day by taking the oath of office in a private ceremony moments before noon on Sunday, with the public pageantry of the inauguration slated for Monday.

Cass, Jordan, and their friends Reg and Myrna Brockman huddled together not far from the Capitol, their breath almost freeze-dried.

"I don't think I can take much more," Jordan mumbled behind the scarf wrapped around his head, already topped by a wool cap.

"It won't be long now," Cass said, stamping her feet against the crunchy grass, coaxing her bloodstream to step up the heat. She'd taken her mother's advice and worn the bulky, ankle-length down coat that visually packed twenty pounds onto her petite frame, though she welcomed its cocooning warmth. If only she'd dressed her feet with as much care, choosing fur-lined boots over the running shoes she now wore. "One more musician and then the oath."

Jordan rolled his eyes and hugged himself tighter, his short, under-insulated jacket no more a match for the weather than Cass's shoes. "If you were the nurturing kind, you'd wrap that king-size coat of yours around us both." His lopsided grin turned to openmouthed surprise when Cass did exactly that. She unzipped her coat and extended one half of it as far as it would reach around him.

"Here, big guy," Myrna said, reaching into her roomy backpack. "I brought an extra blanket." She retrieved a plush throw full of peace signs.

Before extracting himself from the half-cover of Cass's coat, Jordan slipped his other arm inside and hugged Cass to him. "Thanks anyway," he whispered and kissed her lightly on the forehead.

When he released her and busied himself with the welcomed throw, his kiss lingered against Cass's skin, its touch warmer than down. She tried in vain to ignore the implication that it was anything beyond a friendly gesture. Friends kissed each other all the time, didn't they? Had Jordan ever kissed her before? No.

As she watched him envelop himself in the blanket, she heard an announcement from the inaugural platform. Liesl Bower was about to perform. The acclaimed pianist was one of Cass's favorite musicians. "How is she going to move her fingers in this cold?" Cass wondered aloud.

Jordan leaned close. "I hope she's relying on a recording."

"I wouldn't mind if she did. Her talent is authentic."

"How many times have you seen her perform?"

Cass shrugged. "Maybe five. She's incredible." Cass pulled out a pair of small binoculars and looked toward the platform, watching the tall, slender figure of Liesl Bower approach the grand piano placed one tier above and behind the podium where Travis Noland would soon repeat the oath of office. The pianist's long hair draped about her shoulders like a warm shawl. Cass had seen her up close only once, at Carnegie Hall where Cass had volunteered to dress the stage for a Bower concert. "She's very photogenic," Cass told Jordan. "Very gracious." She paused a moment. "There was something tragic in her past, though. Many years ago, she watched someone gun down a friend of hers." Cass didn't take her eyes off the pianist, now seated. She sensed Jordan's surprise but didn't look at him.

"Who was it?" he asked.

"One of her Harvard professors, I think. Not sure of the details, but I've been told it sent her into a psychological tailspin. Made her withdraw from everything but her music." Cass raised her face to the threatening sky, willing a whip of raw air to displace that suffocating thing that had just risen in her. *Get past it,* she told herself. In a lighter voice, she added, "They'd better hurry this along before the ceiling caves in."

No sooner had she spoken than the first chords of an Aaron Copland overture erupted from the piano and through the giant speakers placed around the grounds. Those first notes soon swelled into a heroic passage that hushed the crowds and almost thawed the bitter pall. Cass leaned into the music as if it were a roaring fire. Next to her art, music—no matter its timbre—soothed and empowered her as little else could. And in the hands of this particular performer, the music sprang from something Cass found inexpressible. From a depth Cass herself had never reached, though longed for.

"Look at Noland," Jordan said. "The man of the hour, frozen stiff, I'll bet. No hat. No scarf. Smiling like his face won't move in any other direction."

Cass dropped her gaze to the first level of the platform, watching the president she'd come to admire for his humility. Just below him was the ground-level assembly of the Marine Band, which had performed first on the program and now waited—anxiously, no doubt—for the conclusion.

The moisture in the air further amplified the sound of the piano. Cass trained her binoculars back on the lone pianist in the long black cape, her arms swathed in something soft and clinging, her hands clad in half gloves that left her fingers free to dance along the keyboard. That dance was coming to an end, Cass sensed, its intensity building to such a pitch that the sudden explosion seemed part of the performance—until screams erupted behind them and the music suddenly stopped. All heads turned from the ceremonial platform to see a burst of smoke in the opposite direction, near the reflecting pool.

It was the frantic shouts from the platform, though, that made Cass turn back in time to see a swarm of Secret Service agents descend like a collective cloak over that small, elevated assembly. But not before Liesl Bower sprang from the piano as if it might devour her. What was happening?

Cass saw a hulk of a man in a dark coat lunge for Liesl and haul her to the floor, covering her body with his. Other Secret Service agents did the same with those closest to the piano. Some guests ran from the platform into the Capitol. Those who couldn't move as quickly were physically lifted and whisked away.

Simultaneously, a platoon of agents surrounded the president and vice president, manhandling them out of their seats and up the stairs into the building.

Just then, Jordan grabbed Cass's arm and pulled her against him, his eyes searching the grounds. "I don't know what just happened, but we're getting out of here," he shouted over the rising cries of the confused and frightened crowd. "If we aren't blown up, we'll be trampled."

He turned to their friends. "Let's go!" They fell in behind Jordan, his arm tight around Cass's shoulders, and they all moved as one unit, forging a narrow exit line toward the perimeter of the Capitol grounds. When they cleared a line of trees, they broke into a full run toward the C Street apartment where they'd spent the night. Others ran alongside, wild-eyed and headed down random avenues of escape—no longer spectators but potential targets.

Now came the sirens, confirmation that something, indeed, had happened. But unlike the terrified witnesses fleeing the Trade Center disaster, those who now ran from the Capitol had seen very little. A small explosion. Pandemonium on the platform. And nothing else but the surge of a frenzied crowd.

Something, though, had made Liesl Bower jump from the piano bench and whip around as if confronting an attacker. Is that what had happened? Besides the explosion on the Mall, had someone targeted the inaugural party? An attempt on the president's life? No one spoke as they ran, as if their silence would hide them from an unseen enemy.

Cass was the first through the door of the apartment, its owner a friend of the Brockmans away on business. She went immediately to the television and turned on the breaking news, a barrage of sound bites.

"A malfunctioning explosive device discovered inside the piano . . . first detected by Senator Brad Campbell, who saw smoke seeping from under the lid of the piano . . . this preceded by an explosion of a portable toilet near the reflecting pool . . . one dead . . . nearly a dozen taken to area hospitals . . . one Washington policeman suggesting the explosion was a diversion from what is believed to be an assassination attempt on the president and everyone near him."

"Turn it up!" came a chorus around her, and Cass obliged, watching but not seeing the big-eyed blond newswoman speaking so urgently before the camera. Cass felt gripped by some insurgent paralysis, a numbing down of senses in the aftermath of trauma. Her mind couldn't piece it together.

The remote still in her hand, she hit the mute button and turned to her companions. "Who did this?"

Three sets of eyes rested on her, but no answers issued for a long moment. Then, "Should be obvious," Myrna supplied.

Jordan shook his head. "It's dangerous to assume the obvious, isn't it? I mean, sure, it's easy to call it an Al-Qaeda hit, but it could be some lone-wolf nutcase standing right in front of you with his little bag of tricks."

Cass looked incredulously at him. "How do you get those kinds of tricks past the tightest security in the country?"

No one spoke.

Cass's phone rang. Something both undefined and foreboding lurched when she saw the caller was Hans. She swallowed hard to retrieve her voice, now pinched. "Yes."

"Cass, are you all right?" Hans asked, his own voice laced with panic.

"I'm fine. We're fine." She did and did not want to talk to him. What could he possibly tell her? What was it he had *already* told her? Warned her of? The woman who'd tracked her and Jordan to their homes? She heard Hans's words again in her head. *You don't know who you're messing with.* And why had he insisted she stay in New York on Inauguration Day? Wild, unsubstantiated thoughts took on more solid flesh by the second.

Reg took the remote from her hand and restored the volume on the news. Cass retreated into the kitchen with her phone, catching Jordan's worried eye.

"What did you see at the Capitol?" Hans asked.

She wondered how much he already knew. "The same thing you're watching on TV, I presume. Don't worry about me. We got away quickly."

"Thank God for that," he said.

God? She'd never heard him speak of God before. Almost acidly, she said, "You told me not to come, didn't you, Hans?"

There was no response.

"Didn't you?" she pressed.

"Well, of course I did. The weather is horrible. You should be here in front of our fireplace. Your mother prepared a sumptuous brunch. I'm sorry you missed it."

Why was he so talkative? Why did she even ask the question of him? What did it matter?

But something did. Cass couldn't deny it was there—suspicion, elusive and noxious, like a darkroom negative sloshing about in solution, its image slowly lifting into recognizable form.

She ended the call and returned to the living room. Mustering a steady voice, she announced, "I'm sorry, but I've got to get back to New York right now."

Chapter 12

The White House crackled like a firestorm. Those responsible for the inauguration attacks were still at large, trailing not even a scent. After Wednesday morning's crush of press conferences and debriefings by law enforcement officials, national security advisors, Pentagon brass, and the newly installed Homeland Security director, President Noland had temporarily retreated from the situation room of the White House. Only FBI director Rick Salabane followed him back to the Oval Office, where Noland settled into an armchair and rang for lunch.

Salabane dropped a file containing a faded blueprint and hard-copy diagram of the Capitol complex onto a coffee table, then lowered himself to a sofa in front of it.

Eyeing the contents of the oversized folder, Noland said, "You know we've got a computer file on that, Rick. CADD, or some such thing."

Salabane looked back at the yellowing sheets flung into the manila file. "Yeah, well, call me a dinosaur." He hunched lower over the table and shook his head slowly. "This whole place has been on lockdown for days. How did these phantom bombers get in and out without detection?"

"One of us?" the president asked, running a hand over the top of his silver head. The thought of another traitor in the White House launched him from the chair and into his usual pacing pattern to and from a window overlooking the Rose Garden. At sixty-one, his knees ached each time he pivoted, the arthritis in his joints grating more each day.

Salabane looked grimly at Noland. "Quite possibly, sir. Someone with clearance. Secret Service. An independent contractor aided by a rogue agent. We're interviewing everyone who even breathed in the vicinity of that piano. And those who supplied the toilets. That was the diversion from what was supposed to happen on the platform."

"That's the telling thing, Rick. 'Supposed to happen.' Was it or wasn't it?"

"Our bomb squad claims the piano device was too small to do much damage, except to those closest to it, which would include you, sir, though you were below it. It's just a fluke the thing didn't go off. Or call it what you will. Providence? Maybe. But my people think the bomber was probably too pressed for time or too distracted to set it correctly, and the subfreezing temps may have been a factor as well." Salabane shuffled through more reports and diagrams spread before him. "But to go to all this trouble, why not take out the whole platform? Unless you just want to prove something—that the American giant is helpless to protect itself." Noland let the director's thoughts flow without interruption. "But if that was your intent, you'd want us to know who you were, to claim responsibility, which no one has. No grainy videos from Al-Qaeda, though they might surface yet. No chest pounding from a lone-wolf crackpot. Nothing."

The president stopped midstride. "Well, who wants to claim responsibility for blowing up a porta-potty? Or for botching the piano job?" He rubbed his forehead and looked away.

Salabane reserved comment.

After a moment, Noland went to a cabinet behind his desk and removed a flat, metal box about the size of a legal pad. He returned to sit opposite Salabane and set the box on the table. Lifting the lid, Noland removed the only contents, a *Washington Post* news article about Ted Shadlaw, the White House staffer who just over a year ago had confessed to selling classified information to Russia, and a photograph of pianist Liesl Bower and violinist Max Morozov in concert together.

As Salabane reached for the photograph, a knock came at the door.

Noland quickly returned the items to the box and closed the lid. "Come in," he called. A steward in a crisp black-and-white uniform brought in a tray of sandwiches, fresh fruit, and coffee, placing it on a nearby sideboard.

When the man left, Noland reopened the box and handed the photograph to Salabane. "That was taken not long after young Max led an Israeli commando unit to Corsica, France, and dug up this box from where his father had buried it underneath an old olive press. You know what was inside it then."

Salabane nodded. "A mother lode of evidence against the KGB conspiracy to take over its government. It was all the Russian president needed to stop his own countrymen from assassinating him and the Syrian president." Salabane stared at the empty box, then back at Noland. "Are you thinking our bombers speak Russian?"

Noland didn't answer but instead walked calmly to a window overlooking a slushy lawn. Soon after the inaugural crowds had fled the grounds, the skies made good on their promise to rain ice over Washington. *Fitting*, Noland thought, as he lamented the added weight of weather piled onto the day.

He returned to his chair near Salabane and picked up the photo of the two musicians. "Incredible," Noland said, "that two gentle, peace-loving souls who just wanted to make beautiful music could have brought down such a savage conspiracy on the heads of its underworld Kremlin architects." He paused. "Just a couple of musicians." He looked pointedly at Salabane. "And one of them was seated at that piano."

Later that afternoon, the president summoned Ben Hafner, his young domestic policy chief, to the Oval Office. Ben had been expecting the call.

"Sit down," Noland said as Ben closed the office door behind him. "I want to talk about Liesl."

"I know you do, sir."

"You do?"

"We have to be thinking the same thing, sir. Were they after you or Liesl?"

The two men looked at each other as if they'd just summoned a tempest and couldn't return it to its lair.

"Our FBI director, like most of the talking heads on television, believes that Al-Qaeda is probably behind this attack," Noland said.

"And you, sir?"

"Who can be sure? But the Russians are heavy on my mind."

Russians. In Ben's mind, there was no other explanation for the events on Monday. And now the president himself had said it. The face of the KGB threat this administration had confronted a year ago was leering at them again.

But the media had never uncovered that particular threat or what had really happened in the fall of 2011. All they'd reported was that Russian agents had recruited Ben's own senior aide, Ted Shadlaw, to supply them with unspecified information. The media never knew about the music code Liesl Bower uncovered that October, identifying a Russian mole in the Israeli Department of Defense. They never knew that a secret network of elite Kremlin insiders had plotted to assassinate their own president and seize power, determined to reclaim the might of the Soviet Union. Never knew that the Syrian president had also been marked for death. Never knew the Russian mole in Israel had falsified documents that would "prove" to the world that Israel had pulled the trigger on both presidents. The Russian plotters had calculated that in retaliation, the Arab world would have annihilated Israel while an outraged America turned its back on its Jewish ally.

Ben had known all these things. He and his longtime friend Liesl Bower—his sisterly confidante since Harvard—had ridden the tip of the spear into the heart of the conspiracy. He did it to protect her and the code she possessed, yes. But it was his beloved Israel that had been at greatest risk. And still was, he believed. He would do anything to save his ancestral homeland.

The president elaborated. "I believe it was both a vengeful attack on Liesl and a message to me—'Look how close we can get to you.'" He looked sternly at Ben. "But I'm more concerned for Liesl right now. I'm ordering a security team immediately installed around her."

Ben shook his head. "She won't have it. You know her. Besides, she's got one. Ava Mullins is down the street, every bit the CIA bulldog she ever was. Three big strapping men are in the house with Liesl, and Henry Bower is the toughest protector his daughter will ever have. He didn't get those scars charter fishing that old boat. The Mexican government will never know whose ashes they buried at sea, but it sure wasn't Henry's." Only the slightest grin made a brief appearance on Ben's blunt-featured face.

"Still, I'm asking Rick Salabane to gather security for her and intercede in a possible Russian threat," Noland said. "Again."

"Sir, Director Salabane is a lawman and the best there is. But he's got no bead on the foreign front."

"Which front do you mean, Ben?"

Ben glanced up, that old defensive knot in his belly tightening.

"Russia?" Noland asked. "Or Israel?"

Heat rose in Ben's face, and he hoped it didn't alter his practiced composure. Had he not proven his patriotism, his allegiance, time and again? Had he not single-handedly trapped Ted Shadlaw at the height of his treason against the U.S.? Why did the president keep digging into him? Looking for something?

Noland started to pace. "Ben, people a lot smarter than I am believe Russia is amassing an arsenal of persuasive weapons that have nothing to do with firepower. They're advancing along the path to a new world order, with Russia in control. And they'll do it largely without deploying the first tank or missile launcher." He stopped in front of his desk and sat on the edge, facing Ben. "Russia is trying to buy German power plants that also supply electricity to Central Europe, especially Hungary and Slovakia, which are of strategic interest to Russia. And as Germany phases out nuclear energy, it will rely more on natural gas from Russia. Think of the power Russia can wield with that development."

The president pondered his own soliloquy. "Right now," he continued, "Russia is sidling up next to every regime that's anti-American, especially in the Middle East. They want to halt our missile screen in Europe and cut off our supply line to Afghanistan. Beyond that, though, they'll seize every opportunity to exploit our ailing economy and make a move on U.S. interests wherever they can. This administration is fighting to regain our financial footing before that happens."

Ben jumped in. "But there's more going on than that."

"Much more," Noland said. He gazed into the presidential seal woven into the carpet before him. "It's almost amusing how clueless our leaders can be, including myself. When I first campaigned for this office, my fellow candidates and I waxed so authoritatively on the state of foreign affairs. We were statesmen commanding the stage during televised debates, trying to impress the American people with what we knew about the dynamics of national security and our intelligence agencies. And you know what? We didn't know squat. It wasn't until I took office that the people manning the front lines of our security forces sat me down and told me what was really going on. Things the public, even much of Congress, never knew about—the narrowly averted terror attacks and assassination attempts around the world, military stand-downs, diplomatic crises, deal brokering between countries. And especially our own global covert operations." He shook his head slowly. "Most alarming wake-up call I ever got."

Ben treaded carefully. "And now?"

"Our enemies are bolder. More inventive. They breached our tightest security on Monday, and they're going to do it again." He paused. "It's true, Ben. There's a red storm mounting."

Chapter 13

By late Thursday afternoon. Cass could stand it no longer. She had to get to the Southampton house and into her stepfather's study. She could think of nothing else, certainly not the row of black corn she was propping up for the third time in a week. No, her mind was far down Highway 27 east on Long Island to the cabinetry her stepfather had installed in the third-floor bedroom, which he had claimed as his private domain shortly after marrying Cass's mother. It had been Cass's summer-vacation bedroom until her sophomore year at NYU when her world suddenly teetered on its axis and sent her spilling into the unknown. It was then she had moved into the SoHo loft with no plans for the rest of her life.

That morning, she'd driven to work and claimed the parking privilege she often denied herself. How many stagehands, which she considered herself as much as a set designer, owned two Manhattan parking garages? She wanted nothing to do with the elitism her father had imposed on her. But this morning she needed quick access to her car. The Volvo wagon she'd bought used a few years ago waited in her reserved spot in this high-rise, off-Broadway garage.

She had just unlocked the door when her phone rang. "I'm coming with you," Jordan announced. Cass had finally told him of her meeting with Hans at the diner, of his warnings. She'd also shared her suspicions of Hans and her intention to search his study.

"No, I don't want you to come. I'm leaving now."

"But what if he's there?"

"I just spoke to Mom. They're at home. No plans for the beach."

"Well, go ahead. I'll meet you there."

"No, Jordan."

"Hey, look. Don't forget whose license plate and apartment that woman tracked down. So I'm not exactly incidental to whatever this is. You recruited me, and I intend on serving my time."

Something about that pinched her. Is that all he was doing? Serving time.

"You there?" he asked.

She sighed with emphasis. "Okay, Jordan. If you feel it's your *duty*."

A pause. "I guess I sent a wrong signal. Hopefully, you know better."

No, I don't, Cass thought. *But it doesn't matter. If there's more to us than friendship, I'm not ready for it. Probably never will be.* She settled into the driver's seat and closed the door.

"I'll take your silence as a go-ahead," he continued, "but I'll have to wait until my manager gets back from the dentist."

She fumbled with the seat belt. "All right, here's the address—"

"I know where it is."

Cass halted her efforts to latch the seat belt one-handedly. "You do?"

"Yeah. A buddy from college drove me by the place once."

"Why?"

Silence. Then, "Because that's what you do when you have a schoolboy crush on a girl."

That left Cass speechless. They'd just been lab partners. When had the crush part happened? Still, she didn't have the time or inclination to ponder it at that moment, though something inside yearned to. "I don't know what to say about that, Jordan."

"Don't need to say anything." His tone shifted. "I'll see you soon. And I assume you're spending the night."

"Yeah. I'm taking the day off tomorrow."

"Well, I'll probably come right back."

"No need to. You can stay in the garage apartment." She started the engine, its growl a rumbling echo in the garage.

"We'll see. Drive carefully."

Cass knew he deserved better than she'd just given him.

A leaden sky hovered low over Cass as she drove the well-grooved route along the south fork of Long Island. In spite of the temperature, she cracked the window enough to let in a torrent of air, swollen with the bloom of memories. Many years ago, with the top down on her butter yellow Volkswagen Beetle, she had ferried high school friends from Manhattan to the beach house she most regarded as home. Though her schooldays were contained by the city, weekends and summers at the old house were like throwing back the shutters on her life and letting the salty currents whisk her back to her true self.

Her mind caught a glimpse of one of those long-ago friends, and the memories withered into ashes. The impish face framed by long, wavy hair all but stared at Cass from the pavement ahead. Rachel Norman had been a transplant from the mountains of Vermont and struggled to citify herself in the mold of the savvy Cass Rodino. Shy and insecure, especially about her rounded figure, Rachel had tried to emulate Cass and her confident spirit, her steely self-reliance.

In those days, Rachel was a frequent guest at the beach house. Though she didn't swim, she trusted Cass and her seamanship enough to don a life vest and sail as far offshore as Cass chose to take them.

As she drove, Cass remembered the many parties they'd attended where the guys had pursued Cass and not Rachel, where some of Cass's wealthy Southampton friends had questioned why she always brought her "boring little hick friend" along. That's when Cass began to retreat from those she finally recognized as socially corrupt, their unworthiness lurking just beneath the thinnest gold-leaf veneer of privilege.

The summer after high school graduation, Cass took Rachel to one more party on the island. That's when Rachel met Adam Rinehart. A soccer player from New Jersey, he and his parents had rented a house in Southampton for the summer. Though handsome and pleasant enough to talk to, he strode hesitantly into the pecking order of the local teen society. In hindsight, Cass could see that Adam had found a likewise companion in Rachel, another newcomer the island insiders had snubbed. Soon, though, Rachel and Adam's relationship grew well beyond commiseration. Cass had never seen Rachel so vivacious and animated as when Adam was at her side—almost constantly that summer. Even through their freshman year at NYU, Rachel and Adam continued to date. Near the end of the following summer, though, their relationship ended.

Cass railed against the memory. She couldn't endure it any longer. At the next exit off Highway 27, she pulled into a gas station and got out, letting the blast of air with its frozen fingers slap at her face. *Go ahead*, she thought. *I deserve it.* Then before she slid into the familiar pit again, she threw on her trusted armor and lumbered off in a different mental direction. She would focus on one thing only—Hans's study.

Back on the highway, she sped toward Southampton as the sun waned. Soon, she turned south toward the ocean and the storied lanes of reclusive mansions hidden from public view behind their tall privet hedges, so precisely clipped and postured. Another time and she would tick off the celebrity names attached to the homes she now passed. But not today.

Soon, she came to a house whose weathered cedar-shake walls stood beneath a network of gables, each one rising higher than the next, and pulled into the circular driveway. Well past its prime, its pedigree expired, the house was smaller and plainer than many of its neighbors. Its grounds, though, ran longer and broader than most. As Cass gazed over the rambling lawns, she heard Gerald O'Hara tell his tempestuous daughter, "It's the land, Katie Scarlett. Land is the only thing in the world worth workin' for, worth fightin' for, worth dyin' for, because it's the only thing that lasts." Was that true? Was there nothing more enduring, more constant than this patch of sandy ground? As much as she loved this place, was there nothing more?

She looked out at the grass beneath its salty crust, the color of harvest wheat. The cedars hugging the house fairly bowed their evergreen torsos toward her in familiar greeting. Beyond the house lay the pewter slate of the ocean, its waves relentless, its tides ever changing and never changing. They would never let her forget. Never stop echoing her cries. Had the one who ruled the tides been there that night? Would he ever forgive her?

There was no time to linger on things she couldn't know. She got out of the car and looked toward the top floor of the house. There were other things she intended to know soon.

She unlocked the front door and stepped into the foyer, which instantly wrapped her in its musty embrace. It wasn't a grande dame foyer, more like a kooky old aunt. It, like the living room beyond, was randomly clad in local art—paintings, tapestries, sculpture in no particular era or motif. There were no fine Persian rugs but mats of cotton, hand-dyed in brilliant colors and woven by a Native American artisan in Montauk—the colorful, destination village at the tip of Long Island.

This house had always been the antithesis of the Upper East Side apartment where she'd grown up. Though her parents had lavished their town home with all the spoils of material privilege, they had favored a hair-down, unimposing profile for their retreat by the sea.

Cass dropped her bag and keys on an antique colonial sideboard and turned toward the wall of windows that joined the house to the dunes and water beyond. She paused long enough to drink in the misty blue-grays layered from the back deck to the horizon, then headed for the stairs.

When the room atop the house had been hers, the door to the hall had no lock. For some reason, though, the builder had installed one on the door opening to the small balcony overlooking the beach. When Hans moved into the room, he installed a lock on the hallway door. "I hope it doesn't offend you," he'd told Cass and her mother. "I must keep my clients' records secure and confidential at all times. I hope you understand."

What Cass didn't understand was why her mother didn't have a key to the room. "Oh, you know how fastidious and tight-lipped he is about his work," Jilly Kluen had reasoned. "He won't even let the maids in to clean unless he's in the room the whole time. Then he locks up as soon as they leave. Maybe he's a little overly cautious, but it's his business." It was then she casually mentioned that he hadn't bothered to change out the old lock on the door to the third-floor balcony. And Cass still had a key.

He must have thought the balcony door was unreachable, Cass thought as she climbed the stairs, a smirk on her lips. It pleased her to know that something about the house was still within her control. She first would check the hall door on the remote chance it was unlocked before taking the strenuous route into the room. What Hans hadn't realized was that before his arrival, the balcony door to the room had been very accessible to an athletic young teenager wanting to slip in and out of the house undetected on warm summer nights. Her parents had forbidden her to attend the late-night teen parties on the beach for the very reasons Cass was determined to go. She hadn't forgotten how she did that.

To avoid the creaking stairs, she'd kept a rope ladder in a box of old clothes in her closet. Anchoring it securely to the balcony railing, she would drop it over one side close to the house. After descending, she'd snug the dangling ladder to the house, out of sight—at least to anyone not looking for it, especially in the dark of night. It had always amazed her that no one had ever spotted the camouflaged tieback grips she'd fashioned to secure her telltale escape route. But of course, an aspiring set designer should have accomplished no less. When she would return in the early morning hours, she'd unleash the ladder, climb back up, reel it in, and return it to its hiding place in the closet.

Finding the hall door to the room locked, Cass regretted there was no more dangling rope ladder still in place. So she headed for the garage and the extension ladder no one but the occasional handyman used. It was a heavy and unwieldy thing, impossible for anyone walking the beach not to spot. Struggling to lift the gangly ladder from its wall mounts, she imagined how easily Jordan might do it. As if on cue, the clattering whine of the little Honda suddenly rose above the crash of ocean waves. An involuntary smile sprang to Cass's lips, and she found herself hurrying to greet him, surprised he'd arrived so soon—surprised at how glad she was.

As she rounded the side of the garage, she saw him climb from the car and visually inspect the front of the house. When he saw her, he lifted a hand in greeting. She moved purposefully toward him, though her emotions pinged in disparate directions. She was glad he was here, yet resistant to what might rise between them. Confident of the solitary, work-laden lifestyle she'd chosen for herself, yet fearful of what lay ahead. She swept all of it into that crowded corner of her mind where the troubling things lived.

"You're just in time," she said with a too-big smile. "There's a ridiculously long ladder in the garage we need to move to the back."

"We?" He smirked. "I know which one of us that means."

"Yeah, well, you big guys got that way for good reason, I guess. Moving heavy stuff must be your calling."

"Really? And all this time I thought it was pushing smelly feet into overpriced shoes."

Another time and Cass would have bantered with him, but too much pressed against the moment.

It didn't take long for Jordan to plant the fully extended ladder against the back of the balcony, making sure it was steady on its metal feet. "You've got the key, right?" he checked.

"In my pocket." She'd insisted on scaling the ladder herself.

After an easy ascent, she unlocked the outside door to the study, the inside dead-bolted door to the hall, then the ground-level Dutch door to the back porch. She waited for Jordan to return the ladder to the garage, then led him back to the study.

They surveyed the room's notable scarcity. "Doesn't seem to be much business going on here," Jordan said. "I never saw such empty desktops."

Cass had rarely glimpsed the inside of the room since Hans had claimed it three years ago, replacing her white, cottage-style bedroom furniture with what she now saw. Everything was dark, modern, angular, with lots of chrome. Only a lamp and pencil cup rested on one desk and absolutely nothing on an identical desk across the room. A long, desk-high cabinet ran the length of one wall with a series of doors beneath.

Trying each door, Jordan shook his head. "I think your snooping may have hit a wall." He looked about the room. "Unless Hans has hidden a key to these locked cabinets somewhere."

But Cass had already spotted something she didn't expect to find—her father's old armoire from her parents' bedroom. It was where he'd kept his private stash of chocolates inside a safe he'd had built into the antique piece for storing cash and jewelry, which meant less to young Cass than the candy. She had long ago discovered that there was a key to override the combination lock on the safe, and where that key was kept.

Finding the safe locked as expected, she headed for the open hallway door. "I'll be right back."

Jordan examined that door. "Who locks up a room in his own house and gives nobody the key?" he asked as Cass entered the hall.

"It's not his house," she said over her shoulder. "It's mine."

"Is there anything your father didn't give you?" he called after her.

She stopped short and looked back. "Yeah. A second thought."

Jordan frowned at her. "He thought enough to leave you some prime real estate and a bulging stock portfolio."

From a few steps down, she gazed up into Jordan's wide-open eyes that so often signaled his struggle to understand her, like now. "That's what he left his only heir. It just happened to be me."

On the second floor, she headed for her mother's bedroom and the dressing table where Cass had watched her apply makeup and jewelry before yet another glittering house party in the Hamptons. Cass also remembered exploring the drawers in that old table one evening after her parents had left and stumbling upon the key. Now, she wondered at her own guile and how little it had troubled her through the years. Until that one irreversible moment.

She flung open the second drawer on the left, dug to the bottom, and uncovered the old rhinestone lipstick holder. The key to the safe was still inside. She marveled at how many times she'd stolen into this drawer, then into the armoire safe without detection, relishing the chocolaty and guilt-less reward. She learned never to take enough to trigger her dad's suspicion. She hoped nothing she did today would invite the same from his successor.

Returning to the third floor, Cass went straight to the armoire. "Let's see what old times' sake is good for," she said without explanation. The key turned as easily as ever. She rotated the knob and pulled open the door.

Jordan issued a shrill whistle. "Would you look at that!" The safe was stuffed with stacks of crisp one-hundred-dollar bills.

"But no chocolate," Cass mused aloud.

"No what?" Jordan asked, not tearing his eyes from the cash.

She would explain later. Right now, she gently probed between the bundles of money, having no idea what she'd find. But nothing about the past week had been predictable.

Seconds later, she hit on something that felt different from cold cash. At the back of the safe, her hand closed around a flat, velvet case. Jewelry, she guessed with little enthusiasm. That wasn't what she'd come for. Carefully, she retrieved the bracelet-size case and opened it. Jordan reacted first.

"Someone has to be hiding in here with a movie camera. This is too good." He stared into the case. "You found the key to the key. And I'll just bet this shiny new one opens all those locked cabinets."

Cass wasted no time in testing that theory. Moments later, all five cabinet doors stood open wide. Inside each one was a row of hanging files.

"Okay, so what are we looking for?" Jordan asked.

Only then did Cass feel the gnaw of guilt. She wasn't a ten-year-old on a quest for forbidden chocolate. This was a man's business, his livelihood, his reputation. And more critically, her mother's security. Still, she had to reckon with suspicion.

"Anything that throws a red flag to you," she answered. "Maybe something related to that pair in the UN apartment."

For hours they sorted carefully through files they didn't understand, neither one versed in the intimidating lexicon of high finance. Jordan, too, had inherited his entry into the business world. But unlike Cass, who never dallied there longer than it took to sign whatever her financial advisor occasionally urged her to, Jordan had acquired just enough spreadsheet acumen to run his family's shoe store, one of Manhattan's oldest.

Jordan closed one cabinet and opened another, lifting the first file he came to and a large document tube lying next to the file. In a chair in front of the open cabinet, he quickly flipped through an assortment of tourist brochures and Internet printouts on historic American landmarks. "Well, this is different."

"What is?" Cass mumbled. She was sitting on the floor, her head bent over yet another client file on assets, stocks, and trust funds. Things that were none of her business, and certainly not Jordan's. Why had she let him come? She was almost queasy with guilt over her intrusion into Hans's privacy, beginning to believe she'd let her imagination run amok.

"Nothing financial," Jordan answered. "Just a bunch of travel stuff on"—he waved random pieces from the file one by one—"Ellis Island, steamboats on the Mississippi, an aerial view of a dam." He put down the file and picked up the document tube, removing its scrolled contents. "Hey, look at this," he said, holding up the unrolled sheets. "Why would he have blueprints for the U.S. Supreme Court Building?"

Cass glanced over her shoulder. "Oh, he's always been a history and architecture buff. He and Mom travel a lot. She says he likes to explore places on his own, though. So they go their separate ways and meet for dinner. Strange, I think." She gazed into space and thought about that a moment, then continued her tedious survey of the cabinets, glancing occasionally at Jordan.

He replaced the file and the blueprints tube, then opened a large brown envelope in the next file. After a few moments, he said, "Better come look at this."

"Wait. I'm almost—"

"No, you need to look at it now."

She turned quickly toward him. The set of his face was different. He didn't say anything more as he picked up the contents of the envelope and held them out to her.

"What is it?"

"Just read," he said without taking his eyes off her.

She took the handful of pages, then placed them in her lap. The first thing she picked up was a yellowed *New York Times* article on the 1996 killing of Schell Devoe, a Harvard music professor. He'd been the victim of an armed robbery in his home, the article said. Cass picked up another clipping from about the same time. Displayed prominently in the article was a photograph of Liesl Bower, identified as Devoe's protégé and sole witness to the murder. It was reported that the young student couldn't identify the assailant, whose head was covered by a ski mask. Otherwise, the writer had suggested, the gunman would probably have killed her, too.

Cass was taken aback by the coincidence. She'd just mentioned this to Jordan at the inauguration on Monday, though she hadn't known the details of the story. So this was it. But why was Hans interested enough to save the news clippings? Cass glanced up at Jordan, her eyes squinted in confusion.

"Keep going," he instructed evenly.

She gazed curiously at him, surprised at how unreadable he was at this moment. Her focus shifted back to the pages in her lap. Next in the stack was a small clipping from the *Boston Herald* reporting the death of Devoe's widow. *The same thing again. What's this all about?* Cass read that the woman had suddenly left her husband prior to his death and sort of disappeared into Canada, her whereabouts unknown until her death.

Cass stared at the newsprint, growing more intrigued. *That's what this is. Hans thought it was a good story, too. That's all.*

Then she picked up the next item. Her hands began to tremble. It was a diagram of the inaugural platform.

It wasn't the detailed seating arrangement of the dignitaries, the marked spot where President Noland would be sworn into his second term of office, nor the designated Secret Service positions on and around the platform that struck hardest at Cass. It was what someone had penciled over the diagram. Someone had clearly marked the position of the piano on the upper tier of the platform, the exact time Liesl Bower was scheduled to perform, and a series of lines emanating like a sunburst from the piano. Penciled over that were two words, *TIMED BLAST.*

All sense of space disappeared, and Cass felt herself falling backward into an abyss. Until someone's arms caught her and held her close. "Cass!"

Jordan? She heard his voice in her ear. He was cradling her like an injured child. When her head cleared, though, she pulled away from him. When she looked up and saw the fright in his face, saw him reach for her again, she could bear no more. No one could ever make the grotesque things right. No one ever had.

She shot to her feet, grabbed her jacket, and ran from the room, pounding the worn treads of the stairs to the bottom landing. Jordan followed, but she had wound her way through the house and fled through the back door before he could reach her.

Chapter 14

Cass half ran, half stumbled into the back yard and across the withered grass to the dunes. She stopped long enough to look back and see Jordan emerge from the house, calling to her in a voice she'd not heard before. His soothing baritone now shrieking her name, imploring her to stop. But she couldn't. What had seized her in the study now swung her around and pushed her roughly down the weathered planks that stepped loosely over the dunes.

When she reached the beach, she paused long enough to confront the scolding surf and its unrelenting echo. Then she turned to the old shed, where she and her young friends used to throw back the latch and drag the Hobie Cat from its sandy mooring. In the affected heave-ho cadence of Volga boatmen, the giggling teens would haul the small vessel across the beach and into the breakers, unfurling its sail like a victory flag. They would hop aboard and fling themselves at the Atlantic, feeling it draw them to its risky playground. They feared nothing.

"Cass, wait!"

Feeling his eyes boring into her back, Cass turned east and sprinted down the night-shrouded beach only faintly lit by a lopsided moon. She ran full stride for as long as it took to reach the hurting place. Like an animal that hungrily gnaws its wounds, Cass had returned many times to the spot, to scrape its salt deep into the grain of her sinful flesh. *That's what it was*, she thought as she ran. Sin. The church word that never meant much. Not until it meant everything that she was.

And now, sin raged again. Hans had brought it back home, if it had ever left. Whatever he had done, whatever his connection to that monstrous assault on the steps of the Capitol, it would pull her mother into the abyss, too. She couldn't let that happen. She didn't care what happened to Hans. If he'd visited the shame of a nation upon them, he deserved whatever he got. But not her mother. Cass would stop him. And the others. *You don't know who you're messing with.*

"But I'll find out!" she cried as she ran into the biting wind.

Then something else threw its weight at her. The news clippings, the story, the piano and its bomb. With all certainty, she knew the timed blast was meant for Liesl Bower.

Cass was almost there now. Near the inlet, she slowed and angled toward the open water, hugging her jacket close to her body and feeling her inner garments sponge the sweat trickling down her. She pulled the hood over her damp hair and stood before the filmy curtain of black over the horizon.

She looked toward the inlet waters running swift with the tide. Nearby, a house rose behind the dunes, a security light in its back yard casting sparkles of light over the tumbling currents. She could almost see the fire her friends had built on a night like many others. Just another forbidden, late-night gathering on the beach with friends, but this time, Rachel wasn't there. She and Adam had broken up, and Cass was glad, for right and wrong reasons. She'd caught Adam flirting with other girls behind Rachel's back, though Rachel excused him for it when Cass regretfully reported her observations. "Oh, he's just full of himself, that's all," Rachel once said. "He just wants to make friends with everybody."

Soon, though, it was obvious to all but Rachel that Adam had lost interest in the "homespun mountain kid," as the sleeker city girls had tagged her.

But something else had been working on Cass, something that had made her ashamed, as few things had. As much as she'd resisted it, she, too, had fallen for the handsome soccer player, even catching his eye a few times in unguarded moments of mutual admiration.

The day Rachel finally announced that she and Adam had permanently parted ways, Cass knew it was a unilateral decision. Rachel's tears had told her so, though her words sought to convince Cass that it was for the best. "I would only hold him back," Rachel had said. "He's way too sophisticated and smart for such a homespun twit as me." She'd caught Cass's raised eyebrows. "What? You didn't think I knew what they called me?"

A month later, at the inlet campfire, Cass had found herself on a blanket next to Adam. After several bottles of wine had been repeatedly passed around the circle, he suggested they leave the others and move off down the beach alone. The wine, the lie-down music from someone's guitar, the lulling ebb and flow of the waves answered for her. With the few sober cells struggling for traction in her brain, she told herself that Rachel was through with him and wouldn't mind. Besides, he was bad for Rachel. And for Cass?

Minutes later, it didn't matter to her. She had slipped into his heated embrace and met his every move with her own willing and inebriated body.

The following morning, she was so repulsed by her actions, she wouldn't even take a phone call from Rachel. Nor would she take the insistent calls from Adam, who'd claimed he was crazy about her. She didn't leave the house for days, even once rebuffing him at the door and telling him never to return.

When her sophomore-year classes at NYU began a few weeks later, Cass steered clear of Rachel and Adam, whom she never saw together. Though Adam continually texted Cass, declaring his affections for her and begging her to see him, she never responded—not even the day she accidentally ran headlong into him in a hallway and he seized the moment to wrap his arms tightly around her, causing her to squirm free of him and flee, issuing dire warnings should he ever try that again.

Though Rachel pleaded for Cass to tell her why she'd withdrawn from their friendship, and though Rachel's wrenching hurt was almost more than Cass could bear, she remained aloof from everyone except her biology lab partner. There was no escaping the prevailing presence of Jordan Winslow.

One day after classes, Cass was headed for the subway when she noticed Rachel and Adam sitting on a bench in a small park, facing away from her. She hung back and watched them. Rachel appeared to be crying, and Adam was trying to console her. At one point, he put his arm around her and tried to pull her to him, but she shoved him away and jumped up. Cass couldn't hear her words, but she sensed their hurt. On the way home, she replayed the scene in her mind, trying to understand what might have happened. Then the terrifying question arose. Did Rachel know?

Two weeks later, Cass and her parents had just arrived at the beach house for one last warm weekend when Rachel called. "Your housekeeper told me you were at the beach, Cass. Please let me come see you today. I have something very important to tell you." The voice was light and steady. Cass thought it held a ring of self-assurance she'd not heard before. She couldn't imagine the transition from Rachel's distress in the park to the voice Cass had just heard. With a twinge of hope for reconciliation, she invited Rachel to come and stay the weekend.

Late that afternoon, Cass heard the rumble of Rachel's Jeep in the driveway and went to the door. The familiar face behind the steering wheel was a welcome sight. Cass had missed her old friend but didn't realize how much until that moment. She was suddenly buoyant over Rachel's arrival, enough to momentarily subdue the guilt. Yes, Cass had slept with the man her best friend loved. Nothing would ever change that. But as Rachel climbed from the car and raised a friendly wave, Cass could have burst with joy.

Surely Rachel didn't know.

Cass met her at the car, opening her arms for the usual quick hug and release. Only this time, Rachel clung tighter and longer, the scent of her hair sweet and warm against Cass's cheek, the scent of a beloved sister. Cass vowed never to part ways with her again. When they released each other, Cass led the way to the front door.

"Oh, let's walk around back first, Cass," Rachel suggested. "Maybe we could sit on the back porch awhile before going in."

"Sure," Cass said, eyeing her closely. Then she remembered the important news Rachel had mentioned. "You're being very secretive about something," she teased.

A timid smile curled at Rachel's mouth as she slid a glance toward Cass, but she said nothing. When they reached the back lawn that fell gently toward the beach, Rachel stopped and gazed at the sea. In the slant of afternoon rays, the waters were like agate, their strata of crystal blues and greens flicked with sunset gold. Cass, too, paused to admire what she often took for granted.

"Let's go out there, Cass."

Cass turned to her in surprise. "Now? It's getting late."

But Rachel persisted. "One more ride on the Hobie Cat before winter," she said, her voice calm and persuasive.

"Okay. Be spontaneous, right?" And suddenly the idea appealed to Cass, too. "We'll have to hurry, though. Mom and Dad will be back from shopping in a couple of hours. I'm sure they wouldn't approve."

From inside the shed where they stored the boat, Cass removed two life jackets from the wall hooks and handed one to Rachel. "Your assignment this winter, Rachel, is to learn how to swim at the NYU pool. No more excuses. You can't even dog paddle."

"Okay, I'll do that," Rachel agreed, strapping herself into the bulky vest, then removing her shoes. She was wearing knee-length leggings and a long, plain sweatshirt.

"You did bring other clothes, I hope." Cass looked down at her own cutoff jeans and T-shirt, which she'd often sailed in. Then she pulled two pairs of gloves for handling the lines, something Rachel had always helped with.

"You are going to stay over, aren't you?" Cass added.

"Sure. I'd like that."

The two slid the lightweight vessel from the shed, across the beach, and down to the water. "This will be easy," Cass said brightly. "The waves are tame today." She glanced up at the coral stripes on the sail. "Not much wind, though. We might not get far."

"Far enough, I'm sure," Rachel said. She looked to the west and shielded her eyes from the head-on rays of the setting sun. "It's so pretty, isn't it?"

But Cass was too busy with the launch to notice or respond. She positioned the twin-hull boat into the wind and announced, "Ready to go."

Both girls hopped onto the trampoline deck and grabbed the lines. Clearing the last breaker, they drifted into deeper water, and Cass locked the rudders in place. Her hand on the tiller, she caught a draft and tacked into it. But the wind kept teasing them, rushing at them from different directions, taunting them, and making Cass work for distance.

Soon, though, they locked into a steady current of air and let it carry them into the far reaches of sapphire waters. Her hair twisted into a large clip, her feet tucked beneath the hiking strap, Rachel leaned backward over the edge of the trampoline deck, pulling against one of the sail sheets for support. She clearly relished the ride.

Cass watched her. This wasn't the girl she'd seen in the park with Adam. Cass was anxious to know the important news, but she would have to wait.

An hour later, as the colors began to bleed from the sky, Cass announced it was time to head back. "It'll be dark soon."

"We can't go yet!" Rachel blurted. "I mean . . . I need to talk to you." She glanced toward shore and a few front-row estates. "It's more private out here."

Cass felt the first twinge of unease. And there clearly in the green eyes before her was something out of sync with the light-hearted mood of the afternoon. At least that's how she had perceived their impromptu little voyage. What had just happened?

"Okay, Rachel." She steered the boat straight into the wind, causing the sails to go limp and slowing them to a conversational speed, if that's what Rachel wanted.

Soon, the little boat settled into a peaceful drift, and Rachel fired her first volley. "I'm pregnant."

The words stung like a blast of salt spray, and Cass shuddered, mute with shock.

Rachel's mouth twisted into something Cass hadn't seen on her before.

A snarl. Something raw, as if a mask had suddenly dropped from her face revealing a terrible truth. "It's Adam's child, Cass. I wanted you to know that."

It took Cass just one excruciating instant to read the meaning in her face. *She knows!*

Rachel nodded slowly as if confirming it. "You should be careful."

An involuntary gasp escaped Cass and she struggled for words. "I . . . oh, Rachel, I never meant to—"

"Of course you did."

"No!"

"You set your sights on him long before we broke up."

"No! No! I didn't!"

Rachel raised a quieting hand. "Stop it! I didn't come here for this."

Cass shook violently and had to grab the tiller with both hands to steady herself.

"I discovered I was pregnant after we broke up." Rachel looked away and closed her eyes. "I didn't tell anyone but Adam." She squeezed tears from her eyes and let them run at will down her cheeks. "He was so angry at first. He cursed at me. I didn't hear from him for days." She opened her eyes, wiped them, and turned a suddenly wistful expression on Cass.

"And then, he came to see me. He said he had warmed to the idea of having a family. He promised he'd marry me. That everything would be all right. I was ecstatic." Then the face contorted with the next words. "But one night on a beach, Adam forgot all about that promise . . . and me."

Cass could hardly breathe.

"Then he told me he couldn't possibly marry me . . . when he was in love with Cass Rodino."

A whimper slipped from Cass and she clamped both hands hard against her mouth, against the cry rising inside. And then the words slipped through. "Rachel, I was drunk! I didn't know what I was doing. I hardly knew who I was doing it with. Please understand. Please!"

But Rachel acted as if she didn't hear. "I can't tell my parents. It would kill them." She swiped a strand of wet hair roughly from her face. "No, I can never tell them."

"Rachel, listen to me! I'll take care of you! We'll go somewhere together until the baby is born. Where no one knows us. I can get the money. It'll be okay, I promise."

The green eyes held Cass with contempt. "And that would make you feel better, wouldn't it?"

A sudden wind broadsided the sails and tipped the girls toward each other. Cass grabbed at Rachel to keep her from falling until the boat was turned back into the wind. Rachel looked down at Cass's grip on her arm. "I always thought you were the strong one, the one who always knew the best thing to do." She looked at Cass distantly, a feverish smile stretching her lips. "But now it's me. Now *I* know what's best."

Cass searched the face, the eyes so strangely dim.

Rachel lifted a hand to her hair and removed the clip, letting the shining tresses unfurl in the wind. "There's always a way out, isn't there?" she asked, drawing her feet from under the strap.

"Of course there is!" Cass wailed, hope rising inside her. "You can move in with me and we'll do this together. We'll get you to a doctor, and we'll—"

Rachel suddenly reached to touch Cass's hand, halting her words. "It's okay," she said softly, then slid backward into the water.

"Rachel!" Cass lunged across the trampoline.

But it took only seconds for Rachel to release herself from the vest and begin her descent. Almost as if she'd rehearsed it.

Cass stripped off her own vest and dove in, stroking frantically after Rachel. But the clarity of the afternoon waters had already yielded to the coming night. The deeper Cass plunged, the blinder her chase. The more she thrashed downward, the quicker her breath escaped. Through the sightless waters she grabbed aimlessly for a head of chestnut hair, willing her fingers to lock into its tangled web and find the body beneath still pulsing warm blood. *God, help me!* she screamed inside her skull.

When the searing began in her lungs, Cass knew she would have to choose. Go with Rachel? Accept the fate Cass had brought down on them both? Or go back . . . and pretend to live. Decide quickly! There's no more time!

But then the waters grew so cool. So peaceful. Cass felt them swirl gently around her, pulling her into their embrace, her arms floating up to meet them. Had she made her choice?

No! I can't do this!

Suddenly, her body convulsed. Her legs scissored violently, thrusting her upward.

Exhaling her last breath, her lungs screaming for air, she split the surface and instantly dragged oxygen into her body, forcing the cold knife of air to pierce her.

She could do only one thing now. Scream. Hysterical screams, as if they would raise Rachel from the depths.

Why did she do it? God, why?

Only when her voice failed and the screams died did she observe her surroundings. The capsized boat floated in the near distance, toward the inlet. Two orange life vests floundered in the swells. Could she make it to either? Exhaustion displaced the adrenaline that had fueled her manic dive. Hysteria paralyzed her mind, her limbs. Darkness fell upon her, and she wallowed into a half-conscious float, face up.

Then a sound. What was it? A voice. She managed to raise her head. There! A light coming from shore, bobbing in the waves.

"Cass!"

A familiar voice. *Dad?*

"Grab the ring!"

Just then, something white sailed toward her, and she lifted one limp arm toward it. Missed it. Missed it again.

Then a splash. A man's arms beneath her, lifting. Her dad's voice in her ear. It was over.

Now, as her body slumped against the dune and her sights fastened on that place where the sea had consumed a broken young woman, Cass mourned as if the eight years since that day had never passed. As if she'd never been plucked from the dying waters. *God, why didn't you let me go, too? And why do I keep talking to you as if you're here?*

Cass pulled her knees to her chin and began to rock herself, wishing some kind of oblivion to catch with the cadence of her motion and relieve her pain. Then she stopped. A voice. A light coming toward her. Just like that night.

And again, a voice yanked her from the madness of her grief, snatched her from the brink. "Cass, where are you?"

Jordan! Something hot and smothering lifted from her. She stood and faced the light beam strafing the sand, searching for her. No, she was not going to drown. Another man's arms were about to lift her again. *Jordan, you came for me!*

She ran headlong for him, calling his name, and barely slowing when she reached him. As he opened his arms to her, she leapt at him and laid her head against his broad chest. There were no words. They just clung silently to each other with the surf rolling gently toward them. Cass inhaled the warmth of him and felt herself go limp in his arms.

When she finally pulled away and found her footing on the sand, she looked up at him through the blur of tears. "I'm sorry," she whispered. "I don't know what—"

He ended her words with a finger to her lips, then bent and kissed them gently. When he pulled away, she reached with both arms around his neck and drew him to her again, this time kissing him back with an intensity she didn't understand. She could only lose herself in it, with only the slightest suspicion that it was her temporary escape from torment. But if that's what it was, and nothing more, she would not hurt another soul with her rash and reckless ways. She broke away from him, her guard back and firmly in place.

"Whoa," he said, letting her go. "What just happened?"

She looked sadly at him. "Something that shouldn't have, Jordan. I'm sorry I did that to you."

"Well, I'm not." He grinned down at her. "Want to do it again?" He reached for her.

But she stepped back and laughed.

There in the hurting place, she laughed. Something immovable inside her had just yielded. To Jordan's touch. She looked into the winsome face of this man who had no idea what happened off this beach eight years ago. Someday, she would tell him.

But now, she must leave one horror buried while she unearthed another.

"Jordan, I can't explain what just happened. Let's just—"

"Let's just admit that there's more to us than friendship, and that in our own good time, we'll discover what it is. Is that what you were about to say?"

She nodded slowly. "I truly don't deserve you."

He shrugged. "Probably not. But you're stuck with me. Especially since we're guilty of breaking and entering together." His smiling eyes turned serious. "And since we just uncovered the secret life of Hans Kluen."

Cass zipped her jacket to her chin and shoved her hands in her pockets. "There's only one thing I'm going to do about that right now. I have to warn Liesl Bower."

Chapter 15

A cheerful cerulean sky contradicted the dread Ben Hafner felt as he paced beside Annapolis Harbor that Friday morning. No matter the direction he pounded the splintered boards of the wharf, his line of sight never veered from the entrance to the harbor.

Jeremy Rubin had once again slipped through the security grid to enter U.S. waters, this time inside his own stateroom aboard a sailing vessel of Bermuda registry. Its sails down, the sleek boat finally motored through the turn at the mouth of the Severn River, past the U.S. Naval Academy, and into Spa Creek. Plying the harbor's brisk chop with the grace of a dolphin, the boat finally eased into a slip a short distance from Ben.

No sooner had the boat's crew secured its lines to the dock than the slight figure of a man in a puffy black jacket and knit cap quickly disembarked. He stopped to locate Ben's position, then headed straight for him.

Ben didn't move from his post beside a metal warehouse that leaned precariously toward the water. His hood snug over his head, sunglasses in place, he scanned the area continuously as his brother-in-law walked over to join him. Ben thought it a confident swagger.

Moments later, the two left the harbor in a small sedan, Ben driving, his eyes roving to and from the rearview mirror. There was too much at stake to be careless.

"You're looking well fed, brother," Jeremy snickered, as Ben headed away from town.

"I'm not your brother. Not even your friend. And if I had to live my life as a fugitive outrunning authorities over half the world, I might be as scrawny as you."

Jeremy sniffed derisively. "Oh yeah, this is going to be fun." He looked out the window as if composing what he would say next. Then he turned full-body in his seat to face Ben, who kept his eyes on the winding country road ahead. "Look, we'd better come to some kind of truce because I'm going to be your handler for a long time to come, and there's not much you can do about it. Moscow chose me for obvious reasons, and if you're coming in with us, it's healthier for you and me both if we demonstrate a united front. Kind of like old times in Boston, you know."

Ben glimpsed the conspiratorial smirk on Jeremy's face. "The only thing that's ever united us was Anna."

Jeremy turned to watch the road. "How is my lily-white sister?"

Ben threw a dagger glance at him. "The one whose life you would sell to the highest bidder? Whose husband you tried to disgrace by feeding his past dirt to a traitorous White House aide? That sister?"

"I told you, that wasn't me. I don't know who sent all that stuff to Ted Shadlaw."

"Obviously someone who didn't know I'd already told the president all about my brief tenure with the Boston Bolsheviks. Someone like my clueless brother-in-law, who, by the way, would be the only one who could have supplied the incriminating shot of you and me on that paramilitary charade. Only try to explain to the FBI that the automatic weapon was just a prop."

"That wasn't me, either." Jeremy began to fume. "You don't know what it's like! What they're like! They get their hands on you, on everything you own—including your family photographs! They own all of you."

"Is that why you abandoned your wife? They made you? Or did you love your freedom more?" Ben knew he'd better back off, reminding himself why he was there.

Jeremy ignored the taunts. "Boston was like nursery school. The Boston

Bolsheviks. What a laugh. Just a bunch of Harvard brats in diapers throwing rocks and breaking a few windows. But even then, I did it because I thought I was right and the establishment was wrong. And they *were* wrong!"

"So you turned against your own country and ran off to join the world's brotherhood of misfits, wherever you could find them."

Jeremy's eyes glazed. "It was so good for a while. I belonged. In Paris, London, Istanbul, Jerusalem. Like a secret fraternity." He looked at Ben. "I never belonged anywhere before. You know that."

"You belonged to the Israeli army. Special ops, remember? They trusted you."

"They used me, that's all."

"It's what you call service to your country. Only you don't have a country anymore, do you?"

Jeremy didn't respond.

Ben pulled onto a narrow, rutted lane that ran to the Chesapeake Bay and a sprawling, hilltop house of soaring glass walls. "It belongs to a friend," Ben informed as he pulled into a private drive. "We've got it for the rest of the afternoon."

Jeremy ogled the imposing house, reminiscent of Frank Lloyd Wright designs, blending with its habitat as if it had sprung naturally from the ground.

"It's the spoils of that wretched establishment you hate, Jeremy. The guy who owns it started working in a sheet metal factory when he was sixteen. Lost a couple of fingers. Never went to Harvard like you did. Worked fourteen-hour shifts, and one day bought the company and gave most of it back to the employees. Feel like throwing a rock through his window?"

Jeremy's response was to fling open the car door and stalk up the flagstone path to the front door of the house. There, he waited in a defiant sulk for Ben.

Once inside, Jeremy wandered across a sunlit room to a bank of floor-to-ceiling windows overlooking the bay. He scanned the view, then the room, furnished with modern cubic furniture and hung with abstract paintings. "Your friend did well for himself," he conceded, his tone noticeably disarmed. He was focused on a smaller framed print over a shiny black credenza. "Vincent van Gogh. I hear the Architect loves that guy's stuff." Jeremy glanced at Ben. "He's the one who chopped off his ear, isn't he?"

"Yeah, Jeremy. I'm wondering why you haven't done the same to one of yours. Isn't that the anarchist thing to do? Self-mutilation until you get what you want?"

"You're crazy. I don't know what my sister sees in you." Jeremy's attention wandered back to the print. "Anyway, the guy has this thing for van Gogh. Sometimes wears an ear-shaped tie tack. Freaky."

Ben grew weary of the hostility. There were graver issues before them than their embattled relationship. "Sit down, Jeremy," he said, gesturing toward a brown suede sofa. Ben removed his coat and settled onto a club chair opposite the sofa. "Tell me what I need to know."

Jeremy shed his own coat and cap while studying Ben carefully. "First, are you with us?"

"Tell me why I should be."

"You know why. Israel. It's the only thing you would risk it all for."

Ben brushed his hand along the cushioned arm of the chair. "Go on."

"Noland doesn't care about Israel. But he's desperate to win over the Middle East and all its oil fields. With old hostile regimes falling away and new democracies—or so they call themselves—springing up with inexperienced leaders, your president can influence the paths they take and gain a stronger foothold in the region. *If* he can deliver Israel, or at least defuse her." Jeremy leaned forward, resting his elbows on his knees. "And you can't let that happen, can you?"

There was no word from Ben, no involuntary twitch of the mouth, but he didn't take his eyes off Jeremy, who now sat back to clearly savor the point he'd just scored.

"But there's more, Ben," Jeremy continued, raising his eyes toward the windows. "Something you can't even imagine. Something underfoot in the deep-down of the Kremlin, right under President Gorev's nose. That Maxum Morozov plot last year was just the beginning. Too bad your friend Liesl Bower had to interfere. Don't think Pavel Andreyev and Vadim Fedorovsky have forgotten about that. And don't think they aren't continuing their underground revolt even from prison. They won't be there long, though." Jeremy fairly preened over the letting of privileged information.

"Let me guess," Ben said flatly. "Someone's going to bust them from prison and set them down on a two-seater throne, the Siamese kings of Russia. Right?" Ben felt his emotions slipping into overdrive.

Jeremy eyed him smugly. "Andreyev and Fedorovsky are subordinates." He grinned. "The Architect will rule Russia . . . Europe . . . and Asia Minor." He paused as if for effect. "And the Architect promises to protect Israel."

Ben's brow arched slightly. "Tell me more about this Architect."

Jeremy's dark eyes danced. "You had no idea such a person existed, did you? Bet your CIA hound dogs don't either." He fidgeted with the hem of his sweater and sighed deeply, his face clouding slightly. "Truth is, Ben, I don't know who he is. Some billionaire who rules Russia in ways few others can see. At the appointed hour, he will remove President Gorev, whom he detests, and seize control of Russia. He will build a new empire and take down countries without so much as a single missile strike." Jeremy grinned broadly. "Though, I understand he intends to perform a few acts of, uh, *persuasion* in the U.S., just to demonstrate his powers over you and warn you not to interfere with anything Russia wants to do in her sphere." He paused. "In fact, Inauguration Day was the first salvo."

There it was! Proof. It wasn't Al-Qaeda or a rogue lone wolf. It was Russia! Ben tried not to react but failed. He felt himself tense.

"Well, what do you know," Jeremy said. "I just caught you flat-footed." He crossed his legs. "I am enjoying the upper hand over my sister's big-deal husband."

Ben abruptly leaned forward, his eyes drilling Jeremy. "Was Liesl the target?" he asked savagely.

This time, it was Jeremy who was caught off guard. He stared blankly at Ben as if considering that possibility for the first time. "Of course not," he said, but there was no authority in his voice. "It was the president. That's what we were told."

"Who is *we*?"

Jeremy visibly relaxed, his cocky grin returning. "Besides you, you mean?"

"Answer me."

"I can't tell you that."

"Because you don't know, right? What *do* you know, Jeremy?"

"I know you'd better end this uppity, down-your-nose grilling of me and start worrying about Israel and our families there."

Ben tensed more, his mind spinning. "When are these other acts of persuasion supposed to take place?"

"Soon. That's all I know." He looked thoughtfully at Ben. "Think about it. The U.S. economy is in the tank. Foreign governments hold over a third of Treasury Department–issued securities. China and Japan account for half of that. Other countries are faltering, and Russia's poised to move in and scoop them up."

"But not Israel? Why does the Architect want to protect her?"

"To keep our new White House mole happy. Don't you understand?"

Ben did, and the words repulsed him.

"Now, you're as vital to Russia as Maxum Morozov was. Where the infamous mole inside Israel's Defense Department failed, you will succeed. Your reward—and my reward for recruiting you—is the Architect's promise that he will preserve our ancestral homeland."

"And you believe that? You forget that the Morozov plot was to force Israel's annihilation. What changed?"

"The Arab Spring made the Middle East more vulnerable to Russian influence, without having to touch Israel. But the biggest change was landing you as the mole with the most to offer." Jeremy chuckled. "Too bad you wouldn't come when you were first called."

Ben remembered the voice on the phone, the insistent calls. The voice first dangled unlimited riches if Ben would spy for Russia. Then, when he angrily refused, the voice threatened his family. They would do it again, he was certain.

"But now, you're the Russian eye on the White House. You'll feed the Architect news of Noland's foreign policy strategies. And once the

Architect is officially in power, you'll influence Noland to stay out of Russia's way, so to speak."

Light from the windows grew dim, and Ben noticed a line of clouds had moved in over the bay, snuffing out the sunlight. Such stealth. Was that the way phantom aggressors operated?

Jeremy watched him. "Things are going to happen soon, Ben. You should send Anna and the kids out of the country."

Ben rounded on Jeremy as if he'd just announced a death sentence. But Jeremy persisted. "You don't know what these people can do, Ben. Get my sister out of here."

Chapter 16

Early Saturday morning, the nation's capital stirred beneath the gray covers of low-slung clouds. The sun only threatened to make an appearance, though the few pedestrians on the streets went about their day undeterred. Some who carried newspapers rolled up under their arms appeared focused on the nearest coffee-shop doorway. A few runners, zipped up in NASA-grade spandex, passed Hans Kluen without the slightest glance. He envied the endorphin-induced runner's high he saw on their faces. For them, too, the weather was irrelevant. It was all about the run.

So what was *this* all about? This compromised life he lived. Was it the money? Why not the money? When allegiance and patriotism meant nothing to him, why shouldn't it be about the money? Had it not afforded him the woman he'd yearned for his whole life, alone at night in a cold-water flat in the Bronx? Had it not kept her in the velvety folds of privilege she expected from him?

But sometimes in the night, he would awake and, for a wretched instant, not know who or where he was. In the high bed piled with his grandmother's quilts, next to the window that overlooked a vineyard on the Rhine River? Or was it the iron bed in the Bronx where he first tasted the bile of hatred for his immigrant father and the abuse he wrought on

Hans's mother on the other side of the wall? It was in the Bronx that a gang of Nazi haters bearing an American flag had routinely beat him and his little brother, who died at nine of one last blow to the head. Whatever allegiance Hans had tried to muster for his newly adopted country perished with his brother.

A young couple hunched against the cold passed Hans on the sidewalk, barely looking his way. In a drab-gray trench coat, dark muffler concealing the lower half of his face, a knit cap tight on his head, he was surely forgettable to those who glimpsed him, though they would come to remember the morning well.

Waiting on the corner ahead was a much leaner man in a camel-hair topcoat, black homburg hat, and a soft brown scarf pulled high around his chin. Cashmere, Hans guessed. The formal ensemble was out of step with this early weekend hour. But little about the man was compatible with the world he sought to rule.

When Hans approached, he asked the man, "Where now?"

"I will show you," Ivan Volynski replied calmly, and the two men matched stride as they strolled off together down First Street, passing few other pedestrians.

Hans turned slightly to the man walking beside him. *He's out here in the open with no security,* Hans groaned to himself. *Dressed as if he were already a head of state.* Hans looked away at the city center and the almost-mythical Capitol dome capping the world's most powerful regime. *But no one in this town knows what the man beside me can bring down on their heads. Or who he is. The Architect himself.*

A block before they reached the Capitol, they looked toward another landmark, the neoclassical Supreme Court Building. Then kept walking.

Neither one spoke until they'd crossed First Street and entered the Capitol grounds, loosely inhabited by a few weather-brave tourists. The two men slowed their pace and angled toward a bench near the east side of the Capitol, a resting spot with a clear view of the temple of justice, as the Supreme Court Building was known.

"You will not be surprised to know that Sonya has unearthed nothing of consequence on your stepdaughter and her bumbling male companion,"

Volynski said. "Nothing besides that unfortunate episode of the young woman's suicide. It was Cassandra's best friend, I believe."

Hans had heard only his wife's account of the story. He'd never felt entitled to probe the matter with his insular stepdaughter but was certain the tragedy had devastated her young life.

"I told you there was nothing to worry about," Hans replied. "I've warned her about meddling in other people's affairs. You won't see her or Jordan Winslow again." He attempted a bit of brevity. "Unless her mother gets it in her head that I'm still seeing another woman." His weak smile was met by Volynski's stone-eyed reproach.

"Enough about that foolish girl and her boyfriend." Volynski opened a gloved hand and stole a glance at the pocket watch lying against his palm. Then he looked at Hans. "Because of them, I have had to leave my apartment for another dwelling until we are finished here. You will not find me. But I will find you, Hans. Do not ever doubt that." He looked again at his watch.

Hans chose to ignore the laid-bare threat. "I have been in contact with my man in—"

Volynski lifted a hand. "Quiet," he ordered.

The first two explosions occurred simultaneously, each one gouging a crater in the yards on either side of the grand stairway to the Supreme Court Building. It was a full fifteen seconds before the third explosion tore through the basement, creating a fireball that threatened the entire structure.

Unlike Hans, who'd suddenly leapt to his feet, Volynski remained seated. He hadn't even flinched. With a stoic cool, he noted, "It is true what they say about the perpetrator often watching the aftermath of his handiwork from the crowd of onlookers." He remained impassive. "I only wish I could see that one face when he hears the news."

But Hans was too stricken by what he'd just witnessed to question that remark. If the explosions had been powerful enough to create a percussion wave, it would have hit him no harder than the reality of what he'd just done, or contributed to. It was the blueprints he'd obtained—at great cost—from a contractor working on the building's recent renovations that had made this possible. He looked to see if there'd been any obvious casualties, any bodies strewn on the ground. This attack, like the one on Inauguration Day, wasn't meant to kill or maim great numbers. "Just a few, like Liesl Bower," Ivan had told him. Now, Hans closed his eyes in self-loathing, wishing he'd never met Ivan Volynski. That he'd never been party to the attempted murder of that innocent woman.

Hans took a small step forward, but Volynski stood and pulled him back. "We cannot stay here now," he said, as the mechanical screams of incoming emergency vehicles mixed with the shrieks of fleeing tourists. "Leave quickly," he ordered, raising the scarf higher on his face, "and look for Sonya's signal in the usual place tomorrow morning. If she signals yes, we will pick you up on the river. You know where." He turned and hurried in the opposite direction from the escalating chaos.

Hans watched Volynski sidestep a knot of terrified bystanders watching the Supreme Court spectacle from a safe distance, or so they must have thought. Hans gaped at them. They weren't safe. Not anywhere.

He had to get out of there. If it was true what Ivan had said about the guilty lingering to watch, and if the authorities might act on that, surely he would be questioned. He couldn't let that happen. But neither could he move from that spot. Not out of some perverse thrill at watching his crime unfold. No, it was paralyzing fright like he'd never known before, not even when his attackers had cornered him and his brother in the alleys and waved their bats and lead pipes at them. Because his brother had known no English, the German he wailed only fueled the zealots' rage.

The sound of a helicopter drew Hans back from the long-ago alleys. He looked up to see it close in on the court building, hovering over emergency personnel as they cleared the street for a landing site.

Instead of retreating, Hans shuffled forward in a daze, unable to stop himself. Something had caught his eye, and he no longer cared who noticed him. He'd seen a young woman drop to her knees beside a small body. A child.

Hans pushed his way through a growing crowd that the police were trying to disperse. But he kept moving until he stopped before the young mother now cradling her injured son. *How old is he?* Hans screamed silently. *Could he be nine? Can he speak English? Does this gash in his head and the blood running down his face mean he will die?*

Did I do this? Did I kill this child?

Hans fell to his knees before the unconscious boy and sobbed, rocking back and forth on his heels, his face buried in his hands.

Then something happened that wasn't possible. Not here. Not to him. But it did.

The young woman lifted one hand from her child and reached for Hans. She firmly gripped his chin and raised his face to hers. "Pray for my child!" she pleaded with anguished eyes. "God will answer you if you pray."

Hans lurched back, staring incredulously at her. Him, pray? Was she insane? He had done this! God should strike him dead!

His eyes trailed to the boy, and he saw his brother's face. Without a word, Hans staggered to his feet and ran.

Chapter 17

*H*er forehead pressed against the tiny window, Cass looked down at the foamy mat of the Atlantic. As the jet gradually descended toward Charleston, she wondered what reception she'd get from Liesl Bower. A strange girl comes to her door on a Saturday morning and tells her that it was she, not the president, they wanted to kill. Why shouldn't the celebrity pianist slam the door and call the police? She probably would. Then what? Cass would have to reveal her evidence? Implicate her mother?

Maybe Jordan was right. "Can't you just call her anonymously?" he'd reasoned. "Detach yourself from it?"

She remembered her answer. "I've been detached since I was nineteen years old. Nothing good has come from it." And that was the moment—late last night in her apartment—when Cass told him about Rachel. When she'd finished, she said, "If I can stop a death instead of causing one, I'm going to do it the best way I know how. And that's not long-distance. Or anonymously."

After he heard Rachel's story, including Cass's drunken tryst with Adam Rinehart, Jordan had enfolded her in his arms and let her cry. When she'd finished, he released her gently, wrapped her in a blanket on the sofa, and kissed her forehead. The only thing he'd said before he left was, "It's time to heal."

But Cass believed her wound would never heal. *There's no one to forgive me*, she thought, watching a tanker bob like a bathtub toy far below her. *No one should.* She glanced at Jordan, dozing in the seat beside her. Even after the story she'd told him last night, he remained at her side. There was something so selfless and unconditional about that, and she didn't understand it. She could only welcome it as one gulping oxygen after a painful ascent through drowning waters.

Her hand slipped lightly over his, and he stirred. "We're almost there," she whispered. Her heart swelled with affection for him, and she smiled.

Straightening in his seat, he looked closely at her, then rubbed his eyes and yawned. He glanced back at her and said, "It's a good thing I'm here."

She nodded agreement and was about to comment on his amazing devotion to her when he added, "You've got something blue stuck between your teeth." He pointed at her mouth. "Probably a blueberry from your muffin." He looked away and she could see his cheeks bunch with amusement.

"And this is the kind of help I can expect from you today?" she said, pulling a mirror from her bag and finding no such intrusion between her teeth. Then she looked out the window and grinned.

"See," Jordan said, leaning forward to catch her expression. "It worked. Now we can die with smiles on our faces."

Cass sighed and finally relaxed against her seat. Ten minutes later, they were on the ground at barely eight o'clock.

"I still can't believe you got that guy in the Juilliard office to give you her home address," Jordan said as they deplaned with only one backpack apiece.

"He would have flunked chemistry in high school if I hadn't helped him almost every day after class," she answered, trying to match Jordan's long stride.

"So the debt is paid?"

"He assured me it was. They could fire him for that." After all other attempts to find Liesl Bower's home address had failed, Cass remembered that the pianist occasionally taught music workshops at the Juilliard School in New York. "By the way, have you logged her address into your handheld?"

"Yeah." Jordan pulled out his mobile GPS as they navigated the busy corridor. "Tidewater Lane. Looks like it's in the South of Broad district, which, I understand, is the epicenter of Charleston aristocracy." He steered her into a café. "Let's get some hot brew and food before we go any farther."

They took a seat and ordered. Cass looked around the crowded restaurant, then back at Jordan, who was watching an overhead television screen behind her. "I only spoke to her a couple of times in passing that day at the Carnegie. I wonder what Liesl Bower's really like."

Jordan glanced at her. "You mean on a normal day when no one's trying to blow her up?" He shifted his attention back to the television.

Cass stared at the empty tabletop. "This is nuts," she said in a raspy whisper, not wanting anyone else to hear. "How do we tell her what we know without revealing *how* we know it. She's going to want evidence, and I can't give it to her. I can't do that to Mom."

She waited for Jordan to turn his attention to her. But something on the screen had already captured it. "Jordan, you're not listening to—"

"Cass, look!" he pointed over her head.

Before she could turn in her seat, she heard, "The bombing of the Supreme Court Building in Washington earlier this morning . . ." Cass jumped to her feet and spun toward the screen as the on-scene reporter continued.

"Explosives apparently buried in the side yards detonated about fifteen seconds before the bomb that gutted the basement where maintenance storage, the garage, and the high court's mail-handling facility are located. Two people were killed, a mail-room clerk and a security guard. Only a few bystanders were injured by the exterior blasts, one of them a young boy with a critical head wound. Authorities attribute the few casualties to the early-morning hour, the extreme cold, and to the fact that the building is closed on weekends."

Cass turned fiery eyes toward Jordan, remembering his words last night in Hans's study. *Why would he have blueprints of the U.S. Supreme Court Building?*

Why would he have a diagram of the inauguration platform and the blast pattern centered on Liesl Bower's piano? Cass's whole body went rigid, and she struggled to bend her mind around what was happening.

"Jordan," she said, leaning close to his ear. "This isn't going to stop."

Chapter 18

The old house on Tidewater Lane had been prepped for a day like no other. A wedding day. The caterer, florist, grounds crew, and a string ensemble of Liesl Bower's music students from the College of Charleston would arrive at intervals throughout the day.

But only one person was up when the bell on the sidewalk door rang early that morning. Ian O'Brien trudged down the porch steps in flannel pajamas barely concealed by a woman's pink chenille bathrobe, the quickest thing he could grab on his dash from the kitchen. "Gonna wake up the whole house," he grumbled to himself while scratching his gray beard. He opened the door fronting on the sidewalk and glared at the three men who, at first sight of Ian, seemed to forget why they were there.

"Let me guess," Ian said, eyeing the truck at the curb. "You're the yard crew, right?"

While two of the men stared openmouthed at the pink robe, the third didn't miss the appropriate beat. "And you must be the lady of the house."

As the three men struggled to contain themselves, Ian stepped out in front of them, standing taller and at least fifteen pounds heavier than any of them. The men eyed him carefully. "If you hadn't shown up at the crack of dawn," Ian growled, "I wouldn't be standing out here looking like a ninny trying to make you stop ringing this bell." He looked them square in the eyes. "Now, don't you think it's a little early to be running power tools out here? I got a house full of folks up there trying to sleep, not to mention the neighbors."

The one who'd spoken earlier cleared his throat and pulled a piece of paper from his pants pocket. "Sorry, sir," he said, avoiding Ian's scowl, "but our instructions are to clean up the yards and bring all those potted palms we got there in the truck into the house." He scratched his head. "Guess we could do the quiet part first."

"And which part is that?"

"Well, we can rake without a lot of noise, don't you think, fellas?" he asked, turning to his coworkers. "I mean, we don't have to chant or anything like that."

As they all nodded agreeably, something unspoken tugging at the corners of their mouths, Cade O'Brien emerged from his ground-floor apartment. "What's going on, Pop?" he asked, blinking hard. "And, uh, want to tell me why you're wearing Liesl's robe?"

The three men couldn't take any more. One by one, they shuffled off toward the truck to retrieve their tools, their shoulders heaving. "Shh!" one whispered, looking quickly back at Ian.

"Come on in, Pop. They just don't appreciate your feminine side like I do." Cade laughed all the way up the steps to the main door of the house. It was one of Charleston's iconic single houses. From the front entrance on the sidewalk level, an open-air stairway led to the second-level porch and formal entrance to the living quarters. The stately three-story dwelling had been the Bower family home since the early 1900s.

"Now that's enough!" Ian stomped up behind him.

"Why were you upstairs anyway, Pop?"

"I just came up to start breakfast for everybody when those guys started punching that doorbell. And by the way, it's ten degrees warmer up here. We've got to do something about the damp cold in that apartment of yours. I don't know if I can take another winter down there." They quietly shut the front door behind them and went straight to the kitchen, closing up the two entrances to it as well.

"You don't have to," Cade said in a low voice, focused tightly now on Ian. "After tonight, you're moving up here with me and Liesl." He grinned with unabashed pleasure.

"Nothing doing," Ian said too loudly, and Cade shushed him. In a gale-force whisper, Ian added, "There's already too many people up here. Her dad, her grandmother, and that caregiver woman who talks a blue streak. She's got that long braid wrapped so tight around her head, it's interfering with the on-off switch."

Ian poured coffee for Cade, who moved to a chair at the kitchen table and looked wistfully out the window, unfazed by his grandfather's rumblings. "This is my wedding day, Pop."

Ian clapped a hand on Cade's shoulder, handed him a mug, and settled into a chair next to him, his voice finding its moderate tone. "'And God saw that it was good,'" Ian quoted from the first chapter of Genesis.

"*This* time, you mean," Cade said.

Ian shook his head with conviction. "That first marriage was a travesty, Son. You were ganged up on by that drug-addled young woman, my own money-hungry son, and his drunken wife. And you know what? We're not going to speak another word about those unfortunate souls, not now anyway. They're all gone, and God has brought you the bride of his choice. I know it's true because me and the Lord are always talking things over."

Cade reached over and closed his hand over Ian's but didn't speak. Ian guessed he couldn't. So it was time to return the day to its intended celebration. "Tell you what," Ian said. "Give me time to clean up, then go wake up that bride of yours. We're going to dine fine this morning."

Climbing the stairs to Liesl's room, Cade tried to dismiss his fears for her safety. Liesl had refused to discuss the implications of the bomb planted in her piano just five days ago. "It was only the biggest hiding place on that whole platform," she'd reasoned. "It was the president they wanted." Still, security agents ordered by President Noland himself now monitored the house and all Liesl's comings and goings, much to her dismay.

When Cade reached Liesl's bedroom door, he knocked lightly and waited, but not long. Already dressed in paint-spattered jeans, a baggy gray sweater, and old sneakers, Liesl threw open the door and reached for him. He hugged her to him, inhaling a wisp of lavender soap. "Hmm, you smell good." He set her down. "And I'm certain you're going to look a whole lot better tonight."

After the punch to his arm, she invited him in to see what she'd packed for their honeymoon. An assortment of ski clothes were rolled inside a wheeled duffle bag. Airline tickets to Austria lay nearby.

Cade turned her to him and nuzzled her neck, then found her lips and kissed them. And again. "Remind me why we waited so long," he whispered.

"You wanted to be the chief breadwinner, remember? Had to get Charleston's new metro magazine up and running, pulling in money to feed us and our children." He watched her eyes sparkle at the prospect of a family. At forty, he also was ready. With God's grace, they would both discover what *family* was meant to be.

They heard another bedroom door open nearby, and Henry Bower looked into his daughter's open doorway as he passed by. He smiled at the couple and slipped quietly down the stairs.

Liesl looked thoughtfully after her father. "There goes the main reason we waited," she said.

Cade tightened his arms around her. "It was the right thing to do, Liesl. Your father had just returned from the dead after twenty years. You both needed this time together, to heal. You have. In time, he will, too."

A smile skimmed her face, then disappeared. "But the guilt is eating him alive, Cade. What his drinking did to us all. The accident that killed Aunt Bess. Mom's illness. He believes that was his fault too. I pray every day for God to forgive him and to make him know he's forgiven. That it's done and over."

A gravelly voice came bellowing up the stairwell. "Breakfast will be served on the main deck!"

"And that's the end of that conversation." Liesl grinned, pulling Cade along toward the staircase. "Ian has been so good for Dad. Starting that charter-fishing business with him and giving him a livelihood, a reason to get up in the morning—sober. And making him laugh."

Halfway down the stairs, Cade pointed toward one of the tall, transomed windows overlooking the front porch. "Henry's not the only one drawn to the crusty old sea captain."

Liesl saw Ava Mullins cross the porch toward the door, a party-size coffee urn in her arms and bulging grocery bags swinging from both wrists. Cade went to lend a hand.

"Oh, thank heavens," Ava groaned when he opened the door and took the bags from her. "Someone keeps adding more steps to this porch every day." Though she was approaching sixty, Ava's small form was both girlish and rock hard. And since that day when Liesl had personally ushered her into a new wardrobe and hairstyle, Ava had continued to wear her peppered gray hair cropped in the spiky hairdo that had first rendered Ian speechless. Now, dressed in a black turtleneck and designer jeans tucked smartly into black suede boots, Ava strode purposefully through the door of the house that she, admittedly, had come to love as the only familial gathering place she knew. The former Harvard music professor and now-retired CIA agent was long divorced, and her son was a career marine who seldom visited.

When Liesl approached, Ava gave her the tall silver urn, a quick peck on the cheek, and a cursory appraisal. "Now I know why the groom isn't supposed to see his bride just before the wedding." Her eyes slid over Liesl's attire. "The guy might change his mind."

Cade winked at Liesl as they all headed for the kitchen. "Pop finally found his match."

Liesl's grandmother, Lottie Bower, and her caregiver, Margo Blanchard, were now seated at the big oak table still bearing Liesl's initials, which she'd carved with a fish hook in third grade. Lottie rarely spoke these days, another small stroke pushing her further along a continuum of clouding coherence. But she often smiled and gestured feebly, signaling to those who knew her best that she was glad for their nearness.

"I can't remember the last time I had potato pancakes, Mr. O'Brien," Margo told Ian, who was hunched over two large cast-iron skillets, one bearing the cakes, the other sausage and bacon. Warming nearby were a pot of cheese grits and a pan of scrambled eggs. A platter of fresh fruit was already on the table. "I used to make waffles for my husband before he died of a brain tumor. Well, sometimes he wanted oatmeal to go with them, though I never could understand that combination. But anyhow, he still couldn't start his day without a plate of my waffles. Sometimes I'd put blueberries in them, that is if I could find them when they weren't so ridiculously overpriced, and sometimes I put pecans in them. He loved pecans, and I didn't mind shelling them fresh. And sometimes I wouldn't put anything at all in my waffles. It just depended on his mood, which, as you can imagine with someone afflicted with any brain disorder, was likely to change without warning. Know what I mean?"

Ian turned pained eyes toward Liesl, who'd joined him at the stove and was flipping the last batch of pancakes. "Hurry up and give that woman something to put in her mouth," he whispered. "When she's through eating, we'll use duct tape."

Liesl valiantly choked off a laugh and started dishing food into plates, Margo's first. Soon, they were all talking excitedly around the table. The topic, of course, was final preparations for the evening's wedding at St. Philip's Church and the reception at the house.

Forty-nine guests would attend, but the two friends Liesl wanted most to see couldn't come. She hadn't expected Max Morozov to fly from Israel with his tight concert schedule this year. Before he'd become the first-chair violinist for the Israel Philharmonic, he'd been Liesl's prankster friend and fellow student at the Moscow Conservatory. One of his better stunts had once landed him and Liesl in a Moscow police station.

In the midst of the good-natured exchange at the table, Liesl looked away and remembered another day years after Max's clownish prank in Moscow. It was the day he led an Israeli commando squad to evidence that his father was a Russian spy—the day the light went dim in the heart of Max.

Liesl looked about the table and caught the concern on Cade's face.

And there it was on Ava's, too. Liesl knew why. There was a burn hole in the piano she'd played last Monday, and no one was willing to forget it, certainly not the federal agents who roamed about Tidewater Lane.

She smiled weakly at Ava. The woman may appear to have lost the razor edge of a veteran CIA agent, but Liesl knew that Ava Mullins—even retired and settled into a new life in Charleston—was temporarily back on task and once again running security for her famous charge.

Ridiculous! Liesl refused to believe there was intent to harm her. *That's over.* And she certainly wasn't going to let unwarranted fear spoil the most joyous day of her life. In just hours, she was going to marry the man she loved so desperately, and nothing was going to interfere with that.

Then she thought of Ben Hafner. He and Anna had called the night before, begging her forgiveness for canceling their intended trip to the wedding. "Fallout from the attacks on Monday," Ben had told her. He was dreadfully sorry, he'd said, but there was something else in his voice. Few besides his wife knew his subtle intonations as well as Liesl. Ben had been like a brother to her since their Harvard days. Why wasn't he here?

She recoiled from the mental jabbing that threatened to undo her. *No more of this!* she scolded herself, glancing about the table. *Climb out of this pity hole and be thankful. "This is the day the Lord has made,"* she recalled from the psalms. *"Let us rejoice and be glad in it."*

She looked up to see Cade smile reassuringly at her as if he'd heard her thoughts.

Ava, however, had pulled on her professional mask. Liesl decided she'd put an end to that.

"Ava, we are going to make divinity candy this morning, aren't we?" Liesl affected a buoyant, oversized smile, visibly urging Ava's agent-on-guard countenance to relax.

"I did bring the ingredients," Ava allowed, but her face was still grim.

Liesl brushed her hands together and rose from the table. "Ava and I have serious work to do," she told the group, most of them still lingering over the last crumbs of Ian's potato pancakes.

Later, Liesl was chopping pecans and Ava was measuring out corn syrup when Cade brushed past them and turned on the small television mounted on the wall. "Someone just bombed the Supreme Court Building," he announced.

Ava set the measuring cup down hard on the tile countertop, and Liesl dropped the knife. They both pivoted toward the small screen and latched on to every word. When the reports of the three explosions finally turned from fact to conjecture from contributing analysts—meaning no one was sure of anything beyond the first reports—the three looked at each other, trying to piece together something they couldn't see.

"Just five days after the inauguration," Ava noted. "No one claiming responsibility for that, either."

Without a word, Liesl hurried out of the kitchen. She wouldn't listen to any more of this. Not another horror, not on this day. She would fight her way around it and keep going. Lift another prayer for protection. Then force her way back to peace.

She was pulling on a light jacket, bound for a restorative stroll in the garden, when the bell on the sidewalk door rang. *Ah, the florist,* she hoped. And her spirits lifted.

"I'll get it," she called, her voice rising with expectation. Few things could flood a house with celebration and renewal like fresh flowers. And lots of them, which Liesl had ordered.

But when Liesl opened the ground-level door, there was no florist. Instead, a young couple she'd never seen before greeted her nervously. "Are you . . . Liesl Bower?" said the young woman. Her short blond curls fringed a pretty face with a fresh-scrubbed look. But the face made no attempt to smile.

Liesl tensed. She was used to fans approaching her in public places, but not here. How did they know where she lived? Then she remembered a few tour guides who, since her move back to Charleston last year, had begun pointing out her house to their patrons. That is, until Ava Mullins put a stop to it.

Liesl studied the two before her now. Just tourists, she presumed, then wondered what Ava would do if she knew they'd come right up to the door and rung for admittance.

"Yes, I am," she said with no inflection, looking about for the security agents. "How may I help you?"

The girl hesitated too long and her friend answered for her. "Ms. Bower, this is Cass Rodino, and I'm Jordan Winslow. It's very nice to meet you."

Liesl looked from the pleasant expression on his face back to the severe set of his companion's. Smiling politely, Liesl was about to repeat her question with more emphasis when the girl found her voice. "We need to talk to you, Ms. Bower," she said too firmly. "I have information about the bombings in Washington."

The words tore into Liesl.

"Is there someplace we can talk . . . right now?" the girl asked, her voice tight. "I'm afraid it's urgent."

Liesl stepped back and glared at the two strangers. What could they know? Who were they? She looked quickly around her. It was a practiced move, done too many times. Check the streets, the yards, the parked cars, those passing by. Anything unusual? More importantly, where were the two agents charged with watching the house?

"Ma'am, are you all right?" the young man asked.

"What is it you have to tell me?" Liesl asked bluntly, then immediately reconsidered. Surely she didn't want to discuss such a thing on the sidewalk in front of her house. "No. Never mind. You'll have to come inside." But she looked away and briefly closed her eyes. *I can't invite these people into my home. What if that's exactly what they want? Lord, help me! Tell me what to do!*

"Ms. Bower, I'm so sorry for upsetting you," the girl said. "This is deeply troubling to me, too. But I had to tell you in person."

Liesl wouldn't prolong this another second. It didn't matter where they were. "Tell me what." It wasn't a question.

"I have every reason to believe that . . . that *you* were the target on Monday. Not the president."

At that instant, Liesl's mind slipped through a portal to the past—to retrieve something improbably relevant to the moment. How clearly she now heard her dad's Mayday cry on the marine radio that day nearly twenty-five years ago, heard him hail the Coast Guard, screaming for

help. That Liesl's beloved aunt Bess would soon bleed out from an ac-
cidental spear wound to her abdomen if they didn't come immediately.
The deadly words struck a fourteen-year-old girl eating frosted cornflakes
within earshot of the radio, refusing to believe what she'd just heard. It
wasn't until Liesl saw her aunt's body lifted from a helicopter, fully covered by a gray blanket, that the words were proven true.

Now, the portal closed over, and Liesl refocused on the strangers standing before her. How long would it take for her to believe these words the
young woman had just spoken? Who else would die before she accepted
them as true?

"Please do something to protect yourself," the girl pleaded.

Liesl felt lightheaded, but something caught her eye and anchored her
to the spot. It was just a passing van, a white van with slightly tinted
windows and no markings. *Why is it creeping past?* Liesl looked back at
the girl.

"What makes you believe such a thing?" Liesl hurled the question at
the same time her eyes cut back to the van now turning the corner at the
end of the block and disappearing. She looked once more to the girl, this
time more impatiently.

"That's a bit of a long story," the girl replied, then turned to her companion. "Jordan, would you please get the files from the car?" The young
man headed toward a small sedan parked at the curb a few doors down.

"Are you sure there's no place we can talk privately?" the girl urged.

Before Liesl answered, she looked down the street again. One of her
neighbors had just led his dog onto the sidewalk and headed away toward
the harbor. He passed a postman reaching into his mail pouch as he walked
toward the Bower home. Across the street, a middle-aged couple wearing
matching fanny packs strolled leisurely down the sidewalk, gesturing, as
many tourists did, toward the regal old houses lining the narrow lane.

Any other time and Liesl might have invited this young woman and
her friend onto her porch, but not this time. Something was wrong here
and she wouldn't open the doors of her home to whatever it was. "I'm
sorry but I can't—" Her words fell away.

The same van she'd just watched turn the far corner came roaring down

on them from the opposite direction and lurched to a halt at the curb. The
side door slid open and the driver yelled, "Liesl, get in!" He pointed down
the sidewalk. "That is no mailman!"

But Liesl couldn't move, couldn't focus on anything but the face of the
man in the van.

"Liesl! Get in now!" screamed Evgeny Kozlov.

Only then did Liesl turn to look where he pointed, at the uniformed
postman coming toward them, his eyes locked on her, his hand now pulling something from the pouch strapped across his chest. Liesl grabbed
the girl and yanked her to the ground an instant before a silenced bullet
struck the tree behind them.

"No!" Liesl screamed. She looked back at the house, fearing someone
from inside might appear at any moment. What was it she'd just asked
herself? Who would die before she accepted the truth of what this girl had
just told her?

But it was Evgeny who nailed the answer. "Liesl, they will kill you and
your family! Get in! Both of you!"

Liesl and the girl hurled themselves through the open side door as
Evgeny jumped out, crouched, and fired at the escaping gunman. But the
man ran down a side alley and disappeared. Evgeny lunged back into the
driver's seat.

"Get her out of here!" Cass hollered at him. She slammed the side door
shut and dropped next to Liesl on the floor between the seats as the van
launched from the curb.

"I have to warn my family!" Liesl cried to Evgeny, trying to raise herself
from the floor. "That man's still out there!"

"Stay down!" he ordered. "It is you they want. They will come after us."

"They?"

But Evgeny's attention was no longer on Liesl. "Who are you?" he demanded of the girl, even as he ran a stop sign at the end of Tidewater
Lane. "And your friend behind us?"

Both women turned to look out the back window at Jordan Winslow's
rental car on their tail.

Liesl now glared at the young woman, suspicion rising like an angry tide. "Answer him!" She felt hysteria ride in on that tide and knew she was losing control.

"I'm Cass Rodino," she answered. "Who are you?"

"You would not believe me if I told you. But before I kick you out at the next corner, you need to—"

"Please listen to me," Cass cried. "We know things about the threat to Liesl."

Evgeny narrowed his eyes and studied the girl in the rearview mirror. "Go on," he said as the van skirted downtown Charleston.

But there was something of greater urgency to Liesl. "Please let me warn my family," she begged, not caring how pitiful she sounded.

"Yes, you should," Evgeny conceded. He fished a phone from a bag beside him and handed it to Liesl, who was still wondering why he'd come for her. "It is untraceable," Evgeny said of the phone. "You must use it only. But make no call without clearing it with me first." He looked sternly at her. "It just has to be that way." They were racing up I-26 now toward North Charleston. "And tell Miss Old Lady CIA she had better get to your house quick." Liesl saw the smirk on his face as she punched in Cade's number.

"Are you Russian?" Cass asked.

Evgeny ignored the question.

Liesl tucked Evgeny's phone to her ear and tossed a response to his earlier comment. "Ava's already there."

"Of course," he said mildly. "The wedding police. Well, she has probably reached optimum panic by now. But tell her you are safe with me. She should have no trouble believing that." Liesl registered the sarcasm.

Cade answered, the pitch of his voice too high. "Hello! Who is this?" Liesl could almost see the anxious clench of his jaw.

"Are you okay?" she cried.

"Am *I* okay? Where are you?"

"Cade, keep everybody inside. A man out front just shot at me! Is Ava still there?"

"What! Are you hurt?"

"You have to stay inside the house! Tell Ava I'm with . . . tell her Evgeny

Kozlov just saved me from a killer." Liesl watched the back of Evgeny's head. He was driving hard, though Liesl didn't know where they were going.

There was silence on the other end. Then, "Liesl, that isn't funny."

"It's the truth, Cade. He pulled up in a van and warned me. I'm with him now."

"Where?"

"North of town on I-26."

"No!" Evgeny warned, shaking his head. "Just tell him you are okay and hang up. You can call again later. Much later."

Liesl hesitated and Evgeny turned around in his seat to issue the warning again, but Liesl held up a compliant hand.

"Was that him?" Cade asked. "Tell him I'm coming to get you."

"No, Cade. None of you are safe near me. I don't know when you will be. And Cade . . . this is not going to be our wedding day." Her voice broke.

"Liesl, please!" Cade cried. "Tell me what's happening!" She'd never heard such fright in his voice. Not Cade's. "I love you. Let me come to you."

She couldn't hold back the tears any longer. "Not now," she sobbed. "Stay inside. Ava will know what to do." The words spilled wet and hot. "I'll call you soon. I love you." She clicked off and covered her face with her hands, her body convulsing.

Then someone's arms encircled her and held her gently. "I'll help you, Liesl," Cass said in a voice edged with steel. "You don't know me. And you sure don't know what I've survived. But I *did* survive. And you will too."

Liesl raised a sodden face to this girl who'd also been shot at and now sat on the dirty floor of a van speeding through Charleston, driven by a man she couldn't know was an assassin. And she was assuring Liesl that all would be well?

"This is the day the Lord has made," Liesl had recited just an hour ago. *"Let us rejoice and be glad in it."*

Glad for what?

Chapter 19

*E*vgeny exited I-26 and wound his way into a North Charleston industrial neighborhood that had seen little industry in recent years, the streets edged with weeds and abandoned cars. One more wouldn't be noticed, Evgeny knew, as he drove the van behind a flat, cement-block building he'd discovered the night before. It had once been a metal-fabricating workshop, but now a faded sign hanging on the front door issued a kind of death notice. *Closed.*

Parked behind another building down the street was a late-model Ford Taurus he'd acquired with little effort. An undercover agent who couldn't seize whatever he needed with haste and stealth was eventually exposed. And an exposed agent was often a dead one.

He couldn't afford to take this mysterious young couple to the car he'd hidden. They couldn't describe to authorities what they'd never seen, so he braked sharply behind the metal-works shop and pulled a small handgun from under his jacket. Turning quickly in his seat, he leveled the gun at Cass, drawing a gasp from her. "Again," he said, "who are you?"

Before she could answer, Jordan screeched to a stop behind the van and jumped out. "Open the door for him," Evgeny ordered Cass, who complied.

Seeing the gun pointed at him, Jordan stepped back.

"Get in," Evgeny barked. And soon, three sets of eyes drilled him from the back seat.

"I'm a set designer, and Jordan owns a shoe store," Cass answered hotly. "I hardly think you need protection from us." She looked down at the gun. "And we see those all the time. We're from New York."

"Why are you here?" Evgeny asked Cass, deflecting her anger. His glance wandered to Liesl. *She is strangely quiet*, he thought.

"We found something in her . . . in someone's files," Jordan answered, "that led us to believe someone was aiming for Liesl." He glanced regretfully at her. "It was a diagram of the inaugural platform showing the position of the piano and Liesl's name marked beside it, along with the exact time she was to perform. And . . ." He seemed unsure whether to proceed.

"And . . ." Evgeny prompted.

"Well, there was a drawing of, uh, sort of a bomb blast over the piano. And then we found—"

"Wait just a minute," Cass interjected, looking defiantly at Evgeny. "Why should we tell you anything? Who are *you?*"

"The one with the gun. Keep going." Evgeny's veteran instincts had already told him these two were harmless. But he needed their information.

He watched Cass and Jordan exchange some kind of silent go-ahead. "In this same person's files," Jordan continued, "we found blueprints of the Supreme Court Building."

Evgeny barely contained his surprise. How could such fortune have been handed to him? Again? Nothing had ever come so easy. An inside track to this someone could lead Evgeny to the Architect. These two couldn't possibly know what they'd uncovered.

He steadied the gun on Cass. "*Whose* files?" he demanded.

Cass glared at him, then cast her eyes toward the floor. When she looked back at him, her face was clouded.

"My stepfather's."

The boy's arm slipped protectively around the girl's shoulders.

"Who is your stepfather?" Evgeny pressed.

Cass answered absently. "He used to be a good man. I don't know what happened to him." She paused. "The same thing that drags us all down at some point, I guess." She pulled herself up straight. "But I won't tell you his name. I won't bring my mother down with him." She looked back at Jordan. "Somehow, I have to get her away from him before it's out of my control."

"It already is!" Evgeny snapped. "There are other things about to happen that no mere set designer and a shoe salesman have any control over. Unless—"

"What things?" Liesl demanded. Evgeny looked into the golden brown eyes that three times over the years he'd seen flash with unveiled terror— in a Moscow alley, in Schell Devoe's house after Evgeny had pumped three rounds into the spy, and that night in Liesl's dressing room. Now, the eyes were just angry.

Evgeny finally lowered his gun. "I will not hurt you," he told the young couple. "But you must step outside, and stay where I can see you. I need to speak to Miss Bower in private. And do not be so foolish as to run away."

When the couple had closed the van door and walked a short way off, Evgeny faced Liesl. He saw that she'd drawn as far from him as possible, pressing herself into the door. He looked down at the gifted hands now balled into twitching fists in her lap. He was sorry for the torment he'd caused her so many times over.

"Why do they want to kill me?" she asked plaintively. "I have no more code. I'm no threat to them. Why?"

Evgeny looked deep into the stormy eyes. "My country and yours are in grave danger from one man and his powerful generals who convene in the hidden corridors of the Kremlin."

Liesl didn't move.

"He is called the Architect. He will try again to assassinate our president, and with military forces already secretly moving into his camp, he will take control of Russia. I am convinced that in the process, he will destroy my homeland. His Russia will rule over a new world order. He will sweep through the Middle East at the height of its vulnerability and claim it for a Russia our people will no longer recognize. Then he will turn to devour other countries. But the Architect will work from the inside out.

Infiltrating. To stir fear in the people, topple economies, pit one country against another until they render each other powerless."

"Who is this man?"

"I do not know. Only his generals and loyal soldiers know who he is, though many, I am told, have never seen him."

Liesl looked doubtful. "Well, whoever he is, he can't do these things in our country."

After all she'd been through, how was she still so naïve? he wondered. "He already has! For many years, he has cultivated a legion of sleeper agents throughout the U.S. Some of them are Americans so disenfranchised from their own country that they would do anything to see her fall. Others are Russian plants."

Liesl turned fully in her seat to face him, but remained quiet.

"They are saboteurs in key positions in transportation, energy, banking, the military, communications. They have each been trained in one particular act of terrorism. At the Architect's command, they will act simultaneously. There will be massive devastation. And your country will retaliate against mine."

Her distrust was palpable. "How do you know these things?"

"My contacts run deep, but the Architect's new regime, the one he will fight so viciously for, is quickly outpacing my old comrades. All I know at present is that a series of terrorist acts are planned to convince Washington that when the time comes and the Architect is in control of Russia, your government must cooperate with him, or else he will unleash more attacks. He commands a Red Army already on American soil."

"But how does a dead Liesl Bower figure into this?" she asked bitterly.

"Among the infrastructure and landmarks his secret insurgents are to destroy is one living treasure—you."

The hands jerked involuntarily, and the golden eyes closed.

Evgeny found himself contemptible. Every command he'd obeyed without question, every motive to kill, every pursuit to elevate himself in the eyes of his superiors, every lie he'd perpetrated—all detestable in his sight. Had Liesl Bower done this to him?

"You are the president's favorite musician," he continued.

"He has other favorites."

"But none of them ever crossed Pavel Andreyev and Vadim Fedorovsky."

Liesl gaped at him. "But they're in prison."

"Irrelevant. They remain the Architect's top generals, in full command of their secret forces. And soon, I am told, they will be free."

"They tried to assassinate their own president, and he's going to let them go?" Her voice grew shrill.

Evgeny shook his head. "There is so much you do not understand, and there is no time now to explain."

"Why did you come here?"

He studied the face that had peered at him from the CD cover in the shop window, only this one had lost its radiance. She'd suffered too much. And he was about to hurt her again. "After their failed attempt last Monday, I learned they would try again on your wedding day." He watched her mouth quiver, but he had to make her understand the course of things. "They wanted the world to watch. They wanted your countrymen to see what they could do. That's why they chose the inauguration. Now, they are content to work without an audience." His voice had lost its abrasion. "I could not just call you and hope you would listen. Or alert the police, who still want me for murder. Not your CIA friends, who would love to capture me. I had to come myself, just like your friends out there." He motioned toward the young couple, deep in discussion.

"I don't know them," Liesl objected. "I barely know you. I don't know why you came. Was it just to save me from a bullet? Or is there more?"

How did she know? Yes, there was more. "You must go with me, Liesl."

"What do you mean? Where?"

"To New York. I am quite certain the Architect is there."

"And you believe the two of us can find this man and stop him?" she asked, her voice rising to disbelief.

"I can't involve anyone else, not yet. I have to show *you* what's happening, to convince you. Your CIA friends will listen to you. They'd just hang me."

Liesl shook her head. "This is crazy."

Evgeny lost his patience. "If you do not think you can help me stop this madness and save our countries, then you might as well go back home and wait for the bullets. They'll hit you *and* your family!"

Liesl threw open the door to the van and stomped off toward the deserted street. She ignored Cass asking if she was all right and held up a stand-down hand to Jordan when he made the first move toward her, his arm outstretched as if ready to assist.

Evgeny got out of the van and started after her. "You cannot outrun them," he called, watching her stride furiously away. His head moved side to side, scanning their surroundings. "You must help me end this! But we have to go now!"

Finally, Liesl slowed her pace, then stopped. She turned slowly to Evgeny, who kept coming, kept searching for any unwanted arrivals to this spot. He had learned long ago that no place was completely safe.

"Why should I trust you?" Liesl called to him.

"I do not expect you to, not now. You have seen too much." He stopped. "But trusting me is the only way to stay alive."

She met his steely gaze. "You're wrong, Evgeny. The only one I can trust with my life is God. And if I'm going anywhere with you, I pray he's got your back, too."

She headed back to the van, stopping when she drew even with him. "And by the way, thank you."

He understood.

Chapter 20

*M*ama, what do you do in that place?"

"I'm a secretary, Rudy," Melanie Thompson answered, adjusting her sunglasses.

A swell rocked the boat, and ten-year-old Rudy gripped his fishing pole tighter. "Do you have to work in *all* those buildings?" he asked, looking toward shore.

"No, Son, but I can go most anywhere I want.'" Melanie Thompson cast an amused glance at her husband, who kept watch on his bobber floating on the clear waters of this South Florida bay, but the corners of his mouth curled upward all the same.

Pete Thompson looked toward the sun almost straight up in the cloudless sky, set down his pole, and removed his light sweater, exposing pale arms. "I'll bet your mom is the only secretary in that whole place who is also a brilliant scientist," he told his son proudly. Then he looked at his wife and winked. He picked up his pole and cast the untouched bait back into the water. "It doesn't look like the fish are hungry today, Rudy. Maybe they don't eat on Saturday."

"My friend Sammy says you're not supposed to fish at lunchtime. He and his dad go real early in the morning."

Pete frowned. "Well, I guess I'm not real good at this."

"That's okay, Dad. Math teachers don't have to know how to fish, just how to add and subtract stuff." He looked up at his dad. "But know what Sammy's older brother says?" He went straight to his own answer. "That it's hard to understand what you say in his math class. He doesn't like your accent like I do. I think it's cool."

Pete reached over and lightly yanked on the bill of his son's Dolphins cap, then reeled in his line and opened the cooler. As he pulled sandwiches and sodas from the ice, his wife sat quietly studying the sprawl of buildings before her, making notes and drawings on her legal pad.

Later, Melanie turned to her son. "You like your friend Sammy a lot, don't you?"

"Yeah, we're buddies . . . when he's not bossing me around. He thinks that just because we haven't lived here as long as him, he knows more than me about fishing and surfing and all the stuff other people do here. They even have their own boat. They don't have to borrow one from the marina like we do."

Melanie nodded. "Well, how would you feel if we had to move away from here? Real soon."

Rudy squinted up at his mom. "You mean before baseball starts again?" he squeaked.

"Probably. But what if we moved someplace where there's lots of snow and you could ride snowmobiles and ski?"

"Oh cool!"

"It would be someplace where everybody talks like Dad. Would that be okay?"

"You mean Russia?"

"That's right."

"Would I have to talk like that, too?"

Melanie laughed. "No," she said. "*I* don't. You know that my mother and father were Americans."

"But you grew up in Russia."

She nodded. "Yes, your grandparents were in something called the diplomatic corps. And even though I went to school in Russia, I don't talk with their accent." She reached for a sandwich.

Rudy looked thoughtfully toward shore. "What do they do in all those buildings, Mom?"

"They make nuclear power."

Chapter 21

Confident that the young couple were exactly who they said they were and wouldn't be reporting the van to Charleston police, Evgeny had decided to keep the roomy vehicle, but only after replacing the license plate on the off chance a witness had noted the number during the incident on Tidewater Lane. Now, he and Liesl were driving to New York, public transportation out of the question.

Cass and Jordan had left for the airport and the flight home. They were to await contact from their new friends, the fugitive KGB agent and the pianist marked for murder.

It had been a surprisingly smooth transition. Finally convinced that helping Evgeny was the best way to protect her mother, Cass had divulged her stepfather's identity. She and Jordan then presented their copies of Hans's incriminating files and related Jordan's visit to the curious couple in the apartment near the UN, finally clenching Evgeny's trust that the young couple were not the enemy. Their evidence and naiveté, he'd told them, had convinced him that they were as hapless and confused as Liesl, therefore harmless. Only then had he confided in them as he had Liesl, inextricably drawing them into the hunt for the Architect.

Evgeny had been grateful for Jordan's descriptions of the man and woman he'd confronted, but stopped short of declaring the man the likely Architect. There was too much they didn't know, he'd said.

Later, Evgeny had warned Cass and Jordan not to use their phones, which could be traced. Instead, Evgeny gave them another. Like the one he'd provided Liesl, it was stripped of its GPS locator and as secure a communications device as he could procure on the run.

Plans were made for the four of them to reconvene in New York. There was much to do and the time was short.

Cass and Jordan arrived at their apartment building, the cab dropping them at the side entrance. They carried their backpacks with the evidence against Hans Kluen stuffed inside Jordan's. At this bedraggling hour, they both needed sleep and lots of it.

But the moment she and Jordan stepped from the elevator and started for their separate apartments, Cass suddenly stopped. Lying on the floor just a few feet from her door was an elaborate sketch she'd drawn of the *Wicked* time dragon. She'd kept it in an open portfolio of set designs next to the drawing table in her bedroom. There was no reason it should be lying here on the floor unless someone had dropped it on their way out of her apartment. She looked fearfully at Jordan, who was staring down at the sketch.

"It's yours, right?"

"Yes."

He spun toward her door and advanced cautiously. Over his shoulder, he said, "Hide in the alcove at the end of the hall and wait for me."

She not only refused but was fast on his heels, wishing she had her handgun with her.

Seconds later, Jordan pushed open the breached door and they both stopped to listen. Nothing. But Cass could already see the damage, the contents of her home slung about as if monstrous hands had shaken the apartment loose from the building.

Jordan gripped her arm and whispered firmly. "Stay here. I mean it, Cass."

Against her confrontational instincts, she remained in the doorway as Jordan eased into the room. It didn't take long for him to search the whole apartment. Afterward, he motioned her inside.

She stood at the epicenter of the quake, surrounded by overturned furniture and ransacked cabinets and drawers, their contents spilled and raked. Even the paintings and tapestries had been yanked from the walls and pawed over.

Rachel. Cass wrenched herself from the ruins and spun toward the old oak desk. Its drawers were upside down on the floor, but the framed image of a young girl with rich brown hair sat upright, smiling back at Cass. An indestructible taunt. Would Cass ever be free of it? Would she ever take down the picture she wore like a hair shirt?

Jordan looked past her at the photo on the desk. "Cass, there's enough hurt for today. Let's deal with what's here." He went to the windows and closed all the curtains.

She dropped her backpack on the sofa and wandered about her violated home, unable to summon words. She remembered something she'd read about the *Titanic* survivors taken on board one of the rescue boats. A witness had commented on how still and quiet they were, huddled inside warm blankets, their eyes glazed. They were beyond words, beyond anything that might convey what they'd just endured. Cass understood that.

But Jordan urged her on. "We can't stay here, Cass. They might come back, unless they've already hit my apartment, too."

But Cass was already moving up the steps to her bedroom. It was the sight of her Serengeti oasis that brought the first cry from her. Only the stars on the ceiling remained intact. Her portfolio files with all her designs were gone.

"It's them, Cass," Jordan called from below. "We both know that. That woman knows where I live, and it was my license plate they traced to this building. She was even casing us that day in the rain." Cass moved to the railing and looked down at him. "But this isn't about my visit to them that night," he continued. "These people were looking for something."

He whirled around to survey the mess. "And what is it we have that they could possibly want?" he prompted.

Cass leaned against the railing. "What we took from Hans's study. But how could they know?"

"Unless he told them," Jordan said flatly. "Would he do that?"

"No." Though she'd never loved Hans or regarded him as more than the kindly man who was devoted to her mother, Cass knew he cared deeply for her, too. "No, he would never do anything to harm me. There has to be another reason for this. As far as I know, Hans hasn't been to the beach house in weeks. He couldn't know we were there." She looked at Jordan, his chin propped on a fist, deep in thought. "I think we did exactly what Hans warned me about that day at the restaurant." Jordan looked back up at her. "He said we shouldn't go knocking on strange doors because we couldn't know who might answer, or what they might be in the middle of."

Cass stepped quickly down the stairs. "Jordan, I think we just surprised these people in the middle of something. Made them suspicious that we knew something—even before we did! So they searched us out." Cass sighed. "Hans was right. We did this to ourselves."

"And now they'll think Hans betrayed them to us," Jordan reasoned.

Cass's head jerked up. *What have I done? Again. What harm will come to him because of me?*

Betrayal carried a stench. Like ammonia, it took the breath away and singed the inside of the throat. Cass knew its stinging condemnation. And then it came—a face swimming up from the deep, its convicting eyes, its gurgling voice. *Adam was the one I loved. And you took him from me.* Then the face sank slowly away. Cass felt a cold weight press against her chest, as if this time she had followed the face to its airless crypt. But Jordan's insistent voice pulled her back.

"Cass, we have to get out of here. Pack up whatever you need for a few days. I'm going to check my apartment."

"Wait," she told him, then went quickly to the third step of the staircase she'd built herself. She tugged lightly on the tread, which looked like crudely laid flagstones, and raised it like a lid on a box—which it was. She reached into the hidden compartment beneath and brought out her small revolver. "Take this," she urged, carefully handing off the gun to him. "It's loaded."

He took the handgun, then looked back at her with mournful eyes. "I'm sorry I ever teased you about carrying one of these. I'm sorry you ever needed one."

She looked down at the weapon in his hand, now pointed at the floor. "When I moved out of my parents' home and started working at the theaters, I'd have to come home alone at all hours," she explained. "My father got me into the gun-permit program, bought this handgun for me, took me to the range, and made me learn how to use it safely. Oddly enough, it was one of the most caring things he ever did for me."

"I think he cared more than you want to remember."

"We don't have time to talk about that."

"So we won't. But you hold on to this." He handed the gun back to her and left.

Cass stood like a stone pillar in the wake of him. In the midst of the ruin, there was Jordan. Something strangely warm took hold of her. It seeped through her with surprising speed, thawing the frozen places and thrusting up something foreign through the icy crust. Hope. Just a green tendril of it, but it was enough.

In her bedroom, she shoved clothes, a warm hat and gloves, her old sneakers, and toiletries into a small duffle bag. Everything else she needed was already in her backpack—her phone and the one Evgeny had given them to use, an iPad, cash, credit cards, and IDs. She'd just slung both bags over her shoulders and started down the steps when she heard Jordan calling to her and banging loudly on her door.

When she opened it, he nearly dragged her into the hallway and furiously worked her keys to lock the door again, perhaps in vain. "They're coming!" he cried. He grabbed her hand, and they bolted toward the stairs at the end of the hall.

Cass glanced back at the elevator doors and saw the up arrow flash red. "How do you know it's them?"

As he flung open the door to the stairway, Jordan replied just above a whisper. "I just watched two men cross the street and enter the building.

They left two others hanging back in front of the bakery—a man and a woman. *That* woman!"

They left through the rear of the building, using Cass's service-door keys to relock it, and fled down an alley with their bags and backpacks, like refugees running for the last flight out. A few blocks away, they finally stopped to catch their breath. Leaning against the back wall of a restaurant, they could hear the clatter of pans in the kitchen and its crew bickering in a foreign tongue. Gulping the cold air, Cass looked regretfully at Jordan. "I'm so sorry I got you into this."

He shrugged. "It beats selling shoes." He looked warily around them. "Now let's get moving before we freeze to this wall."

"But where?" She thought a minute. "We can't get to our cars. They'll be watching the garage. How about Myrna and Reg's place?" She thought better of it. "No, we can't invite trouble on them. Maybe a hotel."

Jordan suggested, "Maybe somewhere between the Jimmy Choo boots and the satin pumps."

She knew what he meant. "No, Jordan. They've got to know everything about us by now, including where you work. We've got to—"

The phone in her backpack rang, Evgeny's phone. She answered quickly, then mouthed *Liesl*. Jordan leaned in close enough to hear.

"Are you home yet?" Liesl asked.

Cass could hear road sounds in the background. "We're in New York," she answered, "but not home." Cass told her about the break-in and their escape from the building.

"So you're standing in an alley with no place to go?" Liesl asked with alarm. But then the voice grew calm and firm. "Cass, this is what I want you and Jordan to do. Go straight to West Park Christian Church near Central Park. I'll text the address to you. Go to the small door on the right side of the church and knock. The man who'll let you in is Rev. Francis Scovall." She paused. "He was the one who saved me from . . . the man who saved me today. Ludicrous, isn't it?"

Cass reeled. *Ludicrous? No word can describe this.*

As if hearing her thoughts, Liesl said, "I'll tell you that story another time. But right now, you get to the church and stay there. Rev. Scovall is already expecting the two of us. He'll gladly take in two more, I'm certain of it."

"What do you mean 'take in'?"

"Into the apartment where he lives. It's in the back of the church."

"You mean—"

"I mean you get away from there right now. We'll join you in a couple of hours."

Moments later, with the text bearing the church's address in hand, Cass and Jordan hailed a cab and took off even deeper into the unknown.

"So here we are," Evgeny said, "the assassin and his former prey riding along together as if there were no hard feelings." He eyed her slyly. "But we know better, don't we?"

In the twelve hours they'd been on the road together, Liesl had tried to draw this man from behind his defenses, much like the ones she'd drawn around her own damaged self. It was true, wasn't it? The harder the shell, the weaker the core. The deaths of so many she'd loved and the wounds they'd borne inside her had made her seal herself off from a persistently threatening world. Until Cade had removed the need for those defenses.

But what about this man beside her? He'd murdered Schell Devoe in her presence and then later come after her. He was a man shielded by weaponry and blind devotion to those whose orders he'd never questioned. Until now. What hid within his shell?

Finally, she answered him. "Hard feelings? For the man who came to save me? No. For the man who once tried to kill me? I honestly don't know." She eyed him coolly. "I do know that hard feelings are like the cancer that devoured my mother. God showed me that."

Evgeny scowled at her. "No talk of God. That's for children and old women, for those who haven't seen what I have seen." He shook his head. "There is no God."

Chapter 22

It was almost midnight Saturday when Cass and Jordan got their first look at West Park Christian Church, a few blocks off Central Park. After the taxi pulled away, they remained on the sidewalk, bags at their feet, looking up at the old brick church and its bell tower. Their faces were so weary and forlorn that if there'd been any passersby, they might have thought the pair homeless and looking for help. Indeed, they were.

"When's the last time you were in church?" Jordan asked, gazing up at the tower with its arched openings on top.

"My father's funeral," she said. "The service was long and tedious with lots of holy-sounding words that didn't fit the cheating life of Nicholas Alexander Rodino." She laughed derisively. "My father did use God's name a lot, though. Every time he cursed me and Mom." She looked up at Jordan. "What about you?"

He looked passively toward the church. "Oh, a cousin's wedding, I guess. Can't remember which one. Weddings and funerals, maybe a baptism here and there. That's all the churchgoing I've ever done. I didn't grow up that way. Don't know if I've missed anything or not." He looked up and down the poorly lit street. "We'd better get inside."

They took the sidewalk down the right side of the building and stopped before a plain wooden door. As Jordan knocked, Cass wondered what cosmic order, or disorder, had led them here.

The man must have been waiting just on the other side, for the door opened immediately. Before Jordan could introduce them, the man said, "Come, come," and motioned for them to enter quickly, his face gentle but bearing concern. "You are Jordan and Cass, right?" he asked, locking the door soundly behind them.

A little late to be asking, Cass thought.

"Yes, sir," Jordan answered. "I'm sure this must be a big inconvenience for you."

"Not at all," the man assured them as he gestured for them to sit down in the small vestibule clad in dark paneling. Short benches sat along three walls, and a door stood open in the fourth, though from her angle, Cass couldn't see what lay beyond. Her focus now was on this man dressed in jeans, a pullover sweater, and everyday work boots—not the black robe she had expected. Strands of neatly combed silver barely concealed the pink of his scalp, the same pink that flushed his round cheeks with evidence of a hardy and good-natured soul, or so one might hope.

"I'm Rev. Scovall, and I'm honored that you came."

You are? Cass thought. *Why?*

"Liesl Bower is very special to me, and I'm happy to be of service to her friends." He looked toward the door he'd just locked and smiled. "Perhaps she'll tell you of the night she came bursting through that door in a terrible fright." He turned back to them. "I was seconds from locking it shut, not knowing there was a young woman out there in great danger. But God knew." He paused. "He always knows."

Cass and Jordan exchanged glances but said nothing.

Rev. Scovall eyed their bags. "Now, you'll need lodging and food. I have both. When Liesl and . . . and the man I'm most anxious to meet arrive, you'll all move into my apartment just down the hall." He tilted his head to one side. "You'll find it very modest, indeed, but comfortable. There's a room for the women and one for the men, but you must share a bathroom."

"And what about you, sir?" Jordan asked.

"Oh, I've spent many a night on the sofa in my study on the other side of the church. There's even a small bath nearby." He glanced at his watch. "Ready for a midnight snack?"

Jordan and Cass nodded in unison.

"Good," Rev. Scovall said. "I'd hate for all that food to go to waste." He leaned over and picked up Cass's duffle bag. "Come with me."

Cass looked wide-eyed at Jordan as she grabbed her backpack and fell in behind the reverend. He was of medium height with a few too many pounds packed around his middle, but that didn't seem to slow him down. In fact, he fairly bristled with energy and something even more galvanizing, like a sense of purpose.

When they passed through the door of the vestibule, Cass slowed to a stop and looked around, noticing Jordan do the same. They had just entered the sanctuary. There were no gilded icons or brilliant stained glass windows, but the woodwork was exceptional. The multitiered molding, coffered ceiling, fluted columns, and ornate carvings at the end of each pew spoke admirably of a masterful carpenter somewhere in the past.

But there the visual pageantry ended. The walls were unadorned plaster of pale blue, the windows tall and clear at the top, frosted at the bottom. The mahogany pews were softened with cushions the color of the walls. There was no choir loft and no organ, but a black baby grand piano sat on one side of a raised platform at the front of the church. In the middle of the platform, where a pulpit might have been, stood a single bar stool. Behind it, on a soaring windowless wall, hung a simple wooden cross and nothing else. Cass marveled at the powerful simplicity of the room.

"He was a carpenter, you know," Rev. Scovall said, coming up beside her.

"Who?" Then she realized. "Oh. Him." She didn't know why that embarrassed her.

"I'm told the first congregation of this church wanted to honor that," the reverend added, gazing toward the moldings, which to Cass appeared hand planed. "Now, let me show you to the kitchen."

Cass turned to see Jordan run a hand over the carving of a dove capping one of the pews. She caught his eye and motioned for him to follow. When Jordan caught up, he said, "It's a different kind of place, isn't it?"

She nodded and reached for his arm, less to pull him along than to feel the comfort of him and to watch his face brighten at her touch. She was falling in love with him, though she wasn't ready to. Not now. There was too much to sort out, too little to offer him. *He deserves more than I am.*

They exited the sanctuary on the opposite side and followed Rev. Scovall down a short hallway, through some kind of activity room, and into an adjoining kitchen. "Here we are," he said cheerfully, flipping a light switch. Spread over a long countertop was an assortment of deli meats and cheeses, fresh-baked breads, a couple of pies still in their pans, and an attractive display of fresh fruits. Beyond that were two large casserole dishes, their contents not immediately recognizable beneath a layer of melted cheese on one and sugared pecans on the other.

Rev. Scovall swept his hand over the banquet. "Our secretary and her husband either cooked or gathered this at the last minute. I hope it suits you." Cass and Jordan stared at the food with open mouths. "Mrs. Augustino was here that first night Liesl came to us," the reverend explained.

"Liesl comes here often?" Jordan asked.

"Oh yes. Every time she's in New York, she comes to play for our little congregation." He chuckled. "I'll never forget the first time she sat down at our old upright piano with the cracked keys and plinkity-plunk sound." His shoulders slightly heaved to the beat of his laughter. "We all cringed with embarrassment. That's why we have the baby grand you probably noticed." He paused. "But you know what? She never once complained about the old piano. In fact, she did the most amazing thing the first time she struck those twangy keys." He drew a long breath as if savoring the memory. "She stopped playing, then leaned over and kissed the piano. After that, she proceeded to coax the most beautiful sounds from it we'd ever heard." He looked away a moment, then back at his guests. "That's what happens, you know. Sometimes, it just takes the right touch to restore life."

He looked back at the food. "Well now, enough talk. Please fill your plates. Liesl tells me that this day has been an ordeal for you. I'm sorry for that. I've prayed for God to show you his path through this trouble. You must watch for it." With that, he started for the door, then paused. "I'll leave you now. Liesl and her . . . uh . . . friend should be here soon. I must listen for them." And he left.

It was just after one on Sunday morning when Evgeny parked at the side of the church. Liesl stared out the window at the small, unmarked door before them.

"It will do neither one of us any good to dwell on what happened here," Evgeny said. "That is over."

But trapped behind his scorn was a different sound, a painful plea. Liesl heard it, and she understood. Without a word, she got out and went to the door. As soon as she knocked, Rev. Scovall opened it. Just last week, she'd come to perform for his congregation. Tonight, she'd come to hide. Again.

"Come in," the reverend said, reaching for her and drawing her into a light but affectionate embrace. "Sweet child, you're safe here." He released her slowly and turned toward Evgeny, who'd planted himself a few feet away, his head cocked, his eyes like flint.

Liesl was relieved to see Rev. Scovall make the first move. He walked up to Evgeny and touched the side of his arm. "It's good to see you too, Mr. Kozlov. Please come inside where it's warm . . . and secure."

After a long moment of awkward silence, Evgeny responded, "I should not be here."

Without hesitation, the reverend replied, "Then where should you be?"

Apparently, Evgeny had no answer.

"Please, sir, come with us," Rev. Scovall urged.

Liesl watched the subtle twitch of Evgeny's resolute face. She couldn't help but smile when he turned and followed the reverend inside.

"Your young friends are having a bite to eat in the kitchen, Liesl." Rev. Scovall pointed the way down the hall. "If you'll excuse us, I'd like a word with Mr. Kozlov."

Liesl watched Evgeny go rigid.

"This way, please," Rev. Scovall prompted, offering little chance for Evgeny to decline. When the two men disappeared into the sanctuary, Liesl headed toward the kitchen, wondering what in heaven's name the good reverend had to say to the hired killer.

Cass and Jordan had finished their meal and were cleaning up after themselves when they heard footsteps in the hall. A disheveled Liesl appeared in the doorway. Her hair was bunched into a knot on top of her head, and she wore a bulky jacket that hung below her fingertips. She offered a dispirited smile, then said apologetically, "I hardly know what to say to you."

Jordan didn't miss a beat. "How about 'Pass the casserole, please'?" He picked up a long Pyrex dish and passed it under his nose. "Hmm . . . broccoli."

Cass knew what he was doing, and it worked. Liesl stared at him a moment, then broke into a wide grin.

"Come on and get something to eat," Cass urged. Then she looked past Liesl and saw no one behind her. "Where's the Russian guy?"

"In the sanctuary, talking to Rev. Scovall."

"Do they know each other?" Jordan asked.

"Only by reputation," Liesl answered, eyeing them closely. "I guess you should know what kind of trouble you've gotten yourselves into, and with whom." She waved off Jordan's attempts to bring her food and drink, then sat down in a folding metal chair and stretched her long legs before her. It was the first time Cass noticed the splotches of paint on Liesl's faded jeans. When the jacket came off, revealing a stretched and slightly frayed sweater beneath, Cass remembered that Liesl had escaped with the clothes on her back and nothing more. Cass wondered where she got the jacket. Probably from the Russian.

Liesl released her hair from the elastic band straining to contain it all and shook it free, "Evgeny Kozlov is a former Russian secret service—KGB—agent who, just a year ago, was ordered to capture me for the information I didn't know I had. Then he was to kill me." She paused to let that take root. "He failed miserably, as you can see." She tapped her fingernails against the table and fixed her gaze on Cass.

"It seems you and I share the same proclivity for accidentally knocking over hornets' nests," she told Cass, "then trying to outrun the stinging beasts. I thought I had, until this week." She looked from Cass to Jordan. "There are things I can't tell you about Evgeny, classified kinds of things that have to do with a music professor I once had, a lost code, and an assassination plot that failed because the code was found and translated in time. But I can tell you this. I just spent nearly fourteen hours on the road with Evgeny Kozlov, and I no longer fear him. In fact, I trust him to make sense of what's happening to us right now."

"While he's explaining that," Jordan said, "I hope he won't use words like *proclivity*." He grinned at Liesl as he handed her a stem of grapes. "I want to clearly understand what this Russian hornet has planned for us."

"Why not ask the hornet himself?" Evgeny walked in and stiffly appraised Jordan. Rev. Scovall hung back near the door.

"Well, uh, all right," Jordan ventured. He put down the dishcloth he'd been using and drew himself up tall before Evgeny.

Cass couldn't imagine what he was going to say. "Jordan . . ." she said in a cautioning tone.

"It's okay, Cass," he said over his shoulder. "If this doesn't go well, you can have my car and my stuffed armadillo."

When he turned back to Evgeny, the tone changed. Jordan looked him straight in the eye. "If Liesl says you're an okay guy now and won't be murdering any of us in our sleep, I'll buy into that—until you prove her wrong. And if you do that, well, even this shoe salesman who doesn't like guns too much will come after you."

Evgeny regarded Jordan as one would a foolish child. But that didn't stop Jordan.

"You look around this room. I care about these people. Yeah, I just met Ms. Bower, but I sure do like her. As for Rev. Scovall here, I don't know what you two were talking about, but I hope something he said made you think of that lightning bolt that'll take you out if you mess with one of God's own." Then he turned to Cass. "And this one?" He looked at her with transparent affection. "I like every hair on her head just where it is." He looked back at Evgeny. "I wouldn't want to find even one of them missing." He stared quietly at Evgeny a few more moments, then finally looked away and nodded his head up and down as if confirming with himself everything he'd just said. Evidently pleased, he looked back at Evgeny. "Now, how was your trip? Any trouble finding the place?"

After Liesl and Evgeny had revived themselves with a bit of food, Rev. Scovall said, "I hope you'll be comfortable in my little dwelling down the hall. But before I take you there, would you mind coming with me a moment?"

He led them all, Evgeny included, into the sanctuary and ushered them to a grouping of loose chairs at the back of the room where they could face each other.

"Before you go off to bed," the reverend began, "I want just a few words with you, knowing what you've been through already and having no idea what's to come. Please just listen to this old man who's learned a few things that might sustain you." He looked toward the coffered ceiling, then back at them. "It's almost the fourth watch of the night. In Roman times, that was between three and six in the morning—the coldest, bleakest hours." He peered intently into the faces before him. "That's the sinking hour when Jesus did what I certainly have never seen anyone do. You've heard the story. The storm hit and the disciples' boat began to sink. They'd tried everything they knew to stay afloat, but the elements overpowered them. They had only one hope—their Lord. In their utter despair and helplessness, they finally called to him. In their darkest hour, they called to Jesus. And he came. Over the water, just in time."

The reverend glanced toward some point near the front of the room. Liesl couldn't tell which. She watched the others. Evgeny's face was impassive, Jordan's also unreadable. But it was Cass who visibly locked on every word.

"Sometimes our struggles must take us into the darkest, grimmest hours," Rev. Scovall continued, "to humble us, to teach us. To make us trust. Then God does what no one else can do. Through the drowning storm of that fourth watch, he comes to save us."

Chapter 23

Dane Bruton stood on the back steps of his farmhouse and gazed over the pasture. Its winter stubble stretched to the distant tree line, broken only by the sluggish little creek that wandered off the Mohatchy River. It was one of the last tributaries to cut away from its host waters before the massive, man-made basin downstream sucked the river into containment, otherwise known as Lake Jenowak.

Zipping his jacket against the chill, he watched the eastern sky announce the coming day, its golden palette issuing a peaceful glow at odds with his convulsive thoughts. After all the years of thoughtful preparation, was he ready to do the unthinkable? How many lives would it take? Too few to matter, he told himself, then started for the chicken coop.

Even in the half-light of dawn, he could see the bright rose combs of his dominickers as they strutted their handsome selves about the pen. He'd bred the distinctive birds with the black-and-white barred plumage first for their company, then their eggs. Odd that a man would seek companionship from chickens. But he knew the origin of that. As a boy in Russia, returning home after school each day, he'd always run first to the Orloff pen behind the house. The hardy white chickens with black spots never failed to gather in welcome at his feet, each pushing ahead of the other for his attention. He relished the affection of even these dumb creatures who were more forgiving and caring than the humans who lived in the cold-hearted home of his birth.

When he unlatched the gate and entered the pen, the dominickers recalled for him the simmering hope of his boyhood—to escape the life-less village and attend a university, which he had done. There, he caught a patriotic fever that swept him into a myopic, all-for-Mother-Russia brotherhood of intelligence watchdogs. Fearing a wife and children would only drag him into the smothering restraints he'd grown up with, he was content to journey alone. That made him infinitely valuable to the Architect and the secretive ring of saboteurs spawned in the waters of his underworld.

Waters. He had come to know what power they held. Now an engineer, planted in the United States just ten years ago, he would stir the waters with his unrighteous right hand.

An hour later, Bruton drove his pickup truck down the long, pot-holed drive from his house to the road, his headlights etching the pines along the way. After a decade, he'd come to own the brand of the rural American South—the farm, the truck, the guns and dogs, the livestock, and most of the accent. He'd worked hard to repress his native tongue.

It was fifteen miles to the Lake Jenowak dam and hydropower plant. He could have driven it blindfolded, sensing when to turn and pause along the lakeside route. When he arrived that Sunday morning at the massive structure that held back the river-fed waters, he only slowed at the guardhouse. They knew him. He brought them good-natured greetings and fresh eggs. When they waved him through, he followed the narrow, descending roadway to the base of the concrete dam that rose more than one hundred feet from downstream ground level. From there, it plunged deeper to bedrock.

It was a medium-sized dam. But the river that coursed through the middle of the lake and out the other side of the dam—in critically controlled volume—ran straight to a major city.

Dane grabbed a small tool bag from the back seat and headed for the entrance to the power plant. His usual station was at a bank of computers that controlled many operations, including the flow of water from the intake towers in the lake, through the penstocks, and into the massive turbines of the dam, which harnessed the wild force of the river and converted it to electricity.

But this morning, he stopped at his computer just long enough to log in his security code and shut down a pair of surveillance cameras. Afterward, he went straight to one of the tunnels that led through the belly of the dam. Alone in the tunnel at this early weekend hour, he retrieved a few instruments from his bag, brand new tools ordered online, the kind he'd need to dismantle the plates covering valve heads inset in the concrete walls along the tunnel. He then stopped at three strategic points along the way and tested the tools. When each of three steel plates yielded to his force, he quickly retightened them to their original position, placed the tools back in the bag, and returned to his post at the computers, his heartbeat zinging in his neck as he reactivated the cameras.

Seated alone at his station, his mind's eye saw the charges hidden in weatherproof bags in his barn—enough to deliver all of Lake Jenowak to the city downstream.

Because the town had been built on a high ridge above the Mohatchy, and because the banks of the river from the dam to town rose like cliffs and supported few dwellings, there would be minimal loss of life. But the weapons-grade chemical plant south of town, designed to divert enough river water to cool its machinery, sat on a plain that sloped to the river.

When Dane arrived home that afternoon, he went straight to his chickens. At least they would be safe. He'd leave instructions for how to feed them with the people who'd just bought his farm. Everything was ready. One morning soon, the Architect himself would transmit the signal, and Dane would report to work one last day. He would work late, deactivate the appropriate surveillance cameras, dismantle the plates, conceal the charges inside, time them to blow after the remaining crew had clocked out for the evening, clean out his locker, and head straight to the airport. He should touch down in Moscow about the time the chemical plant slid into the raging flood.

Chapter 24

Despite Jordan's earlier tirade, Evgeny found himself strangely comforted by the company of those so unlike himself. He had never been his own favorite person. In fact, he rather loathed himself. That's why caring for others had been so difficult. But there was something about the unbridled regard these people had for each other that intrigued him. He couldn't relate to them on a normal level, though, so he'd attempted to withdraw from them altogether. When he'd announced to Liesl that she should remain at the church and he would stay elsewhere—in one of the escape warrens he'd dug for himself in the New York underworld—she'd objected. "No. We have to stay together," she'd insisted. He'd never taken orders from a woman, certainly not the mother who bore and later abandoned him. But he remained at the church at the entreaty of one person.

It had been a quick and efficient meeting with Rev. Scovall in the sanctuary that night. Oddly enough, the pastor and the shoe salesman, though separately and in remarkably different ways, had immediately drilled toward the same objective, to probe the intentions of the assassin in their midst. Evgeny had left the reverend with assurance that his only objective was to disarm cataclysmic events whose timers had been set by his own countrymen and were, at that moment, ticking. He also was there to protect Liesl Bower from those seeking revenge against her.

But when Evgeny later tried to leave the church and seek shelter else-where, Liesl pursued him onto the sidewalk and insisted he stay. Not until Rev. Scovall appeared beside her with his own request, though, did Evgeny return with them. The reverend had simply said, "Don't run anymore."

That was all. Had someone just given him permission to live, it might have felt no different. Though he had, indeed, lived on the run his whole life, surely that wasn't living. But what was?

He tried to imagine a different sort of life as he now lay in a tiny room with the snoring Jordan in a twin bed much too close for Evgeny's com-fort. It hadn't taken long that night for Jordan to initiate peace between them, over something as benign as toothpaste. Evgeny had none. "Use mine," Jordan had offered as Evgeny headed for the bathroom. "I guess going off to spy on foreign countries isn't like packing for camp, is it?" Jordan had quipped. "And where's a Walmart when you need one, right?" Jordan chuckled as he threaded a length of floss between his teeth.

His own mouth slightly ajar, Evgeny stared at Jordan for an extended and bewildered moment, then took the proffered toothpaste and went quietly away, wondering how this peculiar union had come to be.

On his return from the bathroom, he paused outside the bedroom as-signed to Liesl and Cass, but heard nothing. Could they have fallen asleep so quickly? It was almost two when Rev. Scovall had ushered them into his private quarters to sleep. Evgeny now felt the tug of fatigue and headed back to his room. That's when he heard Liesl's voice coming from outside the entrance to the apartment. He moved quietly toward the sound.

She was on a phone. "Yes, Cade, in New York. I can't tell you where. . . . No, not now. It's too dangerous for you. . . . I know how terrible this is. I know where you and I should be this night, but please try to under-stand. I've told you all I know for now, everything Evgeny told me about this man who calls himself the Architect. . . . Yes, I trust him. I can't ex-plain why. I guess there's something going on that's so much bigger than we are, something so awful that I have to overlook what he did before. If God brought him to save me from that gunman, well, . . . Yes, I know how unbelievable it is."

Evgeny couldn't listen anymore. He went to bed with the image of himself as pure evil. How could God, if he existed at all, possibly use him to do anything good? He soon fell into the intermittent sleep of one who never relinquishes all consciousness, who must always listen for the uninvited footfall.

So when his phone buzzed just four hours later, he answered instantly. It was Viktor, his friend and informant who prowled the back corridors of Russian intelligence, siphoning up just pieces of whole truth. Evgeny knew this dark labyrinth to be the netherworld of conspiracy, the land where Andreyev and Fedorovsky had once fleshed out their heinous plot to kill their own president and that of Syria, to fraudulently "prove" Israel had ordered both hits, and to watch an outraged U.S. stand by as the Arab world finally extinguished Israel. All the while, Andreyev and Fedorovsky were to seize control of Russia.

Every bit of it according to the dictates of their shadowy commander-at-large, the Architect. But the whole thing had crashed and burned at the feet of a lovely young pianist and the code she found in her music.

When the call ended, Evgeny sprang from bed and shook Jordan awake. "We have to go. Wake the women and tell them to dress quickly, then meet me at the side door of the church. All of you must bring something to conceal your faces. Scarves, hats, sunglasses, whatever you have." Before retiring that night, Rev. Scovall had gathered warm clothing from the church's charity closet, especially for Liesl, who'd fled with nothing but what she was wearing in balmy Charleston.

Jordan mumbled acknowledgment of the orders. In the time it took him to wrestle himself from sleep and finally throw back the covers, Evgeny was dressed and out the door.

Hoping not to wake the reverend from wherever he had bedded down that night, Evgeny slipped out of the church and went quickly to the van. Rev. Scovall had arranged for him to park it in the private space of a church member who lived across the street but spent her winters in Florida.

In the smoky dark of predawn—long before the first parishioners would arrive for Sunday-morning service—Evgeny stopped the van at the curb and watched as three figures approached from the side door of the church. Once they were settled inside, the van drove off at a cautious pace. No need to draw unwanted attention.

"What's going on, Evgeny?" Liesl asked in a sleep-thick voice.

"Cass's stepfather is on the move," he answered.

"What?" Cass asked, startled. Evgeny watched her reaction in the rearview mirror. He needed to know every nuance of this little cast of cohorts he'd been saddled with. He wanted nothing more than to stalk Hans Kluen alone, to follow him straight to the Architect. But Evgeny needed Cass to identify her stepfather, to educate Evgeny on the slippery ways of the traitorous Wall Street banker. He needed Jordan Winslow only to identify the Architect, if indeed that was the man in the UN apartment. But Evgeny couldn't be certain of that if the man stood before him right now. No, it was better to track the known than chase blindly after the unknown. At this point, there were entirely too many unknowns to suit an undercover agent who'd always been sure of his mission, his target.

And Liesl. Yes, her role was critical. She was the credible one, the surest path to those who would release the Architect's maniacal hold on Russia. Still, this wasn't supposed to be a group effort.

"What do you mean he's on the move?" Cass persisted.

"Someone is waiting to signal him. I need to know who and where."

"How do you know this?"

"My contact tells me so. That is enough for you to know."

Cass glowered at him. "You know, we're going to get along a lot better if you stop treating us like unintelligent matter. I have a feeling I wouldn't be here if you didn't need me. You probably don't know what Hans looks like, do you?"

Evgeny squinted at her in the mirror. "That is correct," he conceded.

"Thought so," Cass said. "But here's a better question. What if he happens to see me?"

"He cannot if you remain concealed in the van." Evgeny shifted his focus to Liesl. "You must observe everything, Liesl. That is why you are here. You must record everything you see in order to convince the CIA that we are tracking something real and imminent—as if the inauguration and Supreme Court blowups weren't convincing enough. Still, we must prove the greater conspiracy."

"If everything you tell me is true," Liesl said, "and I have no reason to doubt it, I'll have no trouble convincing Ava and Ben to act on it."

Evgeny immediately swerved to the curb and stopped. "Liesl, I must talk to you alone. Come with me." He looked at the wide-eyed faces behind him, where he preferred they sit. "Please remain in the van," he told Cass and Jordan. "We will not be long."

Liesl climbed warily from the van.

"Please come," he urged her as he walked a short distance away, stopping in the receding doorway of a closed tobacco shop. No one else was on the street when he turned to face Liesl. She was about to speak when he said sharply, "Listen to me and don't interrupt." He ignored her glare. "You will, under no circumstances, contact Ben Hafner or anyone else in the White House. I have proof that the Architect is running an undercover informant inside the Executive Office. Again." He let that sink in, watching Liesl recoil at the insinuation. "This informant works for the president."

Even in the dim light, Evgeny could see Liesl's face redden. "You can't mean Ben!"

"Shh!" he warned, looking around them, then toward the van. "We must go, but first you swear to me you will contact no one until I tell you to. Do you understand?"

She didn't answer, but her body trembled. Not from the cold, he suspected. He'd been too harsh. "Liesl, please. We do not know for certain that it is Hafner, but my contact believes it is."

"Well, your contact doesn't know Ben. I do. He's a good and honorable man."

"Even the good fall, lured by money or ideology. Maybe allegiance to another country."

"What does that mean?"

Evgeny wished he'd ventured no further, but now that he had, he might as well finish. "I, too, believe the White House mole is Ben Hafner.

His own brother-in-law, a longtime insurgent working for the Russian underground, has recruited Ben in the name of their common homeland. Not America, but Israel. Ben's whole family lives there. He keeps a home there. And word has it that he is sending his wife and children to his family in Tel Aviv." Liesl stared at him in disbelief. "I am certain why he is doing that, Liesl. To protect them if he is caught."

He was surprised to see Liesl swipe at her eyes. He didn't anticipate the effect this news would have on her. Now he worried that she might try to warn Hafner. Evgeny would have to convince her of the man's undoing.

When Evgeny and Liesl returned to the van, no one spoke. They rode the distance to Lower Manhattan in an uneasy hush, until they reached the Tribeca district south of Canal Street. "Two blocks ahead, take a right," Cass instructed. "Two more blocks, you'll see an ochre-colored building on the left. That's it."

Soon, the van parked across the street from Jilly and Hans Kluen's apartment building. Evgeny turned off the motor, spewing telltale exhaust plumes into the frigid morning. All eyes watched the glass door of the building where a light from within lit the etched fleur-de-lis design. "You're sure it was *this* morning?" Cass asked.

"Nothing is sure. We will watch. We cannot afford not to."

Cass looked at Jordan, then Liesl, who appeared wholly preoccupied with her own thoughts. Cass noticed that Liesl had tucked all of her trademark hair inside a knit hat and pulled a soft wool scarf over her mouth. Even half concealed, the woman was even more striking in person than in her publicity shots, though just now, Cass noticed, the famous face had pulled into weary lines. Was Cass projecting her own emotions onto Liesl? Probably. There was something almost visceral about Cass's need to share her feelings with another woman. Certainly not her mother. And no longer Rachel. But with the one now yoked to Cass in this dangerous passage.

Cass tugged on the hood of her jacket, pulling it lower over her face, not just to hide but for warmth and insulation against this disturbing time. Just then, she felt a hand on her knee and the gentle squeeze. She looked up into Jordan's caring face and, once again, found the comfort she needed. She cherished his candid affections for her and all the hairs on her head—the ones he'd warned Evgeny never to touch. That made her smile again, inside where no one could see.

Jordan's was an honesty she'd rarely known in others, and she believed some merciful, benevolent force somewhere had set this gentle man down in her path.

Evgeny's urgent voice broke the stillness. "Is this Hans Kluen coming through the door?"

Cass turned quickly to see her stepfather leave the apartment building and turn north along the sidewalk.

"Yes, that's him!" All her senses suddenly returned to the mission at hand.

"He is not hailing a cab," Evgeny observed. "I will have to follow him on foot." He turned to Jordan. "You drive. Stay a safe distance behind me, but not too far. Any communication you need to make with me, remember to use only the phone I gave you."

As Evgeny slipped from the van and closed the door, Jordan scrambled from the back seat to take his place. They all watched Evgeny, clad in black head to toe, with his coat collar drawn high around his face. He crossed the street and took up a leisurely pace a half block behind Hans Kluen.

Cass watched her stepfather's lumbering gait, accentuated by the bulky coat. "I can't believe this is happening," she muttered.

"Do you think your mother suspects anything?" Liesl asked as Jordan pulled the van from the curb and fell in at a discreet distance behind Evgeny.

"Nothing like this. She still thinks he's having an affair. I think she'd handle that a lot better than what's coming."

"What can we do for her?"

We? Something tugged inside Cass. She looked curiously at Liesl. "I haven't thought that one through, but I'll handle it." On her own, Cass knew. She looked at the worn seat fabric between her and Liesl, just a sliver of space separating two radically different lives. Had Liesl just attempted a bridge between them?

When Cass looked up, Liesl was watching her. "I don't know you, Cass," she said in a direct and probing way, "but I sense something very solitary in you."

Cass was too stunned to respond.

"We've been bound together in something too extraordinary to be subtle with each other. Before this is over, we might have to rely on one another for survival. So we should each know how the other is wired, don't you think?" Liesl looked ahead, her sights clearly on Evgeny, who was still strolling casually behind Hans. Then she turned back to face Cass. "I sense the solitary in you because I know it so well. I chose to live that insulated life for many years. I thought it would keep me safe from more hurt. But it just made the pain worse." Liesl glanced toward Evgeny as the van kept a steady pace behind him, the light traffic on the street passing by. "It wasn't until—Jordan! He's turning the corner!"

"I see him." A minute later, the van made a slow right turn. Hans must have slowed after the turn because Evgeny was now too close to him. They watched as Evgeny stopped in front of a pharmacy window and feigned prolonged interest in whatever was displayed there. But Hans took no special notice, though he did turn once to look behind him, at Evgeny and a few others on the street. It was an apartment building on the left side that Hans seemed most drawn to, glancing repeatedly toward a balcony midway up.

"Watch him!" Cass said, rebounding from the awkward and unfinished dialogue with Liesl. "He's looking for something in that building!"

Jordan pulled to the curb near the pharmacy, not far behind Evgeny. "Not something," Jordan said, craning his neck toward the upper floors of the building. "Some*one*! Cass, it's her!"

Chapter 25

The sun had most certainly risen that Sunday morning, though no one in Manhattan had seen anything of it. When Hans left the apartment just after seven, a dusky tarp of clouds covered the city. He'd returned to New York the day before, immediately after the Supreme Court debacle, but couldn't bear to confront Jilly. She wouldn't have known his complicity in the bombing that, according to the hail of news reports, had killed two people and maimed that young boy. Ivan had told him no one would be there, no one in the building, and the outside blasts would be too weak and too far from the sidewalk to injure anyone. Ivan had said it was just a demonstration.

Still, the blood had gushed from the young boy's head, and his mother had asked Hans to pray for her son. How trusting. How absurd.

From JFK, he'd taken a cab straight to his office. No one was on his floor, so he'd closed his door and settled into his calf-leather executive chair with nine-way adjustments and looked out over the city. His expansive office window faced the East River. He'd worked hard and risked everything for the chair and the view, for the tony Tribeca apartment, the European vacations, the Tiffany baubles—all of it for the hand of the woman he'd loved since those early Bronx days when he'd barely spoken English. How quickly she would eject him from her charmed life, though, if she knew what else he had done.

No, he hadn't planted the devices, not personally. Hans the overseer was paid exorbitantly to manage his saboteurs, to recruit and coddle the bomb makers and deliverymen who infiltrated the target sites. For several years, he'd run the Secret Service agent who facilitated the installation of the piano device. Likewise, Hans had shepherded the renovations contractor who'd planted the Supreme Court explosives. Hans knew the man like family and had paid him like an NBA athlete.

Other saboteurs just waited for their fortune. For some, though, it was their chance to stick it to the red, white, and blue. Across the country, they waited for different reasons. But none of it mattered to Hans anymore, not even the money that funded his dream life with Jilly—because he could still see the boy's cranial blood smeared across that mother's cheek. And hear his own little brother's screams at the hands of someone no different from himself.

No, it was all over now.

So on this Sunday morning, it was fitting that the light of day had been all but extinguished. People like him worked best in the dark.

As he strode wearily along the sidewalk, he took note of no one else. No need to. Though surely no one had missed the relentless television recounts of the Washington bombings, who among the viewers could possibly associate those crimes with the man now passing them on the street?

Just a few blocks to go. If the signal was there, he would meet Ivan one last time. Then Hans would arrange for his own disappearance. But how best to do that without drawing incriminating attention to Jilly and Cass? That was his greatest fear.

He regretted wrapping himself so heavily against the weather. He felt hobbled. If he'd had to move quickly—to flee—he couldn't. One more block and he would turn at the corner and survey a certain fourth-floor balcony in the apartment building ahead. In the past, he'd irrationally feared some overly observant local would note the regularity of his visits to the street, every other Monday at half past noon. He rarely had to pause in his casual stroll down the street, only glance up at Sonya's balcony. She was as punctual as he. If she appeared on her balcony wearing solid black, there was no meeting the following night. If solid white, Hans was to report to the apartment. If she wore a matching scarf around her head, the meeting would be aboard the trawler instead, though that was rare. Even though Ivan was often out of the country, Sonya expected Hans's attendance at the biweekly check-ins. Sometimes another overseer would be present.

In the seven years since Ivan had recruited Hans to his network, there had never been a Sunday-morning signal for a same-day meeting. There had never been events such as those in Washington this week. No need for battlefield strategies. Until now.

At the corner, Hans turned and immediately looked toward the fourth-floor balcony ahead. He didn't see her at first and slowed his pace, casually surveying the street. A young woman pushed a stroller ahead of him. From behind, he heard a clanging and turned to see a man raising the lattice security screen from over his restaurant. Farther down the sidewalk, a man dressed in black was window-shopping at the pharmacy.

As he walked, Hans kept looking toward the balcony. Finally, she appeared, stepping from the shadow of the door overhang into the open. In a white coat and matching scarf, she busied herself with the rearrangement of porch chairs, giving no apparent attention to Hans or anyone else in the street below. The color-coded signal meant he would meet the boat that evening. It would pick him up at six, as was customary with river meetings, and return him to the dock before eight. Ivan craved precision. He also craved little games, like making Hans walk to Sonya's porch signal instead of receiving a simple text message. Except for the final signal he would text to his field agents across the country, Ivan preferred the old-school covert techniques to techno-communications, which he claimed were too easily intercepted. But Hans knew that Ivan just wanted to run his agents through their hoops, testing their obedience and endurance, working them like trained monkeys. For his own pleasure.

Traffic was just beginning to pick up. An old white van passed slowly by him, giving him only momentary pause.

At the next corner, he turned down a side street and headed for home. He knew his wife would object to his leaving for any reason that night. There was no excuse he could give that would satisfy her. So it didn't matter what he told her. He would endure her anger and distrust. If she would let him, he would hold her until she uncoiled. He would kiss her tenderly. And he would never return to her.

When Evgeny caught up with the van a few blocks from the pharmacy, he climbed into the passenger seat beside Jordan and told him to drive out of the neighborhood. "I do not want Hans spotting this van again and getting suspicious." He turned to face Jordan. "You are certain that was the same woman from the apartment?" It had been Jordan's immediate call to Evgeny, still stationed in front of the pharmacy, that alerted him to the woman on the balcony.

"Positive," Jordan said. "Who is she?"

"A ruthless old babe who used to hover like a raven over the KGB offices. The fact that she's here in New York means we don't have long. She's a closer." He then turned in his seat and looked directly at Cass.

"In a little while, I want you to call your mother and tell her you are coming over. I need someone inside, watching Hans and listening. We know who just sent the signal to him, but not what it meant. I need eyes and ears on him. Can you do it?"

Cass nodded distractedly, her mind whirling through options for getting her mother out. She could leave the city and move to the beach house, but it wouldn't take long for someone to track her down. Who, though? Who are these people?

"Cass, acknowledge," Evgeny said impatiently.

"Yes, I'll call. But I've got to get my mom somewhere out of reach."

Evgeny looked thoughtful. "I know a place. It will not be up to her standards, but no one will find her. Afterward, you will need a very fine lawyer to prove her innocent of involvement in her husband's crimes."

"Afterward?" Liesl interjected. "What does this afterward look like, Evgeny?"

Cass watched Evgeny turn a surprisingly compassionate eye on Liesl.

Liesl kept going. "I've been in the afterward too many times before, only to find the threat still there. You were that threat once, Evgeny. No, make that three times. And here you are again. Only this time, the threat is from someone new."

Cass didn't move, her eyes finding Jordan's in the rearview mirror.

"If I ever make it home," Liesl persisted, "will Cade and I be walking along the beach one night and hear footsteps behind us? Will there be bullets in this afterward?" She looked out the side window and lowered her head against the pane. No one spoke.

Evgeny turned completely in his seat and pointed to a spot just below Liesl's chin. She flinched as if he'd grabbed her.

"Does that cross you wear mean nothing to you?" he asked sharply.

Cass stared at the necklace, then back at Liesl's colorless face.

"Didn't you just tell me yesterday that your God shows you things?" Evgeny demanded.

Liesl didn't answer.

"Well, ask him what to do with all that fear." He spoke as if Liesl were the only one in the car. "Or don't you trust him?" Evgeny didn't lower his sights on her. "If I believed in a trustworthy god of any kind, I'd believe *all* the time." Then he turned around.

Cass looked away from Liesl, an attempt to offer some modicum of privacy. Then she heard Liesl exhale a quivering breath. "Thank you, Evgeny," she said softly.

The air in the van spread like a hot blanket on them all. Cass stared at the floor, hoping for some spotlight to fall on a way out of this muddled mess of emotion and peril. She wanted resolution—and quickly. Willing to dispel the throbbing vibrations in the van, she turned efficiently to the issue at hand.

"Give Hans time to get back to the apartment, and I'll call Mom," she told Evgeny. "Jordan and I will head there as soon as we can."

"Not Jordan," Evgeny instructed, quickly reverting back to his detached authority. "You'll learn more if there's no outsider making Hans nervous. You must go alone."

"Now wait a minute, Evgeny," Jordan said. "Whoever came looking for Cass at her apartment probably knows where else they might find her. How do you know they're not staking out her parents' place this minute?"

Evgeny gave this thought, then turned to Cass. "Make the call, and I will get you safely inside the building. Then we will—"

His phone vibrated. He listened at length to the caller, then asked tersely, "When?"

The call ended. Evgeny turned to Jordan. "You and Cass will return to the church and remain there. Liesl and I have someplace else to go."

Liesl looked uneasy.

"Keeping secrets?" Jordan asked.

"Of course," Evgeny answered tersely.

"Well, since Cass and I seem to be on your dragon lady's seek-and-destroy list, perhaps you might offer us just a glimpse of your plans for the day. You two going roller-blading?"

Evgeny sighed deeply but didn't budge. "I understand your frustration, Jordan. But for your own protection, there are things you must not know."

"Ignorance has never protected me before."

It was the first time Cass had heard Evgeny laugh. It was more a fleeting rattle in his throat and a crumpling of the brow, but it was genuine. When the face returned to its static composure, Evgeny ended the conversation. "They hunt me for what I know. They would kill me for what I know. You and Cass will wait safely for us at the church, and that is all."

The sanctuary was filled with disparate voices singing a hymn when the foursome returned to the church. Liesl used a key Rev. Scovall had given her to open the side door, and they all slipped into his private apartment unnoticed by the congregation. Liesl would soon leave with Evgeny on the mission he had yet to explain. But she hadn't objected, Cass observed, as if Liesl were numb to all that came hurtling toward her. Cass knew such numbness to a depth that threatened permanence. Only Jordan could fish her from the deadening spiral. She wanted to help Liesl if that was possible. Then Cass caught the glimmer of the cross necklace lodged in a fold of the scarf still loosely wrapped about Liesl's neck. *Maybe she doesn't need my help, after all.*

⤶⤷

Evgeny went straight to the little room he'd shared with Jordan and closed the door. The others could hear him conversing with someone in Russian. Jordan looked to Liesl for interpretation. "I never got the hang of their language," she admitted. "But I trust him. I shouldn't, but I do." She looked at Cass, then back at Jordan. "Do you mind if Cass and I talk privately?"

Jordan looked around as if for another place to go.

"You can stay here, Jordan." Liesl pulled her scarf more snugly about her neck. "But you'll still need your coat where we're going, Cass."

With Jordan settled willingly in a tattered old recliner in front of a small TV, Liesl led Cass into the front hall, whose doors were closed to the sanctuary. They could hear Rev. Scovall's amplified yet soothing voice from inside. Liesl pictured him perched on the bar stool, alone on the stage in front of the crudely hewn cross, delivering a simple message for complicated times.

Near the entrance to the church, they turned down a short hall to a stairway leading to the belfry. Liesl closed the stairway door behind them before they began their ascent. "I have a history with bell towers," she told Cass. "I hope you don't mind indulging me. I do know where I'm going."

Cass voiced no objection, but Liesl could sense her apprehension.

When they reached a landing, Liesl opened a small door to a narrow, spiral staircase, and shuddered at the downward blast of bitter air. After a vigorous climb, they entered the open tower with its four bricked arches, and the cold didn't matter anymore. The tower rose no higher than perhaps a fifth-floor level in another building, but the 360-degree view over this residential neighborhood was engaging enough to dismiss the chill for a while.

Liesl turned Cass's attention to the twin bells above them. "We don't have long before those things announce the end of services."

Cass looked curiously at her. "Why are we here?"

Smiling at the expected question, Liesl said, "Rev. Scovall brought me here the night Evgeny and his men tried to kidnap me. And who knows what else they might have done." She still wondered. "I nearly knocked the reverend down when I barged through the side door of the church, frantic for a place to hide." She looked out over the rooftops and the anonymous lives contained beneath them. "I was always hiding, even on a concert stage." She looked back at Cass. "You're a set designer. You know how grand the deception can be, don't you?"

Cass drew her coat hood about her face and buried her chin inside the collar. "Yeah. I'm pretty good at it, too."

Regretfully, Liesl saw herself in Cass. "Back home in Charleston, I used to hide from my drunken father in the bell tower of St. Philip's Church. Later, I hid in my music, but no longer from him. I hid from hurt, so much of it. Most everybody I loved died horribly, and I couldn't stand any more. So I detached myself from everyone and everything else that might threaten. And you know what?" She didn't wait for an answer. "That was the same as dying."

Cass turned toward her. "Why are you telling me this?"

"Because I wonder if anyone ever has."

Cass looked away.

"Rev. Scovall told me he comes up here alone to listen." Liesl pressed on, not fully understanding her own need to do so. Or was it a prompting?

Beneath Cass's hood, Liesl could see the puzzled eyes. "To listen to God. He said that sometimes when he was just too busy being him, he couldn't hear God's voice inside. And if that was true, he said, what good was he to others?" She hesitated, then added, "I remember wondering what that voice must sound like. Then later, I heard it."

The eyes beneath the hood glistened with silent tears.

"I just wanted you to know that no matter how things look to us right now—how deep into that dark fourth watch we are—God is the one in control. Not some Russian dictator. Not the haunts of our past. I don't know what hurts you, Cass. But he does. Give it all to him."

After a long silence that made her fear she'd overstepped her bounds with this woman she hardly knew, Liesl glanced at her watch, then laid a hand on Cass's shoulder. "These bells are going off in about twelve minutes. We'd better go."

Cass shook her head. "Go on."

"But—"

"I've got twelve minutes, don't I?"

Chapter 26

*W*alter Kolenski stepped off the ferry onto Ellis Island, just like his great-grandfather had done in the century before. Unlike the first of his ancestors to leave Poland, though, Walter had lived past his thirty-eighth birthday. At fifty-three, he had lived longer than his two grandfathers and his father.

He was the only one of his immigrant family to ever have a bank account. As hard as they labored, the others couldn't make enough to support themselves and had to rely on handouts and petty crime to feed and shelter their young. The land of dreams they'd flocked to through the gates of Ellis Island had betrayed its promise. Generations of Walter's family had slipped so far into poverty and despair that they never recovered. One grandfather hanged himself rather than endure the shame any longer. Walter's own father, among the last wave of immigrants to pass through the legendary clearing house in New York Harbor, gave up trying to succeed and sacrificed himself and his liver to whiskey, but not before his wife and children abandoned him. Only Walter continued to see his father right up to his death. For hours he had listened to the man rail against America and its heartless, unfair treatment of defenseless, foreign-speaking immigrants. The elder Kolenski was convinced this country was ruled by gangsters who stole the wages of the helpless and that the devil was in control of the White House. He convinced his oldest son it was true.

Now, as Walter removed his coat, displaying the security badge he wore five days a week, his dad's words returned to him. "America is no good for you, Son. They don't like us Poles. They killed our pride and destroyed our families. Make 'em pay! Make 'em pay!"

Walter had believed it all, even though in earlier years he had made a minimally subsistent wage working as a security guard for a small department store in Flatbush. He was divorced and lived alone. His health had begun to falter, but the insurance his employer provided wouldn't cover preexisting conditions, of which he had many. It infuriated him every time he was denied benefits, which only fed his disdain for the system.

But when his best friend, a Taiwanese laborer with six children, had been killed for crossing a picket line at a New Jersey factory, Walter plunged into a tailspin of rage, venting it to whoever would listen and to some who promptly fled his seething.

Walter hung his coat in an employee locker, thinking about the one person who had listened attentively to his rantings—Cyrus Neale, an old seaman from City Island, where Walter still lived in a cramped and dreary apartment over a grocery store. It hadn't taken long for the two to become ideologically linked. That is, they had fueled each other's hatred for America, drawing attention to their public diatribes in the taverns of City Island.

One night, they were approached by an engaging fellow who floated a proposition before them. It involved spying. "We can do that," Cyrus and Walter both agreed. Sabotage? "Just tell us where and when," they chimed. Money? "Even better." And asylum in Russia, should they desire it. Walter knew he did, but Cyrus wasn't so sure. After all, his soldier boy was buried here.

So Cyrus had his work to do, and Walter had his. In a few minutes, the first boatload of Sunday tourists would descend on Ellis Island. The prospect of destroying that portal to shame and then fleeing the country consumed him. With the help of the man from Russia, Walter had gotten a job as a security guard at the historic monument. He was placed in such duty for one reason. The signal would come, and a day later, Walter would wear a special coat—unusually heavy and stiff—to work that morning. He would hang it in his locker like always, only he would never retrieve it. At the end of his shift, he would pull an identical coat from the same locker—one already in place—and leave the island for the last time.

Just as his father had been one of the last immigrants to enter Ellis Island, Walter Kolenski would be one of the last to leave it . . . intact. A national museum and historic treasure was about to litter the bottom of New York Harbor.

Chapter 27

*W*here are we going?" Liesl asked as Evgeny pulled away from the church.

"My contact in Moscow has hit a vein of communication between the Architect's people here and at the Kremlin. His latest tip is very rich. You will see." And he said no more.

Liesl wondered at her options for dealing with him, finally realizing she had none. She was bound by a peculiar allegiance to this evasive man who cut no discernible profile, only immeasurable contradiction. He was a Russian undercover agent defending America against his own kind, risking all to protect the woman he'd once sought to destroy, waging a battle against this Architect he couldn't identify.

Who is Evgeny Kozlov? Liesl stole a glance at the sunken face that rarely secreted emotion, the eyes now boring through the windshield in what she hoped was no maniacal, revengeful pursuit—with her and that young couple back at the church its victims.

She closed her eyes and conjured images of home, of Saturday's kitchen full of those she longed to hold. To feel Cade's arms enfold her and his lips against hers. To playfully tug Ian's beard. To bask in her father's epic return. To comfort the frail Lottie who'd long been Liesl's refuge. To walk the aisle in a white dress at St. Philip's.

And then she thought of Ava. How curious to find a motherly solace in the hard-wired CIA agent who'd sprung at her after Schell Devoe's murder, subjecting her to a merciless interrogation by a team of CIA and FBI agents. Liesl wondered what avenues the agent might be charging down this moment to locate the one she'd been charged to protect. Liesl regretted the guilt she was certain her friend now suffered.

Retired from the agency and teaching school in Charleston, Ava Mullins still lived on the alert. Liesl knew she had moved to Charleston not for the weather, maybe for the company of Ian O'Brien, but certainly to keep a watchful eye on Liesl. Ava had never trusted that after Liesl's code aborted a conspiracy hatched in hell, that all was well on the Russian front—the one that bordered the old house on Tidewater Lane.

As if a hypnotist had just uttered the word to dispel the rumination, Liesl jerked at the sound of Evgeny's voice. "Listen," he said brusquely, "you must not be recognized. Tuck your hair inside your hat again, keep your scarf high over your chin, and wear your sunglasses at all times." He then pulled the fur-lined hood of his own jacket over his head and dug sunglasses from one of its pockets.

"Recognized by whom?"

He didn't look at her. "You will see."

Jeremy Rubin hugged the wheel of a white Nissan compact like it was a go-cart on a crowded track. This Sunday afternoon, though, the Bruckner Expressway into the Bronx was flowing smoothly, more so than the conversation inside the car.

"I don't know why you're so upset," Jeremy said. "You've gotten your first payment, which should buy all the fine antiques my sister could ever want. Pretty soon, you'll have enough to buy the mansion to put them in."

Ben Hafner squirmed in his seat. "This is not going to happen again, Jeremy. I don't care how much your Russian mob pays me. What if someone recognizes me?" He touched the bill of the baseball cap he was wearing, then adjusted his dark glasses.

"Are you kidding? It's not like you're on *Meet the Press* every Sunday.

Sorry to topple your pedestal, Mr. Domestic Policy Chief, but I guarantee you the people on this road wouldn't recognize your face any quicker than if you mooned them." He chuckled. "Especially where we're going."

Ben clamped his hand around the armrest of the small sedan and pumped, as if the repetitive motion would inflate his mood. It didn't. "Your superiors should be content with keeping me at my job and not gallivanting all over New York with an illegal alien. What if we were stopped?"

"Russian forgers know their stuff. My driver's license, car registration, even the insurance card are as clean as yours."

"And what's so critical about my risking association with you just to meet one of your subterranean rats?"

"Uh-oh. Bad attitude. Wouldn't want that Russian mob, as you call them, to think you're insulting their brotherhood of esteemed saboteurs. Not you, the big man who's going to deliver Travis Noland's administration directly to their pocket—when the time is right." He glanced at Ben. "The whole point of this little meeting today, according to the Architect, is to put a face on the brotherhood for you, to make you see one of its own up close and personal. The boss is just a tad bit queasy about your commitment to him. So he wants to send you up front into one of the trenches to convince you that the battle is real, that it's about to begin, and you'd better be wearing the right uniform. You got that?"

Ben looked at him with contempt. "You know, Jeremy, I wonder if you're really doing this for Israel. Or if you're just getting kicks out of running around in the shadows talking like a B-movie gangster."

Jeremy chuckled again. "You must be really scared. This is what Ben Hafner does when his nerves flare. He finds someone to beat up on. That's okay, Bennie boy, don't be afraid. You're about to meet one of the rats who'll soon bring the U.S. of A. into the right way of thinking."

"How much time have you spent in Russia, Jeremy? What makes you so sure its people are ready to do battle with America?"

His face now open and thoughtful, Jeremy answered calmly. "Fair questions. First answer is four years. Second answer is this. I used to think the Russian people—those outside the power grid—had no voice at all. I knew them to be peace loving and concerned with little more than heating their apartments and icing their vodka. A stereotype for sure, but one I believed. But now I know how restless they are, fed up with the incompetence of their president, with the corruption, with the way their government doesn't seem to care about its people. And now, the loudest voice in Russia is its youth." He looked at Ben as one about to dispense a secret. "Many of them want their Russia to be a superpower again," he said, his focus back on the road. "They want Russia to expand into a constellation again, and they embrace whatever anti-American posture might accomplish that."

"Go on," Ben said with genuine interest.

"There's a political front of Russian youth growing. Very aggressive. Very intolerant, too. They've been compared to Hitler's Youth, though smart people don't say that openly. I hear the Architect has infiltrated the group, stoking its young ardor for his own purposes."

Ben was quiet.

They were approaching the last bridge to City Island. "But that ardor can't compare to what's boiling inside our fraternity of sleepers. You can't imagine what I hear about that bunch. Kooks, a lot of them. But a few of them are big-brained professors like that Schell Devoe guy was. Others are your everyday, shop-at-Walmart spies who go to parent-teacher conferences, for crying out loud." He looked at Ben and frowned. "Are you with me here, buddy? You look like you're about to rip a seam somewhere."

"Just drive. The sooner we get this over, the better."

Jeremy drummed his fingers against the steering wheel. "You know, you'd better start demonstrating that you're Russian goods now because I'm not too sure you've got both feet into this." He popped the steering wheel hard, making Ben jump. "This isn't kids' play, Ben," he said angrily. "You'll see. You'd better see because the Architect's got his eye on you."

With that, Ben turned a square-on look at Jeremy. "What do you mean?"

But Jeremy ignored the question and asked his own. "When do Anna and the kids leave for Israel?"

Ben's pulse began to hammer, and he studied Jeremy without really seeing him. "In a few days." Ben's whole life was his wife and children . . .

and his family in Israel. His mother had moved back to her native land when Ben's father, a New York attorney, died. She was now surrounded by aunts, uncles, and cousins, all of whom clamored for Ben to join them.

"Let's hope that's time enough," Jeremy said.

"Are you threatening me and your own sister?" Ben erupted.

"*I'm* not. But I can't speak for the boss."

"You don't even know who he is!"

"True. I'm fed my orders by an old sow named Sonya. She's the big guy's chief of staff, so to speak. You'll meet her one day, when you're least expecting it. So watch yourself." He only half grinned.

Jeremy was nervous. Ben could hear the tinny quiver in his voice, see his hands tighten on the steering wheel. He'd known his brother-in-law for nearly twenty years, but not really. The first time Anna introduced them, Jeremy turned and left the room, too shy to make conversation with her new boyfriend, twice Jeremy's size and about to enter Harvard Law School. Just a Harvard sophomore, Jeremy was already flunking out. He'd been eager to end his college career and bunk in with the rebel-rousing culture lodged on the fringes of campus.

The two rode in a stewing silence as they headed down the main avenue of City Island, an old yachting village. Only a mile and a half long and a half-mile wide, the main road ran like a backbone through the middle with rib-cage streets running off the sides, with a dead end at Eastchester Bay to the west and Long Island Sound to the east.

"Ever been here?" Jeremy asked, pleasantly enough.

"Yeah. One of my dad's law partners used to keep a sailboat here." Ben knew there was no sense in further tangling with this misfit who called himself an Israeli one day, a Russian the next, and who-knew-what in years to come. If South Carolina decided to secede from the Union again, Ben suspected his brother-in-law would ride a white steed up the steps of the State House in Columbia and bellow "Dixie."

"It used to be a hub for shipbuilding, sailboats mostly," Jeremy informed, a clear retreat from the singeing of their earlier exchange. "The Ivy League teams used to practice sailing out here." He slowed near the next intersection and turned right onto a residential street. It was only a couple of blocks long, ending where a chain-link fence separated pavement from the pewter slab of bay waters that mimicked the dreary, swollen sky. Ben saw small homes lining both sides of the street. It was clear that pride of ownership vacillated house to house. Some in shabby repair stood shoulder to shoulder with a next-door neighbor's freshly painted picket fence and manicured patch of lawn. And there was little more than a patch to work with. The homes hugged the road, offering little ground to landscape a lift to their aging, sagging lines.

Midway down the second block, Jeremy pulled in front of a trim, wood-sided bungalow with new paint, chocolate with bright white trim. Ben immediately thought of brownies and ice cream and wondered how such whimsy found its way into his smoldering mood—which threatened to reignite with Jeremy's next words.

"You're gonna love this part, Gentle Ben," Jeremy said, pulling a black hood with eye holes out of the glove box.

Ben winced as if about to be struck. "No way!"

"You'd rather go in there as Ben Hafner, close advisor to the president of the United States? Is that the recognition you want? Are you out of your mind? This guy's about to commit an unspeakable act of terrorism against the United States. He might be a wee bit nervous about one of the president's staff dropping in on him."

"But he'd feel a lot better about an unidentified guy in a black hood, right?"

"He knows I'm bringing someone. He thinks it's someone like him, another member of his benevolent order of Russian hoodlums. He'll understand the precaution." Jeremy heaved a sigh. "Use your head, Ben. You're Russia's new White House mole. It's time you understood what's happening. You're here to listen to this guy, and that's all. You don't say one word while we're in there. Got it?"

"I thought no one would ever recognize me," Ben noted smugly.

Jeremy sniffed. "Can't take a chance. Here's what we're going to do. You can't walk up to the door wearing this thing and sending some old-lady neighbor tripping over her fourteen cats to get to a phone. No police interference today, please." He looked toward the house. "I'm going in first to keep this guy from seeing you until you get inside and replace your cap with this." He dropped the hood into Ben's lap. "See, it won't even adhere to the contours of that ugly mug of yours. No face, no voice. No way that guy will know who you are, especially in those baggy mom jeans you got on. Where'd you get those things anyway?"

Ben shot up a warning hand. "Enough! Go do what you have to do."

Jeremy muttered something Ben didn't catch, then got out of the car. "Watch for my signal," he told Ben, then closed the door and walked at a hesitant, uneven clip toward the front door of the bungalow. Ben read it for what it meant. *He's scared to death.*

The van crept down City Island Avenue, slowing further at each intersection. "Don't you know the address?" Liesl asked, surveying the unfamiliar town.

"I do. But so do others. We must be careful at each turn." He slid an admonishing look her way. "I suggest you never leave music for spying."

When she turned to him in surprise, he immediately looked away, but not before she caught the upturned corners of his mouth. Could the big bad wolf be in a good mood? She almost hoped. But not for long.

As soon as Evgeny took the next right turn, he pulled to the curb and idled a moment. "You must observe everything, see everyone, search every car, every house and yard. But keep your face covered. I will do the same."

"I don't understand."

"Just do it." Then he locked the passenger door from controls on his own.

"What are you doing?"

"It would be extremely unfortunate if you were to leave the van for any reason." He resumed his cruise down the street.

"Why would I do that?"

"Sometimes we do not know what we do. We just react."

She shook her head in dismay. "Cut the garble, Evgeny, and talk to me straight."

"Okay. I will have to shoot you if you get out of the van."

Her mouth fell open, but she quickly recovered. "You are unbelievable," she crossed her arms and locked them down firmly against her in an undeniable pout, which she instantly regretted.

He looked at her oddly. "You are quite unbelievable, too, Liesl," he said with candid sincerity. And something caught in his face, something she hadn't seen there before. Approval? No, it was more than that. Before he could turn away, she saw it clearly. Affection, though guarded.

In the second block, Evgeny called her attention to a house just ahead. It stood out from the fading little homes strung along the street. It was painted brown with white gingerbread trim. But the most remarkable thing about it was the man just approaching the steps to its front porch. The large man with the deliberate stride, the big hands that hung like hams from the fleece cuffs of his cowhide jacket—the same jacket he'd worn when Liesl last strolled with him down the Washington Mall.

"Ben!" she called and reached for the handle of her door a split second before Evgeny's iron grip caught her other arm.

"Stop!" he commanded. No sign of affection now. "I warned you."

She pleaded with him. "But . . . but I have to—"

"You have to do nothing!" He finally released her and placed both hands back on the wheel of the still-moving van. "This is why I brought you. To prove to you that Ben Hafner is the mole."

Locked hard on Ben, her eyes filled with scalding tears. "It's not true. Not true!"

"Quiet!"

As they passed in front of the house, Ben, now climbing the steps to the porch, turned to give the van a cursory inspection, then went inside. At the end of the street, Evgeny made a U-turn and headed slowly back toward the brown house, pulling to the curb and stopping a few doors away.

Liesl composed herself enough to ask, "Who's in that house?"

"Jeremy Rubin and one of the sleepers. All I know about him is that he was once a merchant marine and now he spends a lot of time in pubs."

In her mind, Liesl grabbed blindly for a reason why Ben would be there. But no reason materialized. She couldn't fathom a single explanation for why he would be in the company of Jeremy Rubin, a man of troubling liaisons whom Ben had forbidden to enter his home.

Liesl turned to Evgeny, then spoke as one grieving a terrible loss. "Why? Why would Ben do this?"

"My source has not provided that information. But I believe, as I have told you, that it is Israel. Your president sends mixed signals about how far he would stick out his neck, as you say, to protect Israel. And there is the money, a great deal to be gained from such work."

"Ben doesn't need the money."

"Then it is Israel."

Liesl knew Ben's devotion to his Israeli family and how much he loved to spend time immersed in their culture. Had he not worked alongside Liesl and Ava to uncover the code fingering the Russian mole in Israel and exposing the plot that might have destroyed that country? Had such devotion become fanatical enough to disable his conscience?

How did I miss that?

Chapter 28

As soon as Ben stepped through the door of the house, he slipped the hood over his head and followed Jeremy's silent directive to sit in a chair near the door. Even through the dense fibers of the hood, his nostrils twitched at the scent of household cleansers generously applied. Through the eye holes, he saw a starkly furnished room with bare wooden floors, a worn leather sofa, two upholstered chairs in mismatched fabric, a scarred coffee table holding nothing but a remote, and the flat-screen television that reigned over the room.

Then he turned to one side and noticed the only cluttered place in the room, a windowless wall paved solid with framed photographs. The same smiling young man peered from most of them.

When Ben was settled, Jeremy crossed the room to a doorway leading to a dimly lit hall. "We're ready for you, Cyrus," he called.

Ben heard a door open and close down the hall and footsteps approach. Then more steps, these the quicker, nail-clicking patter of small canine feet. In quick succession, the two appeared. First, the short-haired little terrier with the Benji face and twitchy tail, then the stocky man with a head thatched in faded black hair that apparently defied combing. The man wore a navy turtleneck sweater over gray sweats and sneakers. There was something distinctly unsynchronized about his walk as he headed

directly for Ben and stopped just a few feet in front of him. "Who are
you?" he demanded. Ben didn't answer.

"Uh, Cyrus," Jeremy said nervously, "remember that I told you—"

"Yeah, I remember," he cut in, still fixed on Ben. "He's just another
mutineer like me. Real important that I don't know who he is. Well, how
come he can know who I am?"

Jeremy measured his words. "There are reasons. But I assure you he is
no threat, just one of our team who'd like to meet the man about to light
the fuse, so to speak.

Cyrus Neale ignored him, still focused on Ben. "So you just want to
meet me, do you?" Cyrus said with sarcastic bite. "Do you want to meet
Charlie Manson? How about the kook who shot that congresswoman in
front of a grocery store? You think I'm a kook, too?"

Ben stiffened but didn't respond.

"Cyrus, I told you not to talk to him. He's not allowed to speak."
Jeremy was growing agitated.

"Well, pardon me for not following directions. I've had a hard time
with that ever since Nam." He leaned over and pulled up his left pants leg,
and Ben understood the limp. It was an artificial leg from the knee down.
"The lieutenant they'd just potty trained and sent to lead our battalion
told me and two others to ferret out a sniper on the other side of an open
field. But he gave us no cover. We didn't make it twenty yards before they
cut into us. I came back without my buddies and half a leg. When I got
home, nobody cared what I gave up for America. Instead, America spat
on me, told me I lost the leg and my friends for nothing and that I was an
idiot to be there in the first place. That's what my country did to me and
the memory of all those mangled soldiers we lost."

He walked solemnly to the windowless wall. "But that's not the worst
it did." He laid a sun-blackened hand over the face of a young soldier in
an army uniform and patted it gently. It was the face repeated frame to
frame over most of the wall. "My boy was in Afghanistan just six weeks
when artillery ripped him into little pieces." Cyrus turned back to look
at Jeremy first, then Ben. "It took our country nearly a year to admit my

boy had died at their hands. Friendly fire. You see anything friendly about that?" he asked no one in particular. He remained near the wall. Jeremy and Ben just watched.

"I have no regrets for what I'm doing," he finally said, straightening into military bearing. "I don't need no army moron sending me where I shouldn't be going. I know exactly what to do. Ain't nothing me and my old tugboat can't do about the death sentences this country hands down to kids like my boy." He moved toward the center of the room and looked straight at Ben. "I'll take care of it all by myself. Do what the man out there says do. Don't know who he is, but I like his style." He grunted with approval.

"What you're doing is merely demonstrating what is to come," Jeremy confirmed, even though, as he'd admitted to Ben, he didn't know the exact nature of that demonstration. "Just sending a warning to the nation. No great loss of life this time out."

"I do what the man says do." Cyrus looked defiantly at Jeremy and snapped his fingers. His dog trotted obediently to his feet and looked up. The man leaned over to pet the scruffy head. "I'm going to miss you, little fellow."

"You aren't taking him with you to Russia?" Jeremy asked, then turned to explain that to Ben. "When this is over, the whole team will leave the U.S. one by one."

"But not this little guy," Cyrus added.

"What will you do with him?" Jeremy asked.

"Shoot him."

It wasn't long before Evgeny and Liesl saw the front door of the house open. From a distance, they watched Ben pause at the doorway and fumble with something on his head. "What is that?" Liesl asked.

"A hood." Evgeny smiled, more a gloat that another of the White House's exalted staffers had fallen so ingloriously. "I could have loaned him mine." He wanted to laugh, but he dared not, knowing that he'd once left his black ski mask dangling like a calling card from a chandelier in Liesl's Washington home. "I'm sorry."

What's wrong with me? he wondered. *I don't apologize. What is she doing to me?*

His attention returned to the two men leaving the house. Ben, with a ball cap now on his head and dark glasses in place, tucked his head and nearly sprinted to the white Nissan. As they pulled away, Evgeny followed from a distance.

Once on the mainland, the sedan sped up, but Evgeny didn't.

"Catch up with them," Liesl urged. "You're losing them."

"Yes. It is okay. We know where to find Ben Hafner. And Jeremy Rubin, I suspect, will not ever be far away. Besides, we have what we came for—your proof." He raised his eyebrows at her, soliciting her confirmation that what he'd told her about Ben was true. But that's not what he got from her.

"You don't know what went on inside that house."

He sighed wearily. "The circumstantial evidence is too overwhelming to ignore. And so we will not."

They could see the Nissan ahead through most of their route through the Bronx, but when they crossed the Harlem River into Manhattan, it went one way and the van another, west toward Central Park and the little church that had become a most unlikely base of operations, at least for Evgeny. If there really were an Almighty, Evgeny was in no mood to confront him.

After leaving the bridge, Evgeny checked his rearview mirror and fastened on the gray panel truck about four cars back. It had been there since City Island. Not good.

Who could possibly have known where he and Liesl were headed earlier that afternoon? Only Viktor. Had his secure phone signal been breached? Who was back there?

At the next light, he took the first of what would be four lefts. A circle. If the truck stayed with him, he would do what he had to do. He leaned sideways and retrieved his gun from the holster under his coat, then placed the weapon in his lap.

"What are you doing!" Liesl shrieked, her eyes blazing on the gun.

He didn't answer. At the next intersection, he prepared to turn left again, his eyes darting repeatedly to the rearview mirror. Seeing this, Liesl turned quickly in her seat and looked out the back window.

"Turn around. I'm watching them."

"Who?" she demanded, still backward in her seat.

"The gray truck that has tailed us from City Island."

He could hear Liesl begin to pant. "Calm down," he told her, then took the left. But this time the truck continued straight through the light.

Liesl whirled on him. "What was that all about?"

"I was mistaken," he lied, leaving the gun where it was. All his instincts told him he'd see the truck again. How soon, he didn't know. His mind ricocheted like a pinball, banking off one scenario after another as he altered course and headed once more toward the church. But should he?

He pulled over and parked at the first open spot he saw. "We're going to wait and see if our friend returns."

Liesl didn't argue. Evgeny saw her focused on the rush-hour traffic as if searching for a lost child. After a while, with no more sightings, he cranked the van and left.

They soon reached the west side of the park and crooked their way back into the handsome old neighborhood with its narrow, tree-lined streets. Many of Rev. Scovall's parishioners probably walked to church on Sundays, Evgeny guessed, trying to suppress the memories of skipping alongside his grandmother en route to the Russian Orthodox church in their village. His grandmother, his sole guardian, died when he was seven. Then he entered the orphanage and, in many ways, never escaped its life sentence.

When they turned the corner near the church, Evgeny slammed on the brakes. The gray truck was parked at the side door.

Liesl gasped. "What do we do?"

Evgeny was about to throw the van in reverse when the driver's door of the truck opened and Ava Mullins stepped out.

"Ava!" Liesl called through the closed window. She looked once at Evgeny—her face alight as he'd never seen it before. Then she reached again for the door handle. "Open it, Evgeny," she said over her shoulder.

"You betrayed me," he accused.

"No! I haven't spoken to anyone but Cade, and I didn't tell him where I was. It's the truth, Evgeny. I don't know how she found us." She looked back at Ava, who stood quite still beside the gray truck, her full attention on them. "Unlock the door, please," Liesl said firmly.

He searched the street around them, seeing no one else but Ava. Then he released the lock on Liesl's door. She jumped from the van and ran the rest of the way to the church. The gun now firmly in his hand, he watched the women embrace, not knowing what to believe. How else would Ava have found them?

Time to go! But before he could turn the van around, Ava raised her hand in a signal to halt, then started for him, Liesl at her side. This was one of those rare times he didn't know what to do. He would make a trophy catch for her. She should be drawing her own weapon, but wasn't. Had she gone daft in her retirement? "Please stop," she called to him. "I'm here to help!"

What?

She was closer now. "Evgeny, let me talk to you," she called.

He stared at her through the window. Surely she knew he was armed and still she advanced on him. Then she stopped at the hood of the van and raised both hands in a surrendering gesture as Liesl bounded toward the front passenger door and opened it. "Please believe me," she implored. "I didn't call her. But she's desperate to talk to you. Please, Evgeny. She means no harm."

He looked from one woman to the other, gauged the dynamic between them, then laid down his gun. A piece of the puzzle had just fallen into place.

Chapter 29

*A*va climbed calmly into the seat beside Evgeny, carrying nothing with her, and rested her empty hands open-palmed in her lap. From the back seat, Liesl watched this stunning détente. Two undercover soldiers from opposing sides, once locked in fierce battle with each other, now looking like Mr. and Mrs. Normal parked beside the church, waiting for Sunday-evening services to begin. Who could possibly guess the truth?

"Either your guard has gone soft from retirement, Ava, or you no longer fear me," Evgeny observed with apparent ease, but Liesl watched the profile she'd come to know so well in recent hours. She saw the jaw clench as if he were biting steel.

"I never feared you, Evgeny," Ava shot back. She sat sharply attentive in her seat, angled slightly toward her one-time nemesis. Liesl was certain she carried a gun somewhere. "I was too busy tracking you."

He smiled thinly. "So you have found me. Let me tell you how that happened. It was you who retrieved Liesl from her refuge in this church that night, the night I chased her down this very street. What affinity she has for it still, the good reverend told me, enough to return to it often. Knowing her, as you so obviously do, and the things that matter to her, you called the reverend, assured him this was a matter of national security and that he was compelled to cooperate with you. And, well, here you are. I admit I did not foresee that. I seem to be losing my edge, as well. What a pity for us both."

"You know, Evgeny, another time and I might try to turn you as we did Schell Devoe."

"And look what happened to him." His flinty eyes remained on her. "But you must know by now that I can never return to Russia. It is no longer my home. It probably never was, but I still fight for her. It is the only reason you are sitting safely beside me now."

"No, it isn't," Ava said confidently. "You didn't come to Charleston for Russia. You came to save Liesl."

Liesl was unprepared for Evgeny's transparent response.

"She had suffered enough."

The silence inside the van threatened to crystallize before anyone spoke again. Then Ava cleared her throat. "We have work to do, don't we?" altering the course of dialogue.

Evgeny eyed her sharply. "The reverend didn't know where we were going today. How did you find us on City Island?"

"You know I can't tell you that." Her face was impassive. "And what I know is too little to arm us."

"Us?"

"Inside the church are two FBI agents who once helped me protect Liesl from you . . . before you decided she had suffered enough." Ava poured grit into that last remark.

The tension suddenly grew palpable. "Get out, both of you!" Evgeny commanded.

"No, Evgeny!" Liesl cried. "Isn't this what you wanted? To prove what was happening to someone who could stop it?"

"That is what you were to do—after I was gone!" Evgeny snapped. "Do not think for a second the CIA would not love to throw a net over me and haul me in."

Liesl turned to Ava. "You can't do that, Ava. He's trying to help and you need him. You don't know the things I've seen." She leaned hard toward Ava. "We saw Ben Hafner enter the home of a Russian spy! He was with Jeremy Rubin. Do you know what that means?" She was still reeling from the sight.

Ava searched Liesl's face. "Yes, I do. And I'm sorry, Liesl. I know that's painful for you."

Liesl reared back and frowned at her. "How long have you known?"

"Never mind that."

Liesl summoned her composure. "Well, what about Cass Rodino? You don't know what's happened to her."

"I do now. I've already spoken to her. I came here to the church first. She told me about her stepfather and the break-in at her apartment."

Evgeny threw up his hands. "What is this, a talk show?" he fumed, rounding on Ava. "Your whole country is about to blow wide open and all you want to do is talk!" He reached for the ignition key. "And I'm not waiting around for my own hanging!"

Just as he turned the key, though, the side door to the church opened and Cass emerged, followed by Jordan and two dark-suited men. Ava instantly sprang from the van. "Stay inside!" she ordered, and Liesl realized she was addressing the two agents. They stopped and stared at her, their hands reaching for weapons. "Stand down!" she ordered again, advancing on them. "Go back inside." The men took obvious affront to the orders, but retreated just inside the doorway. They left the door open and their path to the van clear. They now watched it like hungry hawks.

Ava and Cass drew close to each other, discussing something of apparent urgency. Moments later, Ava returned with Cass to the van, leaving Jordan in the company of two agitated agents.

As soon as the sliding door to the van opened, Cass announced, "Hans is leaving the apartment at five o'clock. I finally reached my mom. She's in a panic to know where he's going."

"Does she have any idea?" Evgeny barked.

"No. But it's already after four. We have to follow him!"

Evgeny looked away a moment, obviously sorting through his options.

"Evgeny, you and I have a job to do . . . together," Ava insisted. "Now, let's get on with it."

He turned and looked severely at Ava. "You come alone and keep your boys away from me. Understood?"

Ava agreed, then raced to the gray truck, grabbed her bag, and returned to the van. "Jordan isn't happy about staying behind," she told Cass as the van sped from the church. "But we've got too many civilians in tow as it is." Then she turned to Evgeny. "I need to order surveillance on the Kluen apartment." She eyed him carefully, as if for approval. "Far away from you," she added, using his words. "But we've got to have it."

He eyed her sternly, then nodded. She grabbed her phone, addressed someone named Mark, and ordered immediate backup and surveillance on the Tribeca building. After the call, Liesl asked, "Was that Mark Delaney?" She remembered the FBI special agent who'd first ushered this mania into her quiet Charleston home. He and his men had callously probed its sacred places in an exhaustive search for the sonata code, mindless of the already fractured soul of the house. But Liesl had finally understood.

"Yes," Ava answered, but her attention was on Evgeny. Liesl watched her eyes probe his granite expression. "There's something you should know, Evgeny," she finally said. "I coerced my way into this operation. Timing was everything. I recently discovered that our intelligence had picked up signals about something huge going down soon within our borders. Then you showed up in Charleston. I entered this equation the instant you grabbed Liesl.

"But there's something else you should know," she added. "I had to convince my superiors that if the things you told Liesl about this Architect—which, by the way, Cade immediately related to me—were true, our greatest assets were you and your contacts. It wasn't an easy task to call the authorities, especially Mark Delaney, off you or get them to allow me to work alongside you."

"Terrific. I have a sidekick now . . . who knows nothing about nothing."

"Don't bet on that," Ava said. "But this isn't about competition between old enemies, which of us knows more. We don't have time for that. If you're real and not some elaborate KGB foil, you and I will have to consolidate everything we know to abort this thing. Can you do that?"

Evgeny took a corner well over safe speed, and Ava grabbed her door handle with both hands, flinging a visual reprimand his way.

"Can *you?*" he snapped.

Before Ava could reply, Evgeny swung into a parking spot near the Kluens' building. It was almost five.

The four of them watched the door to the lobby and waited, but not for long. "There's the punctual man now," Cass announced bitterly. Dressed in a loose-fitting jacket and dark woolen pants, Hans Kluen headed down the sidewalk to an adjacent parking garage. Most notably, he rolled a small suitcase behind him. "He looks like a man leaving home," Cass noted, now with a trace of sadness.

"So he's got a car parked in the garage?" Ava asked.

"Yes," Cass answered. "Hardly uses it."

"But you'll know it when you see it?"

"Big old navy blue Mercedes. The only thing missing are those little foreign diplomat flags on both sides of the hood."

"As soon as you identify the car for us, you must leave us and go to your mother," Evgeny instructed.

Cass pounced on that. "But I want to go with you. Don't leave me out of this."

"That is not the case at all," Evgeny said emphatically. "You are providing a service to us and certainly your mother. If Hans contacts her soon, we need to know what his message is." He glanced back at Cass. "Beyond that, I should think you would want to comfort her."

Cass stared at the floor a moment, then raised her head. "You're right." She grabbed the backpack beside her and looked compassionately at Liesl. "Keep your head down."

"Liesl won't be going with us, either," Ava announced. "Delaney is ordering a security detail around you both."

"Oh, this again," Liesl bristled. "The what-do-we-do-about-Liesl scenario." She leaned forward. "Ava, don't you think I've earned enough stripes in the trenches with you to be treated like one of the soldiers now?"

"Never," Ava replied, turning to face her. "You were never meant to be a soldier. Only a survivor. And I intend to see that you remain one." Her voice dropped somberly. "I failed you in Charleston yesterday. It's not going to happen again."

Liesl fixed on her friend's battle-weary face, at the complexity sizzling beneath. Was this the same woman who'd taught music alongside Schell Devoe at Harvard? Had his treason and her role in uncovering it so transformed Ava Mullins that she'd forgotten where she left her old self?

But as Ava turned back to face the road, Liesl remembered that the woman had once told her, "There is something more powerful than guns and missiles that will save our troops. Something that would have prevented the deaths of thousands on that morning of September 11—information. It's the most critical weapon we have against our enemies."

When Liesl had probed for more, knowing there had to be something else driving the agent, Ava had answered, "My son is a marine serving in Iraq. Every moment, his life depends on the accuracy of information his commanding officers receive from people like me. That's why I never returned to Harvard once the CIA recruited me. You might say the war drowned out the music. . . . I begged the agency to take me on full-time. I had no choice but to protect my son in that way. But now that I know the things I know, I do it for all those who go to sleep at night *not* knowing those things."

Now, Liesl watched Ava's profile, the scanning eyes taking in her surroundings, the raw energy pulsing through every limb. Her CIA personnel file may be stamped *retired*, but her superiors who knew the resilient undergirding of the fifteen-year veteran—especially as she related to the lightning rod Liesl Bower—had ranked her a perennial asset on call.

"Okay, Liesl," Ava said. "You and Cass go with those agents just pulling up now." Liesl watched a dark sedan park across the street. There appeared to be three or four people inside. "You'll wait with them until your escort back to the church arrives. From there, you'll go to an FBI safe house."

Cass shot forward in her seat. "There's the car!"

They watched the Mercedes ease from the garage. "Wait until he turns and cannot see you," Evgeny instructed. "Then you girls hop out and go with your guards."

When the Mercedes took a sharp right out of the garage, three men and a woman emptied from the sedan and approached the van. As the agents escorted Liesl and Cass toward the apartment building, Evgeny merged with traffic and fell in behind the Mercedes, a couple of taxis separating them. Liesl looked over her shoulder at the departing van.

"Feel like yesterday's garbage?" Cass asked as the agents opened the glass door to the lobby and led them inside. "Like once you were vital, and now you're not?"

What's clawing at her? Liesl wondered. She watched Cass push a lock of blond hair off her fine-boned face. Liesl turned to the agents and asked them to wait a moment before taking Cass upstairs, then pulled the young girl aside. "Would you like for me to come with you to your mom's apartment? Maybe I can send my babysitter escorts away when they arrive."

Pressing her lips together, Cass shook her head and smiled weakly. "Mom would freak even more if a stranger arrived while she was having one of her meltdowns." She looked toward the agents, two guarding the door, the other two standing nearby. "I've spent years trying to sugarcoat the hard times for her," Cass continued, a wary eye on their bodyguards. "I just wanted to make her believe things weren't so bad, that my father, her first husband, didn't mean to slap her . . . or me. Didn't mean to bed down every woman he could. When those things happened, I'd take her for walks in the park. We'd go shopping and spend obscene amounts of his money. I'd force her to lunch in the Oak Room, then gorge her with Godiva chocolates—like creature comforts would numb her to the misery at home. But that was a lie, and we both knew it."

Liesl waited a moment, then asked, "But what about you, Cass?"

"What do you mean?"

"Did you tell yourself lies?"

Cass stepped back, and Liesl regretted her ill-timed inquisition. But then the expression on the young face changed. Unexpectedly, Cass broke away and approached the agents. Liesl heard her ask if they'd allow her and Liesl to sit in a back alcove of the lobby. She got the go-ahead.

"Come with me," she said to Liesl when she returned. "We'll keep an eye out for your babysitter." Liesl could see something just behind the eyes, behind the airy talk. And she could hear it, a plaintive cry.

They crossed the black-marble floor and passed near the abstract sculpture at the center of the lobby. "Tell me what you see," Cass urged, nodding toward the imposing form.

Liesl paused to examine the sculpture, the nuance of human form, the fluid lines, curves of slick steel, one inside another. "It's a mother and her unborn child."

For some reason, the shock on Cass's face pleased Liesl. It was raw and honest, concealing nothing.

"Wait till I tell Jordan about this."

Liesl looked at her curiously but kept following. They entered the alcove and settled onto a cane-back settee with a view of the street. Cass squirmed and clasped her hands together. "I'm not sure why I'm telling you this, Liesl, except that right off, you saw me for what I am." She looked down and repeatedly slid the toe of one boot in a tight elliptical pattern against the marble. Then the foot halted. "Maybe my mom and your ride to the church will hold off long enough for me to do this." She placed her backpack on the floor in front of her, her foot on the move again, flexing back and forth against the bag's canvas side. "Something happened between me and a good friend when I was nineteen. She didn't survive. I'm not sure I did."

A time passed that Liesl couldn't measure in minutes, only in layers peeled away from the core of Cass Rodino. As she unfolded the story of Rachel Norman's suicide, Liesl prayed silently for God to embrace this tormented young woman who was reaching for help.

Liesl was new to prayer yet wholly convinced of its powers, the ones she summoned at this moment. Soon after Cass ended her story, Liesl told her, "You've mourned far too long. You're convinced you are to blame for this girl taking her own life. But that's what *she* did, not you. It was her choice, and she didn't have to choose death. It's very likely that something else was working her to that point, something besides her boyfriend's betrayal—and yours. Maybe it was shame over her own indiscretions. Maybe fear of her parents' outrage and rejection. I don't know. But what I do know is this. You're looking for forgiveness, and I'm glad. That's the only thing that will heal you. It won't come from Rachel, but it will come from God if you'll ask for it."

Cass started to speak, then faltered. Finally, "I don't know how to do that."

"You start by just talking to him. He's as real and close to you as I am right now. So just talk. It's not hard. It's—"

"Ma'am," one of the agents called to Liesl. "Your escort just arrived. Please come with me, but wait inside for them."

Liesl grabbed her bag. "We'll talk again soon," she told Cass, who rose to accompany her to the front of the lobby.

"We'd better be sure it's FBI in that car," Cass warned as they approached the window and looked out. "Will you recognize them?"

When Liesl didn't answer, Cass turned to her. "Will you?" she prodded, but still no answer. "What's the—"

Liesl suddenly cried out and flew to the door before the agents could stop her.

"Cade!"

The man who'd just climbed from the charcoal-gray sedan at the curb turned and stretched out both arms. Liesl rushed headlong into them and buried her face against his neck, not caring that a trio of bodyguards hovered nearby. Her tears streaming, she tried to speak, but he quieted her.

"Don't talk," Cade whispered. "Just hold."

She clung to him as if she might slip into some bottomless crevasse if she let go.

When he finally lowered her to her feet, his arms still wrapped snugly around her, he looked deep into her eyes. "From here on, no matter what comes our way, we confront it together." Behind his declarative words, she heard the pleading. She slipped a gloved hand to his cheek and caressed it, running her fingers over his lips. He lowered his face to hers and swept her mouth with a fevered kiss. Then more. When he finally pulled away, he looked back at the car parked beside them. "Mark Delaney must be on broil by now."

"That's Delaney?" she asked, turning to look inside the car.

"It is. The guy's really ticked that he had to bring me along. He must be spitting tacks over this public display of ours. We'd better go." He pulled her rapidly to the car, flinging open the back door and climbing in behind her. "Agent Delaney, you remember Liesl Bower."

Already turned in his seat, Special Agent Mark Delaney cocked one hard-line brow at Cade. "I don't run a dating service, Mr. O'Brien. You don't jump out of my car like that and draw the subject into the open, then proceed to make a spectacle out of her. Don't you understand that there're people out there who want to kill her?"

Liesl felt Cade's body jerk. "Agent Delaney," Liesl began, "I'm the one who forced that little scene, and I'm sorry. Now, can we go?" Just then, though, she remembered something.

"Agent Delaney, may I go inside for just a moment? I need a word with Cass."

He shook his head and motioned for his driver to go, then turned and looked through the back window, issuing a terse reply to Liesl's request. "No. They're taking her upstairs now."

When his eyes lingered on a spot behind them, Liesl and Cade both turned to look that way. There was a car fast on their bumper and another just pulling up alongside. Delaney's driver signaled for that car to move ahead. Now, they were sandwiched in an FBI caravan and picking up speed.

Delaney's phone rang. Liesl watched him glance at the screen. "Delaney." Pause. "That's right. To the church. Full alert."

Chapter 30

*H*ans parked his Mercedes at an isolated dock on the East River. Used mostly for trips to Southampton, the car sat like a prince among paupers on this squalid stretch of waterfront, sulking beneath the hostile glare of the spotlight. Hans could only hope it would be intact when he returned. He would need it more than ever then.

In the trunk was the suitcase he had packed while Jilly took her afternoon nap. When he reached the beach house that night, he would gather everything else he needed for his departure. He would remove the vile man he'd become from the lives of those he loved.

Promptly at six, a rusty trawler pulled alongside the dock, and a young man in heavy-weather gear jumped from the stern with a line in his hand and tied it into a snappy figure eight around a cleat. From on board, the captain tossed the bow line to the boy, and he repeated the maneuver at the other end of the boat. When he finished, he stood almost at attention as Hans boarded.

Hans was used to the military bearing of the young man and his middle-aged captain. He had made this jaunt upriver several times before, whenever Ivan felt the need for greater privacy than the UN apartment allowed. Hans anticipated a debriefing of sorts and a pump-up-the-troops review. He wasn't prepared for what happened.

Descending the steps to a well-furnished salon below deck—incongruent with the grimy exterior of the boat—Hans cordially greeted Ivan and Sonya, seated and waiting for him. It appeared there was no one else in the room. He was wrong. From behind him, someone grabbed both his arms and pinned them to his sides while an accomplice wrapped a heavy cord about him, shoved him into a metal chair, and strapped him to it. Hans cried out and tried to wrestle free, but to no avail. The boat was moving.

"Anything else, sir?" one of the assailants asked Ivan.

"No. Leave us."

Hans jerked his head toward the two men. Then he turned raging eyes on Ivan. "Have you gone mad?"

"No. You have." Ivan stood up and moved toward Hans. "Insanely reckless! Or was it deliberate?"

"What are you talking about?"

"What happened in Charleston yesterday?" Ivan demanded.

Hans gaped in confusion. "Charleston?"

"You pretend very well, comrade," Sonya sniffed.

Hans pulled against the straps.

"Be still!" Ivan commanded. "Anyone else would already be in the river."

But Hans kept struggling against the straps. "I don't know about anything happening in Charleston."

Ivan remained unimpressed. "No. You were not supposed to. It was not your affair. So I am wondering how you knew."

Now Hans was angry. "If you keep talking in riddles, we'll never get anywhere! Tell me what happened in Charleston! " His assertive tone changed the course of the conversation. Ivan turned to look at Sonya, whose acrimonious expression now turned inquisitive.

Ivan brought a pensive forefinger to his lips as he seemed to gauge Hans's sincerity. Then he lifted a briefcase from the floor and retrieved something from inside. "This was taken yesterday morning."

The photograph Ivan shoved in Hans's face made him blanch. Sweat trickled from his scalp as he stared at the clear and unmistakable image of

Cass standing beneath a moss-draped tree with Liesl Bower. Hans's mind spun like a roulette wheel waiting for the ball of reason to drop solidly into place. But there was no reason behind what he saw.

He looked up into Ivan's seething face, at the eyes that watched him back, judging Hans's reaction. But his astonishment was genuine.

"Your stepdaughter is what happened in Charleston yesterday," Ivan said, bending over Hans as if he were an unruly child. "Somehow she knew Liesl Bower was marked for death. And somehow, she managed to prevent it. How did that happen?"

But that was just one of two questions pounding in Hans's head that instant. Momentarily suspending his incredulity over Cass's involvement, he looked Ivan steady in the eye. "You tried to kill that woman again?"

Ivan straightened and strolled confidently back to his chair, lowering himself onto it as though it were a throne. He gazed arrogantly at Hans. "How I choose to deal with my enemy is none of your business."

"Liesl Bower is not your enemy! I was glad when that piano bomb didn't go off!"

Sonya leaned forward in her chair. "Do you think a great power rises without spilling blood? That the assets of our enemies are off-limits to us?"

"She's just a piano player!" Hans charged. "That's not a wartime kill. It's murder!"

Ivan jumped to his feet. "You should be shot for insubordination! You should be hanged for treason against Russia." He moved menacingly toward Hans again. "What was Cass Rodino doing in Charleston?" he demanded. "And who were the men with her?"

Cass went to Charleston to save Liesl Bower? Impossible! Hans refused to believe such a thing had happened. "If I didn't know anything about this, how could she?"

"Then explain this photograph!"

"I can't," Hans replied emphatically. "Besides following me that night to your apartment, purely at the whim of her mother, she has absolutely no knowledge of our operation. No access to—"

The thought struck like lightning—*The beach house! The files in my study!* Had Cass gotten in? Why would she? Then he remembered their conversation in the diner and later in the park. Had his warnings only ignited her curiosity, and the inauguration attack fueled it? Yes, it was beginning to make sense.

He caught himself too late. He'd waited too long to finish his sentence.

"You know something more," Ivan prodded. "Tell me!"

"I don't know anything."

"Well, I'll tell you what we know," Sonya said, her words slithering through tight lips as she stood up. "Your girl got into something of yours that led her to Liesl Bower. Perhaps she knows about the court bombing, too. Your files, a carelessly placed note to yourself, something. Whatever she has, we'll find it before it reaches the wrong people." She bent to look Hans in the eye. "We just missed her last night, but we will find her again." She taunted him with obvious pleasure.

Hans didn't disappoint her. He lunged against the restraints. "If you hurt that girl, I'll—"

"You will do nothing!" Ivan's voice boomed. "You are now powerless. Sonya will take over your duties as overseer. We will find your stepdaughter and end her threat to us."

Hans lurched forward, almost upending the chair.

"It is a pity our man in Charleston could not take care of her and Liesl Bower at the same time," Ivan droned on as though for his own amusement. "Andreyev and Fedorovsky eagerly await news of Miss Bower's death. And I must accommodate my generals' lust for revenge. It was she, you recall, who brought them down." Ivan nodded toward Sonya.

"You will write two letters," Sonya instructed with cold detachment. "One to your wife, telling her you are leaving her. Because of our generosity over the years, she will not want for anything except, maybe, her husband. Then again, perhaps she has already tired of you." Her lips curled with satisfaction. "The other letter goes to your employer, announcing your immediate resignation."

Hans's chest grew tight, and he dug his fingernails into his palms.

"We will return your car to the garage," Sonya continued. "We want no meddling from the police should it be found abandoned at the dock. And then, you'll remain our guest until we see fit to dispose of you permanently." She shook her head. "We simply cannot tolerate your carelessness."

Ivan looked regretfully at Hans. "You would have enjoyed living in Russia. In just days, our American comrades will complete the tasks they have trained long and hard for, then immediately escape. You would have received a hero's welcome." He motioned for Sonya to join him as he moved toward the doorway.

She left the room, but Ivan paused and looked back at Hans. "You would have enjoyed the irony of what I am about to do. And who I am."

The van waited in the dark, snugged against the side of a warehouse within sight of the dock. Evgeny and Ava had watched Hans park his Mercedes and wait at the end of the dock. Soon, an old commercial trawler approached and a young man stepped from inside and secured the boat to the dock. Hans Kluen boarded promptly, and within minutes the boat pulled away.

Ava alerted Mark Delaney. "Better get a marine detail out here now to tail this boat." She gave him a brief description of the vessel. "We don't know who's on board, but this isn't a routine evening for Hans Kluen. Something's up. Could be our man waiting for him on board. Maybe not. We can't afford to chase him off and lose our link to his sleepers. . . . No. We're staying put. Kluen's Mercedes is still here. I suspect he'll return." A pause. "What's that?" She looked sideways at Evgeny. "I know. Bizarre, isn't it? But he's behaving himself right now." She ended the call.

"You know I will never let you take me in," Evgeny said calmly, not meeting her eye.

"Is that a threat?"

"Call it what you want." He knew she was regarding him carefully.

"You're not the first murdering spy I've worked beside."

He didn't take offense. That's what he was.

"I can intervene on your behalf, though," she continued. "You saved Liesl's life and warned us of disaster. Still, I can't guarantee your freedom."

"No, but I can." His answer was swift and sure.

The long awkward silence between them finally broke when the trawler returned. "It's too soon!" Ava fretted. "Delaney hasn't had time to scramble help."

They watched as the same young captain's mate jumped from the boat, walked briskly to the Mercedes, unlocked it—presumably with Hans's key—and drove away.

"Kluen is either on board or in the river," Evgeny said with certainty.

He fought the urge to follow the car, knowing the greater catch was probably aboard the trawler. Could it be the Architect himself? If it was, how far should Evgeny pursue him? Shouldn't Evgeny the fugitive disappear soon? He had accomplished his mission. Now, the CIA and FBI were on the trail of this man who would destroy Russia with his imperial insanity. Could Evgeny trust them to stop it? He was beginning to doubt that.

He looked through the frosted windshield at the boat tied to the end of the dock. When someone else hopped from the boat and cast off the lines, Evgeny moved quickly. "Let's go," he said and quietly opened the door. Ava followed.

They skirted the warehouse and ran down an overgrown path to the river in time to watch the trawler head into the channel. With night already fallen, it was hard to identify any markings on the boat. But inside the wheelhouse, something glowed orange. "A lamp or something on the instrument panel," Evgeny guessed.

Ava was back on the phone, describing the orange-lit wheelhouse. "Hurry," she urged. "Fly!"

Ava and Evgeny kept watch on the river, the trawler now out of sight. After awhile, they heard the racing motors of two small powerboats coming upriver—and the unmistakable percussion of a helicopter advancing from the same direction. But they'd come too late to suit Evgeny. The trawler could have stopped anywhere along the river by now and discharged its passengers.

"Come on," Evgeny said. "We'll keep up." He outran Ava to the van and threw it into drive as she climbed in. "You will have to guide me," he said. "I do not know these streets." But eventually, they lost sight of the boats and had to rely on crackling reports to Ava from the pursuing vessels, manned solely by FBI.

"What about the chopper?" Evgeny asked.

"It's NYPD. They'll communicate directly to the boats, not me."

"And Hans Kluen?"

Ava shook her head. "I don't think he's in good standing with his superiors right now. Something tells me he didn't willingly give them the keys to his car."

Evgeny brooded. "I do not like this. The cowboys in those boats and chopper might scare Kluen and his boss into hiding where we will never find them. And I believe the hour is near."

"The boys on the water know what they're doing. They've been ordered to find the boat but not confront it. As for the NYPD chopper, that's a familiar sight over the city. Even your Architect shouldn't be spooked by it, if he's in the boat."

Chapter 31

*A*gent Delaney deposited Liesl and Cade at West Park Christian Church with a hefty accompaniment of attending agents. "I'm so grateful you're back safely," Rev. Scovall said, hurrying toward the door and locking it behind them. Just like before, Liesl remembered. "We've been so anxious to know how you were."

"Anxious ain't the word for it," said the old man just rounding a corner of the narthex. "Try spittin' mad."

"Ian!" Liesl cried.

Despite his contrary words, the old man's face beamed bright at the sight of her. "Come here, darlin'," he said, reaching for her. She welcomed his bracing hug.

"You smell like home," she told him, sniffing the collar of his shirt. "Like bacon and eggs."

"Good, I was afraid you were going to say magnolias." He squeezed her once more, then loosened his hold, keeping one arm lightly draped about her shoulders. He turned his attention to Cade. "Son, you ever tried to talk to an NYPD cop?"

"Oh no," Cade moaned.

"Well, hear me out," Ian continued. "Since none of you folks had the consideration to call and tell us what was going on, and I couldn't reach any of you, I did a bit of investigating on my own."

"Oh boy," Cade muttered, squeezing his eyes shut.

"So I called up one of those precinct numbers and asked the young man who answered if anyone had reported a van load of people in an accident, that one of them talked Russian and might have a gun and another one was a CIA agent with one of those sticky-out hairdos and a lot of miles on her. Or if a car with an FBI agent named Delaney in it and a big guy who thinks he's Rambo had overturned somewhere."

"You didn't," Cade said with only faint hope.

"And you want to know what that guy said to me?" Ian's face was getting redder.

"Not really, Pop."

"He asked if he could talk to one of the nice ladies who took care of me. Imagine that. So I asked him just how many nice ladies he had taking care of *him* and that it seemed to me he might need a few more."

Before anyone could summon a response of any kind, a loud rapping came at the front door, and one of the agents headed for it. "It's Delaney!" came from the other side, and the agent unlocked the door. Delaney entered with a phone to his ear, and everyone remained expectantly silent while he pulled his agents aside, issuing what appeared to be hasty orders.

Meanwhile, Jordan Winslow came bounding down the hallway and headed straight for Liesl. "Glad you're okay, Liesl. Where's Cass?" There was no mistaking his priorities.

"We left her at her mother's apartment. Hans was already gone."

"She's there alone?" Jordan asked with alarm. "What if someone comes looking for Hans?"

Just then Delaney joined the group. "I've got four agents at that apartment right now," he told Jordan.

"What about Ava and Evgeny?" Liesl asked him.

"I can't discuss that. For now, though, we're getting you and Jordan out of here and into a safe house. It'll be a little cramped with your . . . entourage in tow." Delaney was clearly irritated.

"I never been called an *en-tour-age* before. Have you, Cade?" Ian snipped sarcastically, then met Delaney eye to eye. "But I'll tell you what, Mr. FBI, when it comes to protecting Liesl, you'd better hope your pedigree agents can measure up to me and my boy. It's us mongrels who are most loyal . . . and the quickest to dismember anyone who threatens one of our own. Just thought I'd point that out to you."

Liesl looked away, stifling a grin.

"Mr. O'Brien, my apologies," Delaney said as he stepped away. "But if you will, sir, please gather your things—all of you, you too, Jordan—and wait here by the door. We'll be leaving soon."

Jordan touched Liesl's arm. "I'm not going with you," he whispered. "Don't tell the Nazi, but I'm going to Cass." He didn't wait for her to respond, but slipped back down the hallway.

Liesl rushed after him, catching up with him at the side door to the church. "Jordan, you can't leave. It's not safe. Those people who broke into Cass's apartment know you, too."

Shouldering his backpack, he paused long enough to hug Liesl. "No one came gunning for me. It's you they need to protect. And it's Cass who needs me. At least, I hope she does."

As he ran out the door, Liesl called after him, "Jordan, be careful!"

Chapter 32

Riding the elevator to her mother's apartment with the four agents, Cass could think of nothing but the conversation she'd just had with Liesl in the lobby. To her, Liesl was still an unknown. Perhaps she would remain one, even after this critical hour in both their lives.

When Cass arrived at the door, two of the agents remained in the hall, and the other two started to enter the apartment, but she stopped them. "Please wait out here. My mom has no idea what's happening. You'll only terrify her. I'll call if I need you." The agents hesitated, but did as she asked.

"Mom!" Cass called as she passed through the living room.

There was no answer.

"Mom, where are you?" Cass scolded herself for not coming up right away, for placing her needs before her mother's. Just then, she heard something heavy drop to the floor. The sound came from the master bedroom. Rushing into the elegant boudoir, Cass found her mother on a step stool in the walk-in closet, where she'd dropped a suitcase to the floor. "Mom, what are you doing?"

"Leaving. I won't stay here anymore, whether he comes back or not. I'm through with this. The cheating. The other woman. The place he goes at night. You think there's nothing going on, but there is. He's not the same, and I know why."

Cass braced herself. "No, you don't, Mom. You don't know at all. But I do."

Jilly turned slowly and looked accusingly at her daughter. "You've been keeping something from me?" she asked, then stepped to the floor. The flowing caftans and lounging pajamas she liked to wear at home had been replaced this day by bulky sweats, top and bottom, that hung in unflattering folds about her slim body.

"Come sit down, Mom." Cass led her into the bedroom and patted the down-filled comforter on the king-sized bed. "Right here."

As Jilly hesitantly sat down, Cass saw torment in the eyes. She lifted one of her mother's slender wrists and clutched the hand that used to smooth back the unruly blond ringlets on a little girl's head. The same hand that used to cup the small chin and nuzzle nose to nose, drawing peals of laughter from her daughter. Cass fastened on the face that once peered from magazine covers across the country. How many other daughters had looked at that face while standing in the grocery checkout line with their mothers and wished for such beauty? But had beauty ever sustained Jillian Kluen?

Cass looked into the sorrowful eyes and told as much as she knew about Hans's double life, about the files she'd found in his study, about Liesl, Ava, Evgeny, and why FBI agents were now posted outside the door. When she finished, her mother leaned forward and rested her head in her hands. Cass stroked her back. Then, her face smudged with spent tears and her breath faltering, Jilly asked, "How did I fail him?"

It struck Cass that her mother's first reaction wasn't anger over what her husband had done to her, but fear for what she might have done to him. Cass looked at her mother as if seeing her for the first time, marveling at her sense of selflessness. She embraced her mother and rocked her gently as if she were a child. "Mom, I think God might protect us and lead us out of this."

Jilly pulled back and looked at her. "I've never heard you speak that way."

Cass removed her arms from around her mother and gazed into the delicate silken weave of the comforter. "I'm not sure, Mom, but I believe he's here. Just like you taught me when I was little. Then we both forgot."

Jilly looked at her daughter with swollen eyes, studying her for too long. Cass started to speak, but Jilly stopped her. "Listen to me, Cass. Not everything I taught you was true."

Cass looked curiously at the face now drained of color. "Like what?"

Her mother got up and asked Cass to follow her into the living room. When the two reached the mahogany sofa table, Jilly pointed toward the display of photographs. "What do you see here?" she asked Cass.

Impatient with the ill timing of whatever lapse in focus this was, Cass looked at her watch instead of the photographs. "Mom, this isn't the time to reminisce."

"Just answer me, Cass."

Cass hoped her mother wasn't suffering some mental lapse brought on by shock. "Okay, Mom. I see photos of you and me at the beach, Grandma and Grandpa teaching you to snow ski when you were little, you and your sisters in a swing." She looked blankly at Jilly.

"Did you ever wonder why there were no photographs of your stepfather's family?"

But Cass clearly recalled asking Hans about that very thing a couple of years ago. "He told me he didn't have any pictures. That his mother had kept them all in a big box that his father, in one of his drunken rages, set fire to. Isn't that true?"

The answer was a long time coming. "No, Cass. What's true is this. If you had seen photographs of his family, especially his mother, you would have seen yourself."

Something quickened deep inside Cass, as if some detached intelligence within her had recognized the truth before she did.

"It was the shape of her face," Jilly said, her eyes now glistening, "her small mouth and strong chin." Jilly laid a gentle hand on Cass's shoulder. "Your grandmother's face."

There was no sound or feeling where Cass was at that moment. No up or down, no bearings, no support to grab for. Only swirling images of Hans Kluen and his courtly manners, his pleasant face, soft hugs—and his warnings. Now she knew. He'd asked her to the diner that day to warn her away from those who might hurt . . . his daughter.

Cass felt as though she were stroking upward through sluggish waters, struggling to reach the surface. She looked back to the sofa table and her mother, who'd kept such a ponderous secret for so long. Only now did she feel her mother's hand on her shoulder and turn. The stricken face before her pleaded to be heard, the full-lipped mouth working through words to say. Cass could only wait for them to come.

Now it was Jilly's turn to reach for Cass's hand and lead her to sit and hear a story. On the sofa, Jilly plumped pillows and wedged them behind her daughter. Cass let her.

"Hans and I were in high school when we fell in love. My family was well-off and nurturing; his was poor and broken. When my father got a seat on the New York Stock Exchange, we moved from the Bronx to Manhattan, and my whole world changed. My family discouraged me from seeing Hans anymore. My father said that such an unfortunate immigrant's son would never amount to anything. He didn't know I was already carrying Hans's child." Jilly bent her head and stared into her lap, but kept talking.

"I was desperate. I had to marry right away. So when my father brought Nicholas Rodino home for dinner one night and later encouraged me to snag his rich new client's eligible son, I saw my chance. I practically seduced Nick, and a month later, we were married.

"I thought he believed the child was his. But after you were born, he confronted me, demanding the truth. He'd been suspicious from the beginning, he said. But I never told him your father's name. Later, it didn't seem to matter to him anymore. He was determined to punish me anyway. I never understood why he stayed with me. Perhaps he loved me a little. I'm certain he loved showing me off, or so he said. And I'm sure he grew fonder of you, though not until he rescued you that night in the water when, well, you know." Jilly stroked her daughter's hand. "That kindled his compassion for you."

Cass began to fidget. She released her mother's hand and removed several pillows from behind her, pushing herself deep into a corner of the sofa, just short of a full retreat.

"It wasn't until Nick's funeral that I saw Hans again," her mother continued. "He was living near Wall Street, where he'd worked for many years, building a war chest, he told me later. He'd married and divorced. After that, he said, he could think of nothing but winning me back—with cash, if that's what it took." She looked around the room and smiled. "The luxuries are so nice, and I've been terribly spoiled. But I know in my heart, I would have loved Hans if he'd still lived in that sad little flat in the Bronx. I never forgot him through all the years with Nick."

It was time for Cass to ask, "How long has Hans known I was his child?"

"Since our wedding day. And when I told him, well, that was the happiest I've ever seen him, before or since. He was positively jubilant. Clapping his hands together and hugging me so hard." A shimmer of elation stole across Jilly's face. "But he didn't want me to tell you about him. Know why?" She shook her head slightly. "He didn't want you to think badly of me. And he didn't want to rob Nick, even in death, of his fatherhood, of his place in your life." She reached to finger a curl falling loosely over her daughter's forehead. "Do you see Hans a little clearer now?" She pinched the space between her eyes, and tears flowed through her fingers. "Because I do. And I think he may have done this terrible thing for money, to keep me and keep me happy." She hid her face in her hands and sobbed.

"No, Mom. I don't believe that's all of it." Cass inched closer to her mother's crumpled body and hugged her tightly. Then she thought of the files. Maybe there was something else there, something they'd missed. Suddenly, Cass was up and moving. "We have to leave here."

"But why? Hans will come back. I'm sure he will."

Cass wasn't sure of that at all. "Mom, we're going to Southampton."

A knock came at the door, which opened slightly. "Ms. Rodino," a voice called. "It's Agent Corley. There's a Mr. Winslow out here. Do you know him?"

"Jordan!" Cass ran to open the door, and his guileless face smiled down at her. Without so much as a glance at the four agents behind him, she wrapped both arms around his neck and touched her cheek to his.

"Oh, yeah, this is nice," he said, returning the embrace.

"I'm so glad you're here," she said, her voice breaking slightly.

Releasing her embrace but holding tight to her hand, Jordan turned to the agents. "It appears that she knows me. So I guess it's okay to go in, right?" Though he looked to them for clearance, Cass grabbed his arm and pulled him inside. Before closing the door, she thanked the agents for being there. "And," she added, "I don't know how close you're supposed to stick to us, but we'll be leaving for Long Island in a little while. Better tell Ava Mullins."

As the agents swapped confused looks, Cass closed the door. Jordan was greeting Jilly when Cass announced, "Jordan, there's a lot I have to tell you, but we've got to get to the beach house in a hurry. Can you get my car from the garage?"

As they were discussing the logistics of that, another knock came at the door. "Ms. Rodino, it's Agent Corley again."

Cass went to the door. "Yes?"

"Ma'am, Agent Mullins wants to talk to you." He handed Cass his phone.

"Cass, why Long Island?" Ava asked in a rushed tone.

It occurred to Cass that things had happened so rapidly since Saturday morning that Ava Mullins might not know much about her and Jordan or the beach house. "I know Jordan and I are strangers to you and—"

"I know more about you both than you'd be comfortable with, Cass. We also know it was your bloodhound sniffing around that blew this wide open. So tell me what else you think is at the house. And be quick, please."

Where are they? Cass wondered, then answered Ava. "Jordan and I didn't have time to search all the files in Hans's study. There might be something else there. Something to lead us to these people."

"I hope that's what Hans is doing for us right now. So stay where you are. Get some sleep. If we need to search more files, I'll send for you. And Cass . . . don't leave that apartment!"

Chapter 33

Ava clicked off the conversation with Cass to take a call from the tracking boat on the river. "They've located the boat. It's about to dock," she told Evgeny and directed him through a maze of streets winding north. It was almost nine.

"The Russian mob is all over this place," Evgeny informed offhandedly, steering the van into a warehouse district. "You know that, don't you? The waterfront, the airports. Everyone thinks it's the Italian mafia that dominates there. Wrong." He shot down a straightaway running along the river, which they could glimpse intermittently between metal buildings squatted against the wharf. Suddenly, he braked and backed up. "There!" He pointed, stopping the van in the middle of the street.

In the misty dark, a gauzy orange light lit up the wheelhouse of a boat just turning off the main channel and heading for a dock. "I see it," Ava said. "Cut your lights and get as close as you can."

Evgeny eased the van to the edge of a parking lot that ran between two buildings. "And that must be your boys drifting slowly behind. Not much use, are they?"

"They're following orders," Ava insisted. "To watch and wait."

"You wait. I'm moving in."

Before Ava could stop him, Evgeny climbed quietly from the van and ran low against the metal shell of a building. He was thankful that the water-rat gangs had seen fit to shoot out a few spotlights, opening a fairly dark corridor between the van and the incoming boat. When he reached a dumpster that reeked of something putrid, he had no choice but to shield his nose and take cover there.

He pulled his jacket up over his nose and watched a young man hop to the dock and tie down the lines. Evgeny could see the captain at the helm, cast in orange light and turned toward someone behind him. The captain threw up his hands in what appeared to be an angry gesture. He cut the engines and disappeared from view.

A few moments later, the same man slid open a wooden door and stepped onto the side deck facing the dock and called to the guy just finishing the lines. "Go find us some beer," he ordered, then looked down the dock toward the parking lot. Seemingly content with his surroundings, he went back inside, and his crewman headed Evgeny's way, scuffing his shoes along the pavement as he walked. Evgeny had no way of warning Ava. Surely she'd seen or heard the guy coming.

He watched as the crewman gave no notice to the van parked where he now could see it plainly. But he walked past and kept going, down the street and out of sight. Seconds later, Evgeny heard, "Pssst." Then again, "Pssst." He didn't even have to look. He just waved her on, and Ava slipped up beside him, her weapon drawn.

Sensing her unspoken question, he held up two fingers for the two men he'd seen on board and whispered, "So far." They heard voices from inside the open doorway of the boat. The captain and another crewmate emerged, engaged in a dispute. Evgeny was too far away to understand their words, but there was no doubt about the angry tone. Then the crewman hopped off the boat and stormed down the dock, looking once behind him and calling, "It could be days before he calls. You know where to reach me."

That's when Evgeny knew the Architect wasn't on board. But what about Hans? Could they have deposited him elsewhere before coming in for the night? Where?

When the captain went inside—leaving the door open, Evgeny was pleased to see—he motioned for Ava to stay as he crept from behind the dumpster. But she grabbed the back of his coat and pulled hard. "No!" she hissed under her breath. "Wait!"

But he just smiled patronizingly at her, released her hand from his coat, and took off, knowing she'd have to follow. He understood her dilemma. Were the U.S. top cops really going to let a KGB hit man hold the reins in such a critical operation? Could they afford to ignore the things he knew and they didn't? His Russian contact was feeding him, not them. But then the nagging thought returned. What had led Ava to City Island?

He heard her behind him but didn't slow. His own handgun firmly in his grip, he moved with surprising speed for a man his age, then turned to see Ava matching it. He focused on the orange-lit wheelhouse, still empty.

Careful not to upset the balance of the floating vessel, he stepped gingerly over the gunwale and plastered himself against the side of the boat, listening. No voices.

He motioned for Ava, who'd just repeated his moves, to stay. It occurred to him that they'd been telling each other to do that all evening, and neither one had. He hoped she'd obey this time. He'd hate to see her take a bullet.

When he heard music from somewhere below, he knew he'd have only seconds to surprise whoever was there, probably the captain. Even one creak-inducing footstep above would surely summon trouble from below. He looked once more at Ava, then moved inside the cabin. At the door to the steps, he paused and listened again. No movement. *Maybe the captain thinks it's his crewman back with the beer.*

Bingo.

A voice called up from below. "That was quick. Bring it down here. I've got the—"

The sight of a gun pointed at his face choked back the rest of the man's words. He dropped the skillet in his hand, slinging hot grease down his pants, which elicited a fury of profanity. Evgeny moved too quickly for the man to recover his defenses, though his hand had shot toward a knife behind him on the galley counter. Evgeny knocked the blade out of the man's reach and steadied the gun at eye level.

"Sit down!" Evgeny ordered, shoving a small stool toward the man and looking quickly about the well-appointed salon. The pieces were fitting. Who would suspect this old clunker to harbor such a sleek hideout below deck. *Nice move, Architect.*

In seconds, Ava was beside him, training her own gun on the captain. "Where's Hans Kluen?" she demanded.

The man only sneered at her. Evgeny picked up the knife from the floor. Without delay, he leaned over and sliced through the pants where hot grease had saturated, knowing the skin on the thigh below was already painful. Another shriek from the captain.

"Now we will make the question harder," Evgeny said calmly. "Where is Hans Kluen *and* the man you work for?" He lowered the blade toward the man's other thigh.

"Wait!" The captain raised a trembling hand. "I didn't sign on for this." He paused to gather what Evgeny hoped was the truth. "We took them all across the river and dropped them off."

"Who?"

The captain cursed Evgeny, who raised the knife over the now bleeding leg. "Don't!" the man cried. "I'll tell you. My Russian boss and that big woman . . . and that Wall Street guy they hauled out of here all trussed up like a pig. Then we went back to move his car."

"Where did you take them, and where were they going?" Ava demanded.

"A dock in Brooklyn. I don't know where he goes when I drop him off. There's always a car waiting." Evgeny made a move toward him. "I swear it!" the man yelled. "He's got a house somewhere over there, a big place like a museum or something, his driver told me. Lots of art."

Something flared in Evgeny's memory. He leaned close to the man. "What kind of art?"

"Don't know. Just art. The driver says he's crazy about it."

"Antiques, too?" Evgeny pumped, drawing an inquisitive stare from Ava.

"I don't know about no antiques, buddy. All I know is he likes art. Period." The man dabbed at his bloody pants. "Hey, you gonna do something about this bleeding?"

"You ever pick this guy up around the South Street Seaport?" Evgeny asked, ignoring the man's question.

"Yeah, a few times. He's got a place down there, too. He's got 'em all over the world, I hear. Must be some big mobster. Don't know."

"What kind of car meets the boat?" Ava jumped in, still eyeing Evgeny curiously.

"Big black Beemer. But sometimes it's a black Range Rover. The guy's got money."

Evgeny wasn't listening anymore. He remembered the night Pavel Andreyev had summoned him to an apartment near the South Street Seaport. Evgeny had heard it belonged to an arts-and-antiques dealer who used to work at the Kremlin.

"And now the bigger question," Ava continued. "What does he look like?"

The captain thought. "Not too tall. Kind of skinny. Not a lot of hair. Nice dresser."

Evgeny sorted through a mental file of former Kremlin types. No matches surfaced right away. But now he had landed on a more promising lead. The Seaport apartment. The FBI had already searched the UN apartment Jordan Winslow had directed them to, finding no shred of evidence.

"Get your boys in here to take care of this guy and the others," Evgeny told Ava. "You and I have someplace else to go."

Ava raised a questioning brow.

"I'll explain later. Better make your call."

It didn't take long for the agents on the river to swoop in and take charge of the captain and his vessel. Evgeny knew they would wait for the beer runner to return, then hunt down the third member of the crew. As for the black vehicles belonging to the Architect . . .

"Do you know how many black BMWs and Range Rovers there are in this metro area?" Ava asked as they left the boat. "And records don't show which ones belong to Russian expats." That had quelled Evgeny's urgings to track the cars. He had a more urgent pursuit anyway.

Back in the van, Evgeny told Ava about the Seaport apartment and his brief connection to it. "That's where I went to report to Pavel Andreyev the night I failed to capture Liesl." He wouldn't look at Ava. "I knew he was just a guest there, that the owner traveled a lot—just some vague being I never gave thought to." He fumed. "It has to be him!"

"Can you find this place again?"

"Hang on."

As Evgeny swung the van onto a southerly route to Lower Manhattan, Ava called Cass at the number attached to the phone Evgeny had provided. That piece of logistical planning had impressed Ava, who still hoped to bring Evgeny in and convince him, in whatever way it took, to apply his considerable spy craft to U.S. interests.

It was nearly eleven, and the flight from Charleston earlier that morning seemed days ago. Ava tried to ignore the creeping fatigue in her body, preferring to picture herself asleep against Ian's shoulder through most of the flight. *Ian.* Almost sixteen years older than she, he'd captured her heart without meaning to. No one knew how much she loved him, including him.

"Yes, ma'am?" Cass answered in a sleepy voice.

"Okay, Cass. You're on. Tell the agents to take you to the beach house right away and get started on those files. You'll have to let them oversee the search."

"Can Jordan and my mom come, too?"

Ava grimaced. Jordan would be a help, but she wasn't sure about the mother.

"I can't leave her here by herself, even with bodyguards," Cass insisted.

"Okay, but hurry. And Cass, we have reason to believe Hans is being held captive by these people. It's critical that you stay close to your security detail. At this moment, the people who took Hans are probably looking for you."

Chapter 34

*T*he black BMW pulled up to the two-story Brooklyn house. Two men hauled a still-bound Hans from the back seat as Ivan and Sonya followed them inside. Ivan was angry that Sonya had left the front drapes open, inviting anyone with a flashlight to look inside. Though the former estate was walled with gated entrances that were usually locked, Ivan had been surprised before by curious neighborhood kids. More than once, they had scaled the brick wall and set off to explore the abandoned buildings of this long-closed arts college. He was sure they'd been drawn by that ridiculous cow outside the front gate. "An already warped sense of art gone utterly haywire," Ivan had complained to Sonya.

"Take him to the basement," Ivan ordered the men, two of his most trusted aides, neither of whom spoke more than a smattering of English.

"Are you so sure we were not followed, Ivan?" Sonya asked before heading to her upstairs bedroom.

"Go to sleep, Sonya," he responded impatiently, dismissing her fears. When she left, he retreated to the small study from which his friend Boris had once managed the affairs of the college. "A euphemism, for sure," Boris had once admitted. "No accreditation. No diplomas. Just a small colony of artists joyfully engaged. And filthy rich!"

Ivan remembered the times he'd come to America with fabricated papers and headed for this isolationist compound in the midst of teeming Brooklyn. He and Boris Reznik had fled Russia soon after the collapse of the Soviet empire. Boris, a Russian Jew with wealthy American friends, had reveled in the artistic and financial freedom that America, and his generous students, had afforded him. He had repeatedly chided Ivan for clinging to dreams of a Russian resurgence. "Your new world order is foolishness," Boris had scoffed. "Noble but foolish. Come and luxuriate here with us. We want nothing more than to live as we choose and savor each decadent morsel of American life." Then he'd bellowed with laughter and handed Ivan another glass of ice-cold vodka.

The old oak floor squeaked beneath the antique rugs as Ivan crossed the study to the fireplace. He added a handful of kindling, two fat logs, then struck the match—much like the orderly progression of sabotage. And revenge. *Such a satisfying word*, he thought, tumbling the two syllables about in his mouth.

As the dry tinder caught, he poured cognac from a nearby decanter and lifted it to the flames, watching the fiery liquid dance inside the crystal snifter. "Wrong, Boris," Ivan said to the flames. "I do *luxuriate* in ways you couldn't know."

Now an invalid living in Manhattan with his daughter, Boris had never asked how Ivan had acquired his wealth. The truth was, the Kremlin insider, before abandoning the sinking Soviet ship, had helped himself to government funds he believed he was entitled to. In the chaotic aftermath of the Soviet Union's collapse in 1991, certain accountants were too busy treading water to notice the grievous imbalance of their books. Ivan wondered if they ever noted the disparities but dared not insinuate blame. He'd invested the confiscated capital wisely and multiplied it many times over.

Besides his strategically located residences around the world, his private plane and helicopter, his boats, his Savile Row suits, and his well-paid troupe of strong-armed attendants, the luxury Ivan enjoyed most was his front-row seat at the rise and fall of an American president. It was coming soon.

As he swirled the cognac in the sparkling glass, he remembered the cracked pottery on which his mother had served him food as a child, with never enough to satisfy his hunger. She'd scrubbed the homes of the

Kremlin elite and tended their thankless broods, then returned to care for her young son in the hovel they shared with another family. Then Ivan simply turned off the offending memories and let them drain away, like the foul-smelling sulfurous water that trickled from the faucets of his childhood. There was work to do.

He lifted his phone and summoned the photographic signal that would launch the next stage of attacks on this gluttonous country. With his fingertip, he traced the image of the bandaged ear, the haunted eyes of the artist who'd indulged the thrashings of his own mind, of his own knife-wielding hand. Ivan wondered what had drawn him so to Vincent van Gogh's fatalistic self-portrait. Even though supposition held that the artist's self-mutilation had sprung not from the toxicity of his genius but from the unintentional ingestion of lead paint.

Still, Ivan preferred to look upon the image as the glory of an injured warrior, even though the battle raged within himself. That, Ivan could relate to. And so he'd chosen the famous painting as the final signal to his loyal troupe of saboteur-spies spread across this land. When they received the text and opened the image, they would know exactly what to do. The death rattle of American dominance and Travis Noland's reign would begin.

Ivan looked at his watch. Captain Cyrus Neale would launch the massive, coast-to-coast strike with one shocking opener, a horrific teaser of what was to come. He and Sonya would watch the spectacle from shore. Seconds later, his chopper would whisk them away and deliver them to a safe haven. Ivan had many from which to choose.

The door to the basement opened, and one of his men advised him that the captive below was demanding a word with him. *Why not?* Ivan considered. *The man hasn't long.* "Tell him I will be there in a moment." Ivan first needed to confirm the coming afternoon's pick-up time by the boat crew who'd just deposited him, Sonya, and Hans in Brooklyn.

When the aide left, Ivan dialed the captain's phone but got no answer. He dialed again, then again. He had demanded they be available at all times for his call. Now he was angry. He dialed another of the crew. Still no answer. His instincts released a sudden charge. He revisited Sonya's question. *Are you so sure we weren't followed?*

Ivan sprang from his chair and hurried to the basement. He charged at Hans. "What have you done?"

Hans turned bleary, red-tinged eyes on him. "Evidently something else I'm not aware of," he moaned sarcastically.

"Did someone follow you to the dock?"

Hans sighed. "I don't know," he droned. "I seem to have a deplorable lack of knowledge, wouldn't you say?"

"Straighten up," Ivan commanded.

But Hans was tied to a chair. "Why don't *you* straighten up, Ivan!" he cried, the sound of one resigned to his fate and no longer fearful. "You've had your fun. Now why don't you take your fat friend upstairs and get out of here. You make me sick."

The blow across his cheek came swiftly from Ivan's own hand.

Hans absorbed it but kept charging. "That's the coward's way. Hit the man who can't defend himself. Shoot at the innocent piano player and go after a man's child because she dared to interfere with your noble plans." Hans looked fiercely at Ivan. "What drives you, Ivan? Are you really such a Mother Russia patriot? Or just a lunatic?"

Ivan raised his hand again.

"How about the other cheek this time?" Hans jeered, turning his head the opposite direction.

Lowering his hand, Ivan eyed him savagely. "Where is your step-daughter?"

"Make that *daughter*." Hans preened with a mixture of triumph and pain. "And didn't you hear yourself tell me she was in South Carolina? If anyone followed me, it wasn't *my child*."

Sonya's agitated voice sounded at the top of the basement steps. "Ivan, come quickly!"

With the door to the basement left open. Hans could hear the conversation Sonya began with Ivan.

"Cyrus Neale just phoned. His house is being watched. He is sure of it."

"Rubin took Hafner to that house today, did he not?"

"He did, sir."

There was a long silence. "Get Rubin on the phone."

"That contact information is on my flash drive with everyone else's. Give me a minute."

"Where do you keep that?"

Hans strained to hear. "In a cigarette case inside my purse."

"That is no place to keep such critical information."

"We have moved around too much to keep it in the safe at my apartment. But don't worry. I will secure it once we reach the boat, where I also have a duplicate."

Ivan returned to the basement. "When was the last time you spoke to Cyrus Neale?" he asked Hans.

Hans decided it was best to cooperate. He needed time and opportunity. "He called me this afternoon."

"What did he say about Jeremy Rubin's visit?"

"That he didn't trust him or his friend."

"Why have you not told me this?"

Hans looked down at the straps around him. "Something about being slammed into a chair and tied up put a real damper on conversation."

Ivan ignored his sarcasm. "Why did Cyrus not trust them?"

Before Hans could answer, Sonya called for Ivan.

"Get up and come with me," Ivan told Hans, then turned to the man guarding him. "Untie him and bring him upstairs."

When the man released Hans from the chair, a sharp pain radiated through his right shoulder and he winced. Ivan watched him carefully but ignored the show of discomfort. "You might be of use to me yet. Cyrus has never spoken to anyone but you and Sonya. I don't think he likes her. Imagine that." Hans knew the ruthless woman was feared, even hated, by many within Ivan's network, though she remained fiercely loyal to the cause. "You will speak to him now."

Upstairs, Hans was directed to a chair at the kitchen table and shoved into it by the man still holding a gun on him. Instantly, Hans's full attention was drawn to the open handbag across the table from him. Taking his seat, he leaned forward as far as possible for a better look inside, then shifted his eyes quickly away before the guard took notice.

Sonya inserted a flash drive into a laptop on the kitchen counter and pulled up the necessary contact information.

"Get Cyrus on the phone first," Ivan told her, and turned to Hans. "You are his overseer. He will speak more freely with you."

Sonya closed the laptop. Hans saw the flash drive still protruding from the side. She punched in the number and hit speaker, then handed the phone to Hans.

The man picked up immediately. "Cyrus here."

"This is Hans. Tell me why you think someone's watching you." He looked up at Ivan and Sonya hovering over him.

"I've seen the same car in different spots on my street," Cyrus said. "Then it leaves and another arrives. It's been going on all afternoon."

Ivan mouthed the word *Rubin*.

"Tell me about your visitors today."

"Didn't like either one of them, especially the guy with the hood on his head. He didn't even speak. I know he's some kind of big-deal spy of yours and couldn't let me see him. But it gave me the creeps."

"What about Jeremy Rubin?"

"Okay, I guess. Kind of nervous."

"What do you mean?"

"He kept watching the other guy and fidgeting, you know." He paused. "Hey, are you ready to do this thing or not? Tell that big boss of yours I've got the explosives all loaded up and ready to fire. Good thing I decided to dock my tug someplace else. Whoever's watching the house probably doesn't know where it is now. But I tell you what, I'm plenty tired of waiting for the action. Fish or cut bait!"

Ivan mouthed a word that made Hans's pulse quicken. *Tomorrow.*

Hans relayed Ivan's message and reminded Cyrus to keep his phone on him at all times and watch for the signal. The call ended, and Sonya retrieved the phone.

Ivan abruptly walked into a study off the kitchen and closed the door. Sonya looked after him, her face clouded. Hans didn't take his eyes off her as she retrieved the flash drive and returned to the table. Feigning disinterest while cutting his eyes toward the purse, he watched her open a flat, silver cigarette case, drop the small drive inside, then shove the case back into her purse. She was about to snap it shut when Ivan flung open the door and announced, "Call Rubin now! Tell him I want to meet with him and it is imperative he bring Ben Hafner. Make certain he understands that. Then give him very clear directions to the warehouse. Tell him to be there promptly at noon tomorrow."

A highly agitated Ivan motioned the guard to come into the study as if any further threat from Hans had been suspended. Now, only he and Sonya remained in the kitchen. Hans couldn't believe such an opportunity had been handed to him. He would have to act quickly. Any minute, Ivan might regain his better judgment and order Hans retied.

His eye on the purse, he asked, "Sonya, may I have a glass of water, please?" Then he slowly stood as if to retrieve it himself, all the while listening to the conversation inside the study. He heard only sentence fragments from Ivan. "On the roof . . . first sign of backup . . . call immediately."

"I'll get it," she barked at Hans.

Hans risked further movement toward the purse, but Sonya was too preoccupied with calling Rubin to notice. Closer. Almost within reach now. He stopped suddenly when she turned and handed him a glass with barely a splash of water in it, then clamped the phone to her ear.

Hans remained where he was and drank slowly, gauging his risks.

After a moment, Sonya turned away and spoke briskly into the phone. "Jeremy Rubin?" It was, and she proceeded to relay Ivan's exact orders, taking great pains to make them clear.

This was the moment. Hans backed slowly to the table, one hand on his glass, the other behind him, reaching, searching inside the open purse. When his fingertips fell on the flat, cool metal, in one fluid motion he slid the cigarette case out of the purse and into his right back pocket.

In the midst of her instructions to Jeremy Rubin, Sonya turned sharply toward Hans as he calmly placed his empty glass on the table and returned to his seat, careful not to put any weight on his right hip.

When she ended the call, she shot one wary glance toward Hans, then walked swiftly to the study. His heart slamming against his chest, Hans pulled the silver case from his pocket, removed the flash drive, slid the purse toward him and plunged the case inside, careful to leave the purse open as before. He had just pushed it back to its original resting place and leaned back in his chair when Ivan entered the kitchen.

"You have been of service to me after all," Ivan told Hans without expression. "But you will remain here under guard until I tell my men what to do with you." Ivan ordered his aide to retie Hans.

Hans quickly slipped his closed and sweating hand into his right coat pocket and released the flash drive as the aide approached him. "So tomorrow is the day?" Hans asked, straining for calm.

Ivan scrutinized him through narrowed eyes. "You were never cut out for this, were you, Hans? I should have realized that long ago. But you tried. And some of your efforts will pay off for us. You will have your revenge, and I mine. Perhaps you will hear the explosion from here. After that, the whole country will run to ground for a hole to hide in." A trace of regret flitted across his face. "If you had not failed me, you would fly away with us tomorrow, over the flaming river and out to the ship."

Chapter 35

*W*hat will your courts do to the Architect if you bring him in alive?"
Evgeny asked Ava as they cruised toward the South Street Seaport.

"That's for all those people with law degrees to figure out. Not a music
teacher."

He hitched a half grin at her. "Oh, so that's what you are now? No longer the CIA doyenne, the stainless-steel spymaster? You think you can just
crawl back into your old life of pleasant little concertos and forget what
you saw out here?"

Ava stared straight ahead. "Forget? No, I never will. But I'm trying.
Music has always helped me do that."

"What sort of music do you think the Architect listens to while he plots
mass murder?" He felt her scrutiny.

"What's on your mind, Evgeny?"

He turned hard eyes on her. "He must not live long enough for court
of any kind."

It was almost midnight Sunday when they parked beside the Rococo-
style apartment building. Evgeny remembered the acidic meeting with

Andreyev there just over a year ago—and the humiliation of failure. Now, he was glad Liesl Bower had escaped him that night. He'd been blinded by patriotic promises from men whose mighty words had soon rung shrill and hollow, whose motives had spun out of control.

He'd had Liesl clearly in his sights that night. Three men on her heels, certain of the capture. Then she turned the corner and disappeared. "God held that door open just long enough for me to escape." That's what Liesl had told him. Would he ever believe it?

"What floor?" Ava cut into his thoughts.

"Fourth."

When the elevator opened onto the small lobby, still wrapped in ruby-flocked wallpaper, Evgeny went straight to one of four doors and listened. Ava reached for her handgun and stood to one side of the door, her back to the wall. Evgeny knocked lightly. No answer. Then again. Still no response. He retrieved a slim, flat rod from his bag, telescoped it a couple of feet, then slid it under the door. The camera on the tip of the rod picked up no movement, no sign of occupancy, at least not in an area dimly lit by one floor-level night-light. With two more instruments from his bag, he tediously unlocked the door.

Silently, they moved as one unit into the foyer of a fanciful dwelling clad in velvets and satins. The prisms of an elaborate pink chandelier caught enough lamplight from the street to cast a rosy wash over the living room—wholly inconsistent with the mission of those who'd passed through.

After a room-by-room sweep, Ava lowered her gun. "Looks like a brothel," she said finally, fingering a purple lampshade trimmed in gold fringe.

Evgeny was too anxious to begin the search to respond aloud. *A house of ill repute*, he thought. *How fitting.*

As he handled the Architect's belongings, he tried to imagine the mind of the man. Was it as deliberately pretentious as this apartment? A mere confection? At what point did it shift into cold blood?

Careful not to turn on lights visible from the street, should Ivan approach, Ava searched the living room and kitchen by flashlight while

Evgeny headed for the two bedrooms. After a while, they still hadn't found anything of substance. While Ava sifted through linens and toiletries in the guest bath, Evgeny tackled the closet in the master bedroom. They had no profile of what they were looking for, just anything that would identify and help locate the man they hunted. En route to the apartment, Ava had requested an FBI search for the deed, tax records, utility billing, and any other lead to the apartment's owner, which she suspected was a dummy corporation, as with the UN apartment they'd already investigated. Evgeny was certain the effort was futile and had told her so. The Architect might have light-headed taste in decorating, but he was no dummy, corporate or otherwise.

In the master closet, Evgeny rummaged through a footlocker that held an assortment of tourist information—maps, menus, sports schedules, Gray Line tour routes, shopping guides, historic-site pamphlets, and a printout of a website for a heliport on the East River. Evgeny sat back on his heels and stared at that last item, then turned it over. Handwritten on the back were the words *Bell helicopter 429* and a serial number. From there his eye landed on a scribbled date. Tomorrow's.

Hearing Ava approach, he quickly folded the paper and shoved it into his coat pocket.

"Anything in here?" she asked as she entered the room.

"Nothing," he called, emerging from the closet. "We should go."

But she remained where she was. "Is this the last lead you have?"

"What do you mean?" He knew exactly what was on her mind.

"Do you know of any other connections this man has to the U.S.? Any other lead at all?"

He eyed her carefully. "You mean, have I reached the end of my service to you?"

"I didn't say that. You have been—"

"Save your words. It is time to go."

Back on the sidewalk in front of the building, Ava took off in the direction of the van, parked around the corner. Evgeny kept pace with her at first, then stopped before reaching the corner. She turned quickly back to him. "What's the matter?" she asked.

Another time and he might have toyed with her and the alarm he saw in her face. But this wasn't the time. "I know what is waiting for me around the corner. The same spooks you have had following us ever since you got into the van at the church. Did you think I had lost all my skills? That I did not see them shadowing our every move?"

She stared straight up into his face but didn't answer.

"They were there all the time, even when we boarded the trawler," he said. "If I had not handled the situation to your satisfaction, you would have called them in, no doubt."

"You've lived up to your reputation, Evgeny," Ava said, her voice tight, unsure.

He watched her eyes dart about, appraising her situation. Her safety. Why now? After all her time alone with him—her protectors just out of reach—why was she suddenly on guard with him?

"I am not going to hurt you, Ava. I have grown rather fond of you, in fact. But I will not go with you. Surely you know that."

"And surely you know we couldn't let you just walk away. Murder one. Attempted kidnapping. Assault with a deadly weapon. Espionage."

He smiled resolutely. "It is what I do."

She nodded acknowledgment. "And what I'd like to do is bring you into the fold, to work for us."

He reached for her hand and held it lightly, surprised that she let him. "I belong to no one," he assured her. "Not anymore." He released her hand, then turned and walked away.

Ava watched him go, unable to summon those who, indeed, waited around the corner to apprehend Evgeny Kozlov. When she couldn't see him anymore, she returned to the van.

Chapter 36

*T*he Oval Office is the loneliest place on earth, Travis Noland and presidents before him had declared. The chilling truth of the statement ran like ice water over Noland's aching bones this predawn Monday. The leader of the free world sat alone at his desk, hours before the West Wing would surge to life. Spread before him were intelligence reports gathered by those in climate-controlled CIA offices with their earpieces tuned to the back-alley chattering in places like Tehran, Kabul, Istanbul, and Moscow. And by those agents in the field who played catch-as-catch-can, snaring whatever shreds of intelligence they could uncover through their global scavenging. It was no way to protect 313 million Americans, yet sometimes it was the only way. What lay before the president this morning was like a parachute shot full of tiny holes, just a semblance of solid information, but you couldn't risk a test jump. You couldn't accuse Russia of the inauguration attack or the Supreme Court bombing or plotting more acts of terror—not with intelligence as riddled as this.

From the consolidated, up-to-the-minute reports—compiled and analyzed by the pros at Langley, Quantico, and the Pentagon—Noland knew a ring of proficient subversives was in place in the U.S., that a massive terrorist plot was on countdown toward the destruction of key infrastructure and national monuments across the nation. The whispering shadows had signaled that the plot was a warning to leave Moscow alone.

The president agonized. *What does that mean? Alone to do what? Who is this person—this Architect?*

This wasn't a front-room Kremlin conspiracy, the president believed. Relations with President Dimitri Gorev, though tenuous, had been progressive and mostly respectful. No, this didn't carry his signature.

A light knock came at the door. The president's secretary, Rona Arant, had reported to the West Wing simultaneously with the president at four this morning, awaiting the visitor who'd just arrived. "Sir," Rona announced, "the director is here."

"Show him in, please . . . and Rona, thank you for losing a night's sleep over this."

"As did you, sir." She stepped aside and ushered Rick Salabane into the office.

The president rose and came around his desk, extending his hand to the FBI director and gesturing toward the twin yellow damask sofas. "What happened last night?" Noland asked, taking a seat opposite Salabane and wasting no time with perfunctory greetings.

"We followed the boat to a small industrial slip upriver. My men were watching it, but Ava Mullins and Evgeny Kozlov boarded and surprised the only guy on board, the captain. Now we have the crew of three. We've been interrogating them all night. So far, the only useful thing we've gotten is a description of their boss and the false name he uses with them. It's the same description Jordan Winslow gave us of the man he saw in the UN apartment. Again, though, we don't know if he's the man we're after or not. But we got a rather crude rendering based on those descriptions. We're running it through our database for a matchup. If this guy's never blipped the radar, though, we won't get a hit. And we can't broadcast the rendering and send him deeper undercover."

The president nodded, his mind surveying the treacherous terrain of this crisis, landing on another old nemesis. "Kozlov, huh? What a preposterous ally that is."

"But if intuition is worth anything, sir, I trust Ava's and my own. I think this guy might very well be one of our greatest assets right now. Ava and Liesl Bower are convinced Kozlov is as driven to stop this thing as we are. And he did go to heroic efforts to save Miss Bower's life on Saturday."

"We can't trust his motives to align with ours, though. We don't know his, not really. Now, what about Ava? You feel good about bringing her back in?"

"The CIA sure does. Director Bragg hasn't forgotten the job she did, finding the code and keeping Liesl Bower alive at the same time. She can run the off-radar op we need better than most. You see, sir, we can't ramrod our way through this. Capturing this person, if it is just one, has to happen without forewarning. His finger is on the switch."

The president looked back at the files on his desk. "And where is Liesl?"

"We took her, her fiancé, and his grandfather to a safe house last night."

The president nodded. "Very good. But keep her away from Hans Kluen's stepdaughter and her boyfriend. I've read the reports on them. Innocuous enough, but we can't be sure. We don't know what allegiance she might have to Kluen. And where is she?"

"Searching through Kluen's files at the Southampton house, for whatever else they turn up. Jordan Winslow and the mother are with her. We've got plenty of protection around them, and one of my agents is supervising their search."

"And if Hans Kluen shows up there?"

"We're prepared to deal with that, sir."

Noland shook his head and stood up. "You never know what's ticking inside the guy next door, do you?" He walked to one of the windows and looked into the darkness, punctuated by spotlights trained on the grounds. "Our country is under attack. The people are afraid. And the media has gone crazy. Who rigged the explosives at the Capitol and why can't anybody find them? Our people need answers. The Supreme Court is bombed, and nobody is even a suspect. Heaven help us if this new plot twist leaks to the press and we're still flat-footed." Noland paced back and forth in front of the window. "Washington is on lockdown. New York is fast behind. And we still don't know whom or what we're dealing with!" He made a fist and pounded it into his other palm. "That's got to change!"

Salabane rose to face the president. "One thing we do know, sir. Either the bomber or the person who slipped him in and out of the Capitol security grid . . . is one of ours."

Noland's eyes almost squinted shut. "Secret Service?"

"We're digging deep, sir. We should know soon."

"Not soon enough. Now, Bragg will be here in a few minutes, and I'll ask this question of him. But I want your gut reaction. What are the chances that Pavel Andreyev and Vadim Fedorovsky are behind this?"

"Excellent chances, sir. Those two are still running their underground network even from prison. President Gorev knows it, too. There's a reason why he hasn't already executed them for plotting his assassination. I believe Gorev knows the Architect and is scared to death of him. Do Andreyev and Fedorovsky know who the Architect is? Absolutely. Do they answer to that person? Absolutely. That's what I think, sir."

After Salabane left the Oval Office, the president returned to his desk and continued his study of the files. He had half an hour before Bragg and the Homeland Security chief arrived.

He lifted one folder and removed a handful of reports, his eyes scanning swiftly through the first one. He had almost finished when he landed on one small paragraph, just one incidental fragment of information that snagged a trip line in his memory. He gripped the page with both hands and brought it closer, his eyes boring into just two sentences. "It seems that the man known as the Architect is also an art collector. He has a particular fondness for Vincent van Gogh and has been known to wear a tie tack in the shape of an ear."

That's all it was. That's all the president needed. He knew who the Architect was.

Noland jumped from his seat and called through the closed door for his secretary, bypassing the intercom system. She came right away. "Rona, call the State Department and get Shelton Myers over here. Tell him it's urgent!" His mind was sorting furiously through another era of his life.

"It's very early, sir. Shall I try his home first?"

"Yes, please. And hold off my next appointments."

When she closed the door, Noland sank to the nearest chair and raked through memories of a time nearly thirty-five years earlier. He'd been recruited straight from Yale to the U.S. diplomatic corps, assigned to London. He hadn't fooled himself into believing it was his scholarly and student-leader achievements that had earned him such a soft yet prestigious post. Though convinced it was his father's long and luminous tenure with the U.S. State Department that steered the assignment his way, young Travis eagerly accepted it. To follow in his father's footsteps wasn't at all distasteful. Though the man was regarded as overbearing and ruthless by those who'd found themselves across the world's treaty tables from him, he was a patriot. An absent father, too, spending weeks at a time in hot spots across the world.

Just a year after his relocation to London, Travis Noland joined a trade delegation to Moscow, billed as on-the-job training. There he met a young Soviet Army officer who'd risen quickly through the ranks and now held a position of influence inside the Kremlin. Though Noland was in the company of more senior U.S. and British diplomats during that short stay in Russia, the young Soviet had shown particular interest in Noland. In a group, the Russian repeatedly singled out Noland to discuss the most sensitive issues, then took obvious delight when the neophyte diplomat stumbled in his answers. Humiliated, Noland returned to London with misgivings about his future with the corps and bitterness over his mistreatment at the hands of Ivan Volynski.

Noland's intercom buzzed. "Sir, Mr. Myers says he'll be here as quickly as possible."

"Thank you, Rona. When he arrives, bring him right in. And get Salabane to send me the rendering he just told me about. Quickly, please. Thank you."

Shelton Myers was ready to retire. He'd served the State Department his whole adult life, often rejecting a higher-profile post, preferring the backstage, in-the-trenches negotiations for which he was considered brilliant. After that first inglorious trip to the Kremlin, Noland had returned twice more over the years, each time in Shelton's company. In time, Noland, too, had reached veteran status with the department before entering Congress, then the White House. But Shelton Myers had remained

Noland's most trusted adviser and confidant. Just two days ago, Noland had confided in Shelton the threat of imminent terrorist acts orchestrated by a billionaire Russian revolutionist known as the Architect.

When Rona finally ushered Shelton into the Oval Office, the dark still clung opaquely to the windows. "Shelton, I'm sorry to call you out so early. Please sit and help yourself." The president gestured toward a tray of coffee and danish on a nearby sideboard.

Shelton waved it away, dropped his briefcase and jacket onto a sofa, and remained standing. He was fit and energetic for his sixty-plus years, a few inches below Noland's six feet, and immaculately dressed for one summoned on such short notice. But he had a Basset hound droop to his face, which had always fooled adversaries into thinking he would be a pushover in negotiations, just plodding and compliant. They didn't know a pit bull lurked beneath the surface.

"What's up, Travis?" Alone, they were just two old friends who'd fought Capitol Hill battles together too many years for formalities.

"Let's sit down. This might take awhile." Noland poured coffee for them both and took the cups to the table between the matching sofas. Handing one to his guest and taking a seat opposite, he dove straight to the issue. "Do you remember Ivan Volynski?"

Shelton's drooping face lifted slightly. "The KGB stiff neck? Who could forget the guy? Made of serrated Soviet steel." He chuckled. "Speared you with it a few times, didn't he?"

"And with pleasure." Noland searched his old friend's face and its network of hard-won crevices. "Shelton, there's something I never told you about that first return trip to Moscow I made, with you and the others." He paused to gather his thoughts. "You remember I didn't want to go. Hated the thought of confronting that man again. He was just nine years older but postured himself as an elder statesman, out to rid his country of any interference from young Westerners like us."

"I remember well. Go on." Shelton picked up his cup and leaned back.

"After our first meeting, at which I said next to nothing, he approached me and suggested I might like to visit his office." Noland shook his head and sniffed. "I don't mind saying it scared me. But I went, too curious not to." He sipped his coffee and replaced the cup solidly in the saucer, pausing a moment more. "Volynski closed the door behind us, and the first thing I noticed about the office was the framed print of van Gogh's self-portrait, the one with his bandaged ear."

Shelton grimaced. "I can see how that would serve as inspiration to a guy like that," he offered snidely.

"There were paintings by other artists, but mostly van Gogh's." He paused again. "He asked me to sit across the desk from him. I knew it was the old superior-subordinate game, but I didn't object. He rambled on and on about the mercurial state of the Soviet Union, that if it ever fell—which it did four years later—it would return. He said he would personally guarantee that. I dismissed it as the bluster of a colossal ego."

Shelton returned his own cup to the saucer on the table and leaned forward.

"I should have paid more attention." Noland paused. "I believe Ivan Volynski is the Architect. That he's in the U.S. and ready to strike."

For all his years on the front lines of international disputes and power plays, Shelton Myers looked genuinely stunned.

"But there's more," Noland added, moving closer to the edge of the sofa. "When he finished his diatribe on Soviet Russia that day, he pulled a letter out of his desk drawer. He handed it to me and told me to look at the pictures inside, then to read the letter.

"They were old snapshots. Three of them. My father was in each one with his arms around a woman I'd never seen before. Then I read the letter. It was in my father's unmistakable hand, telling things only he could know."

Noland locked eyes on his friend. "Ivan Volynski is my brother."

Chapter 37

Evgeny Kozlov had long suffered the moniker of KGB rabbit. He could dig a warren quicker than anyone else, most of the time on the run and needing a handy hole—such as that very night, after fleeing Ava's ambush near the Seaport apartment.

He'd found a very suitable camper van with draped windows in a parking garage near Wall Street and helped himself to it. For the rest of the night, he'd done what he'd been trained to do—defend and prosper his country by stealth and with swift, uncompromising judgment of others. Only this time, he answered to no one but himself.

That night, using tools he could work as easily as his own appendages, he'd disarmed security systems and entered a half-dozen stores and storerooms around Manhattan, preparing for the coming day.

By five o'clock Monday morning, he'd finished his work and longed for sleep. Like the rabbit, he burrowed into blankets he'd found in the back of the camper and slept for an hour. He was parked outside the gate to a heliport on the lower East River.

The broad aviation dock was populated by a flock of sleek corporate birds that flew their privileged owners to and from their next million-dollar deals. Now awake, if not sufficiently rested, Evgeny had his eye on one bird in particular, a seven-passenger Bell 429, its serial number matching the one scribbled on the back of the printout he'd found in the Seaport apartment.

Two fresh guards at the gate had replaced the one Evgeny had circumvented earlier that night. It hadn't been difficult since the old man's snoring surely could be heard up and down the river. Evgeny had come prepared to tranquilize a guard dog or two if necessary, but none were on duty.

As the famous skyline behind him slowly emerged in faint relief against a creeping red dawn, Evgeny glanced about at the few cars parked nearby, then back at the guards. Content that the camper had drawn no undue attention, he settled back with his doughnuts and coffee. He had no idea how long he would have to wait. The few groceries he'd stashed in the back would have to suffice. He'd even provided himself with a chamber pot of sorts. There would be no leaving the site.

He wondered at his incredibly good fortune. It had been just a date written in pencil. It might have been someone's dental appointment, and all his efforts would have been pointless. But written on the back of a heliport printout? Next to the model and serial number of a chopper? No, it smelled too much like a travel date.

Where are you going, Architect?

Chapter 38

*T*ravis, who else knows that Volynski is your brother?"

"Half brother," Noland corrected. "I never told anyone. Never even confronted my father. Later, when all those other photographs implicating him arrived at the *New York Times* and the scandal broke, I knew who was behind it. They were different from the ones Ivan had shown me, the ones of his mother. He wouldn't drag her into it. The pictures he sent the *Times* showed my father with a couple of different women—both purported to be spies for their various governments. I never believed they were. I was so angry with my father by that time, though, I had trouble mustering sympathy for him—only for my mother. She didn't deserve to suffer like she did."

"Your father never knew you'd met his illegitimate son?" Shelton asked incredulously.

Noland shook his head. "No. I wanted to protect him."

"Who?"

"Ivan."

That took Shelton by obvious surprise.

"My father was very powerful. I didn't know what he'd do if I told him about Ivan. I'm not sure why I kept the secret all these years, even after my father died. Survival instinct, I guess. But I always feared Ivan would pounce again. This time on me."

"Did you ever see him or talk to him after that day in his office?"

"I tried to reach him many times, but he wouldn't return my calls. I really wanted this guy to know how sorry I was for what my father did to him and his mother. But Ivan would have nothing to do with me. I saw him once more at the Kremlin years later. I approached him and asked if we could talk. But he just looked me dead in the eye and walked away.

"Not long after the Soviet collapse, Ivan left Russia and left no trace of himself. No one on either side of the U.S.–Russia divide knew anything about him, reportedly. But you'll remember, after we uncovered the plot to assassinate the Russian and Syrian presidents, a buzz started. When Andreyev and Fedorovsky—whom we thought masterminded the plot— went to prison, we started picking up chatter about someone else out there. Some mystery man working Andreyev and Fedorovsky." Noland looked toward the ceiling, then back at Shelton. "I never made even the slimmest connection to Ivan." He picked up the telltale file. "Until this."

Shelton read the report, then looked away, visibly processing it all. "So now we know what this man looks like."

"You and I do."

"And the FBI doesn't."

Noland shot up from his seat. "I have a photograph!"

Chapter 39

By eight Monday morning, Cass and Jordan were still rifling through files in Hans's study. They'd slept only a couple of hours at the Kluen apartment before Ava dispatched them to Southampton, and their search had grown almost robotic. When the agent sent to oversee them stepped out to make a call, they fought the temptation to curl up on the floor and give in to weary defeat.

Instead, they trudged on with their search. Jordan closed one cabinet and opened another. He picked up a small envelope containing a black-and-white photograph. "Look at this," he told Cass. It was an aerial shot of a walled complex with one large house and a few smaller outbuildings.

Dropping the folders she was searching, Cass took the photo from him. "It doesn't look familiar." She turned it over. "There's something written lightly on the bottom edge. *Brooklyn house.*" She looked up at Jordan. "Hans doesn't own any property in Brooklyn that I know of."

"Ask your mom."

Cass hurried from the room and down the stairs. She found her mother in the second-floor master bedroom, sitting like a propped mannequin on the velvet chaise overlooking the ocean. "Mom, are you okay?"

Jilly Kluen wiped tears from her face and reached for her daughter.

Cass sank onto the soft blue velvet next to her mother. "What is that?" Jilly asked, pointing to the photograph.

"Do you recognize this place, Mom?"

Jilly studied it. "No. Where did you get it?"

"In Hans's study."

"Well, it might be useful, dear. I just don't know." Cass knew her mother had slipped into some distant realm, someplace where the window shades on reality were half closed.

"Did he ever own a house in Brooklyn?"

Jilly thought a minute. "I don't think so."

Cass tugged at her mother's shoulders. "You okay down here by yourself?"

"I guess I'd better get used to it," Jilly said with enough resolve to lift Cass's hopes for her.

"We're going to be fine, Mom. I don't know how I know that. But I've been . . . asking God for help."

A pleasant surprise lit Jilly's face. "Oh, really. When you have time, I'd like to talk about that."

Cass kissed her mother on the cheek and returned to the study. She grabbed Evgeny's phone and called Ava about the photograph. "Excellent!" Ava exclaimed. "I'm here at headquarters. Now do just what I say as quickly as you can. Use your phone to photograph the image as large and clearly as you can, then send it to Delaney." She gave Cass the number. "He can run it through aerial inventory for a footprint match and give us an address."

"Is this where Hans is?"

"We'll see. Now get to work."

"Where are you?"

But Ava had already hung up. A little later, though, she called back and asked for Jordan.

"He's right beside me," Cass answered, catching Jordan's eye.

"Good. I'm sending you a photograph. I need to know if this is the man Jordan spoke to in the apartment near the UN. Got that?"

"Yes. But how did you get a picture of him? Do you know who he is?"

"Too many questions, Cass. Just tell Jordan to stand by. I'll need his answer immediately."

They both watched the phone as if it might burst into flames. When the image finally appeared, Jordan cried, "That's him!"

Chapter 40

Liesl opened the blinds and looked out at the harbor. "So this is a safe house," she said. "On top of a high-rise in handshaking distance from FBI headquarters."

"All the better to watch you, my dear," Ava teased from the kitchen. "Short of parachuting onto the roof or climbing the outside walls, the only access to you is one express-elevator ride up with no exits along the way, plus the stairwell. And you've seen the number of guards posted at all those points."

"I can't live this way, Ava. Not anymore."

Ava came up behind her and touched her back. "I know. Not much longer, I hope." Then she returned to the coffee she'd just poured for herself.

Liesl turned slightly. "Did you get any sleep?"

Ava nodded. "A few hours at headquarters. I'm okay. Just needed to check security here this morning. I can't stay long."

"Then where will you go?"

"Got a few things working."

Liesl waited. "And that's all you're telling me, right?"

Ava nodded.

"Well, can you at least tell me where Evgeny is?"

"Can anybody?" Ava asked rhetorically. "He's a ghost. Nothing to hold on to. He disappears in plain view. But I'm confident he'll reappear for one reason—you. He cares a great deal for you. Who would have believed that a year ago?"

As Ava busied herself with phone messages, something Liesl had read in the book of Romans returned to her. *We know that in all things God works for the good of those who love him, who have been called according to his purpose.* She closed her eyes. *Lord, look at all the ones you've brought to me, who've taught me to love again, and to forgive.* She opened her eyes and looked on the streets below. *I forgive Evgeny. Will you?*

"What are you so thoughtful about?" Ava asked, pulling on her coat.

Liesl turned from the window and smiled at the woman she'd come to love as a trusted friend. There hadn't been many of those in Liesl's life. Just then, the image of Ben Hafner burned inside her, and the fumes of betrayal rankled the air around her. She fought to hold back her anger, knowing how quickly she could bolt back into the world of her own human grievances.

How could you do this, Ben? she silently railed. *I loved you like a brother. What happened to you?*

Ava's voice jerked her from her gloom. "Liesl, try to pull out of this mood you're in. None of us can afford the luxury of self-pity. Not now."

The words caught in Liesl like grappling hooks. Is that what this was? Was it all about Liesl? Again? She straightened herself against Ava's bluntness but couldn't fault her for it. Because it was true.

A bedroom door opened, and Cade walked out, fresh from a shower. He went straight to Liesl, who leaned into him, hoping his love would refresh her. He embraced her and stroked her hair.

The same bedroom door opened again, and Ian loped into the living room in overalls. "Uh-oh," he said, looking toward Liesl and Cade still wrapped in each other's arms. "Since it's getting all cooey in here, I'm going outside to talk to those marines in the hall."

"They're NYPD, Pop. And there's no cooing."

"Yeah, well you kids deserve some privacy." He looked at Ava, answering her phone. "Hold your fire," he announced as he opened the front door. "The only weapon I've got is a toothpick." His voice trailed as he closed the door behind him. "Hey, you guys know how to play canasta?" Liesl welcomed the chance to laugh. "I'm so glad you brought him." She looked thoughtful. "I hope Dad was okay with staying behind. He was my unseen protector through all those years." She was still dumbfounded by his admissions that in Boston, Washington, and New York he had watched over her. Because he'd always disguised himself, she had passed him on the street several times and never known it.

"But your grandmother needed him more," Cade said. "Him and the Charleston police patrolling the house."

Liesl grimaced. "What is it about us Bowers?" she asked. And there it was again. Self-pity. She recoiled at the touch of it, then thought of Cass. She had suffered as much.

"Liesl," Ava said, approaching with the phone in her hand. "You have a call." Her eyes fairly danced.

Liesl took the phone and answered. "Hello?"

"Hey girl."

Surprise brightened her face as she looked back at Ava. "Max!"

"So you just couldn't stay out of trouble, could you?" he teased.

She didn't respond right away.

"Liesl?"

"I'm here, Max. Tell me how you are."

"Still fiddling around and anxiously awaiting my appearance on stage with the lovely Liesl Bower."

"I wish we could fast-forward to next year, Max."

"It'll come soon enough. By then, surely you and Cade will arrive at the Nuremberg Music Festival as husband and wife. I regret that little white-lace ceremony has been postponed."

Wishing to change the subject, Liesl asked, "Max, have you heard anything about your father?"

"Ah, the renegade Russian mole who had to flee Israel for his disgraceful life? The underground Russian insurgent who schemed to kill his own president and wipe out my whole country? That father? Well, just when I think he's met President Gorev's firing squad, rumors surface about a

Maxum Morozov sighting somewhere in the Urals. Or is that urinals? I get them confused."

"Max, be serious."

"Do you realize how long you've been telling me that? What you don't realize is that I'm deadly serious too much of the time. Something about juxtaposing the philharmonic violinist with the Israeli intelligence officer in the same body. It's enough to make me seriously schizophrenic."

Liesl envisioned her wiry friend with the unmanageable red hair. "Just talk to me, Max. Tell me you're all right. And your mother, too."

"Oh, Mom's having the time of her life. Freedom from tyranny, from the brutal reign of Maxum senior. She didn't grieve his abrupt leaving too long."

"And you?"

"A far-too-complicated subject. I'd much rather talk about your own harrowing life. How are you holding up?"

"I'm okay, but do you know about Ben?"

There was a long silence. "I learn of too many things in my intelligence role. Some things I wish I didn't know."

Liesl waited for more, but it didn't come. She pressed. "What made him turn on us, Max?"

"I can't answer that, Liesl."

Again, she waited for more, but Max divulged nothing. "Ava told me he just sent Anna and their two girls to Tel Aviv," Liesl confided. "Like that's going to spare them the shame of his treason." Liesl lost her battle against anger. "After seeing what that did to Dr. Devoe and his wife, how could Ben do this to his own family? I thought I knew him!"

Cade reached to steady Liesl, gesturing for her to calm down.

"Liesl, I wish I could make this easier for you, but I can't," Max said gently. "And now I have to go. Try to behave, and do as you're told."

Liesl swallowed against the lump in her throat. "Be careful, Max."

"Always." He hung up.

Liesl cupped the phone and lingered over the voice now gone. But seconds later, it rang again. She gave it to Ava and returned to the window. There was so much to sort out and so few answers. She looked over her shoulder and saw Cade in the kitchen, opening a box of cereal. Then she caught some of Ava's words from the bedroom where she'd retreated with her call . . .

"Something's not right. Why there? Why now?"

Soon after Ava returned to the living room, her phone rang again. But this time she just listened and said, "I'm on my way."

Liesl saw something she didn't like on Ava's face. "What's wrong?"

But Ava only waved a hand behind her as she dashed out the front door. Liesl moved to the windows overlooking the alley behind the building. Moments later, she watched Ava run from the building and hop into the back seat of a waiting car.

Liesl leaned her head against the glass as the car sped away. *How much more?*

Chapter 41

At the wheel of the white Nissan, Jeremy talked distractedly about what a momentous occasion this was. "Ben, you're about to meet the Architect! I mean, savor it, man. The big guy wants to shake your hand." Jeremy finally looked back at the road, but the ebullience continued to bubble. "I mean, he never asked to meet me. But I'm okay with that. You're my brother. Close enough."

Ben sat slouched in the seat that was too small for him. The bulk of his jacket wedged him in even tighter. But that was the least of his discomforts. Unlike Jeremy, he couldn't take his eyes off the road. Its borders might as well have been the never-intersecting lines of eternity, routing him toward a point he couldn't see, a fate without end. And it was all his doing. No one forced his decision. The president's trusted advisor was about to personally profess allegiance to an enemy of the state. Had Ben Hafner gone completely mad?

At least Anna and the kids were safe in Israel, though he realized the irony of that notion. No place in Israel was safe. At least they wouldn't have to suffer a media feeding frenzy if he was compromised.

Checking his GPS, Jeremy routed them into a Brooklyn industrial park with too many empty, overgrown buildings to suit Ben. "He couldn't have found a better place to meet?"

Jeremy grinned at him. "You would have preferred the lobby of the Waldorf Astoria?"

Ben didn't feel like dueling with his brother-in-law. But there was something he wanted to know. "You still don't know what job Cyrus Neale is supposed to do for this guy?"

"Not yesterday. Not today. The Architect believes the less any of us knows about the other, the better. My only job right now is to get you settled into the network. When you're ready to start transmitting the information we need, I'll show you how to do that. Simple."

Jeremy slowed and checked his course.

"You've never been here, I take it."

"No. The Architect has property everywhere. This was once a legitimate business, I believe. You know he's still an arts dealer."

"But you don't even know his name."

"Don't need to. All I need to know is that he's going to protect Israel . . . and keep my paychecks coming." Jeremy laughed, then slowed into the last turn. It was a dead-end street that led to a two-story metal building with barren tree branches scraping against its sides. When the wind rose, the fingernail-on-blackboard screech made Ben's skin crawl.

"I don't see any cars." Ben checked his watch. They were ten minutes early for their noon meeting.

Mark Delaney and three other FBI agents ran low between two buildings. Half a block away, hidden from anyone approaching the industrial park, plainclothes officers in unmarked NYPD cars waited to assist.

Delaney led his team within sight of the white Nissan, now parked in front of a lone warehouse at the end of the street. The agents crouched behind a line of bedraggled shrubs and watched the car's two occupants. Delaney raised his radio close to his mouth and reported their position to the backup teams.

A young man stationed at an upper-level window overlooking the entrance to the industrial park spoke quietly into his phone. "You were right, sir. The cops are everywhere."

"How far from Mr. Rubin?" Ivan asked.

"Four of them about fifty yards. More cars waiting behind."

"Are he and Mr. Hafner parked close to the warehouse?"

"Right in front, sir."

"Very good. Stay where you are."

Ben glanced at his watch. "They're fifteen minutes late. I'm not happy about this."

Jeremy shifted nervously. "We can't just leave. If we passed them on their way in, it would look bad."

"They should be here already, waiting on us. After all, aren't I the prize mole?"

"Ben, you've got to—"

The first bullet pierced the driver's side of the windshield with hardly a sound. Jeremy's head snapped backward with the force of it. The arterial spray hit Ben full in the face, clouding his eyes and choking off his scream.

Ben lunged toward the floor an instant before the second shot plugged the back of his seat. Blindly, he felt for the door handle above him and yanked. Shoving the door open, he rolled onto the ground and scrambled on his belly across the pavement toward an old shed.

But it was too far. He was too slow. He didn't even hear it when it came—when the bullet entered his chest. When another sliced through his neck. He heard nothing as life's sweet serum poured from him. Would Anna hear? In a fading, gurgling whisper, he spoke to her. "Anna . . . I . . . love . . ."

Chapter 42

Sonya called Cyrus Neale's phone repeatedly, desperate to abort his mission. "He doesn't answer," she reported to Ivan. They were alone in the study of the Brooklyn house. Hans's arms were now tied again, though not to the chair this time. One guard roamed the property, and another remained inside with Hans.

"Keep trying," Ivan said. Walking to the window, he looked out at the barren yard that even a dazzling midday sun couldn't brighten. His friend was too old and sick to tend the property anymore, and the students had long since abandoned the walled commune of their youth. What about Ivan's youth? Would its residual zeal carry him through the coming years? Before he might be too old and sick to care, like Boris.

But not yet. The fire still burned. Like sulfur. He could smell it again, running putrid from the kitchen sink through all his early years. Now it was time for someone else to pay. What a stunning coincidence that Travis Noland should occupy the White House at this precise moment in the history of the new Russian revolution. *How perfect*, Ivan thought, trailing back in time.

When Ivan's mother first told his father that she was pregnant, the visiting dignitary from America who'd taken advantage of the fetching young chambermaid merely flung a handful of money at her and moved on to another willing paramour. When Galina Volynski repeatedly asked for her lover's help, F. Reginald Noland threatened to accuse her of extortion and certain imprisonment. In the years that followed, the woman taught her young son to hate the arrogant Americans and one family in particular. She died before witnessing her son's first strike on the house of Noland.

All it had taken to dethrone the elder Noland was one large envelope of photographs sent anonymously to the *New York Times*. Taken over many years, the images recorded the statesman—routinely entrusted with highly classified material—cavorting with two different females whom the sender of the package had documented as spies. Though an investigation proved the evidence inconclusive, and even some news headlines suggested a frame-up, the damage had been done. Noland willingly resigned from his venerable post. Soon after, his wife divorced him. The evidence had been conclusive enough for her. Ivan had so delighted in what he'd wrought, he didn't even mind when the son overcame his father's ruin to reach the pinnacle of power. All the better to bring him down.

Ivan now checked his watch. Just thirty minutes since his men had reported both targets had been eliminated at the warehouse. It gave Ivan no satisfaction to do such things. They were young men who might have been of greater value one day, but Ivan couldn't afford whatever compromise they had made with the enemy, whatever carelessness had left a trail for federal agents to follow. He wasn't sure which of the two had been to blame. It didn't matter.

"I have him!" Sonya announced. She handed the phone quickly to Ivan.

"Cyrus, you must not go today," Ivan ordered. "I am postponing your mission. You were right. The Americans are watching you."

"Not anymore. I got away. I'm already at the tug, and we're going to do this thing as planned. All you need to do is watch."

"Cyrus!" Ivan cried, but the line went dead. Ivan could feel the heat in his face as he turned to Sonya. "The fool! He is going anyway."

But Sonya was steady and cool in her response. "So be it. If he succeeds, we win. If he doesn't, we lose nothing."

Ivan held her words, examining them closely. "You are my sensible comrade," he told her. "You are right. Nothing would be lost." His spirits brightened. "If Cyrus is successful, I will give the signal to all the others. And it will begin. The power plants, the dams, the historic landmarks, the computer networks—they will all go down."

"And if he isn't successful, send the signal anyway," Sonya reasoned. "The feds have no way of stopping the others. They don't even know who or where they are." She smiled triumphantly, her large hands coming together in silent applause.

Ivan raised a hand to his chin, his thoughts spinning. Then he checked his watch again. "We must go soon." He glanced toward the kitchen. "I doubt our weak and out-of-shape friend in there will require more than one guard to stay here with him."

"I suggest we rid ourselves of him as soon as possible," Sonya said icily.

"I will make that decision once we reach the ship. I don't want any entanglements to delay us. From there, we'll launch the entire operation."

"Are you sure one man is enough to leave with Hans?"

"The others will return soon. They have already eluded the trap set for us at the warehouse." He hung on one sobering thought. "If not for our man Cyrus's suspicions, for his simple observation of that car on his street, we might have suffered a great setback today."

"And what about Cyrus's fate? Can we be sure of his intentions? Are you certain he's prepared to sacrifice himself?"

Instead of answering, Ivan strolled into the kitchen and stood before Hans, noticing how tightly his arms were bound in front of him. "Are you in pain, Hans?"

Hans raised his head, his drooping eyes clouded. "Not the kind you would understand, Ivan. That would require a conscience."

Ivan laughed but his eyes didn't. "And mine is a calling you would not understand. But there is something you might know. From all your contact with Cyrus Neale, are you convinced he wants to end his life today? No second thoughts about asylum in Russia?"

"Who knows such things for certain, Ivan? He says he is ready. He's made arrangements to dispense of all his belongings. Even buried his dog in the back yard."

Ivan inspected the beleaguered face once more, silently and with regret that he'd failed to win the allegiance of this man he'd once admired. At that moment, he decided what must be done with Hans. But not right now. That would be one kill he had no interest in watching.

Chapter 43

*A*fter Cass, Jordan, and Delaney's agent had finished their exhaustive search of Hans's study, finding nothing else they considered worth reporting, Jordan closed the last cabinet and remained seated on the floor, staring into space. The agent was now in the front yard, talking to security officers on duty there.

"What's the matter?" Cass asked, replacing the last of the hanging files and struggling to stay awake.

"Let me see that photograph of the house again," Jordan said. "Something's been nagging at me."

He studied it a few moments. "I don't know why I didn't catch this before. Look at this."

Cass plopped on the floor next to him and leaned toward the glossy aerial shot.

"Is that a cow?" he asked.

"A what?" She took the photograph from him and squinted at the spot he pointed to. "It could be. Hard to tell from this angle. Why?"

"Did you ever drive by that old arts school in Brooklyn? The one near Owls Head Park and the bay?"

"I once knew a set designer who took classes there, long time ago. But I've never seen the place."

"I've passed it only a few times," Jordan said, "but I remember this big plaster cow near the front gate. The students used to paint wild designs all over it. Something different every time I saw it." He tapped it again with his finger. "I'm pretty sure that's the cow."

"Then we'd better go see." Cass was already off the floor and heading for the door with renewed energy.

Jordan balked. "Oh no. You call Ava first."

"And tell her what? That we can't be sure, but we think we see a familiar cow?"

"But what if that's the place where they are holding Hans, and lots of guys with guns are just waiting for two clueless sleuths to show up at the door? Again."

"Well, we've got a gun, too."

"Cass, be serious."

"I couldn't be more serious. We're going. And I'm not pulling the FBI off their computer search for the place to join us on a wild . . . cow chase. Let's go." Cass was heading for the stairs. "We'll have to sneak out of here. They'd never let us go, and we're better off on our own anyway."

"One problem, Cass. We don't have a car."

"A friend of mine down the beach will loan us one. We'll go out the back."

Jordan finally quit arguing and fell in behind her.

Before they left, Cass slipped into her mother's room to tell her they were leaving, but Jilly was asleep. Cass scribbled a note assuring her that all was well and they'd return soon. Almost an hour later, they were headed to Brooklyn in a borrowed Mercedes, surely one of the first produced, Jordan had noted glumly.

During the drive, Cass decided to unleash the news of her biological father. When she finished, Jordan reached for her hand, his gaze shifting between the road and her. They rode in silence for a few minutes more, his hand still on hers. Then he squeezed it gently and said, "As if you haven't been handed enough to process already, here's one more thing." He glanced her way, then back at the road. "I love you, Cass Rodino, or whatever your name is. I love you something awful."

Cass unbuckled her seat belt and leaned into him. She nuzzled his cheek and kissed it softly. "And I love you," she whispered.

He nodded. "Now we're getting somewhere. Put your seat belt back on. I've waited too long for this to lose it before the next traffic light."

She laughed out loud. It felt good and cleansing. Why couldn't it last? The good times never had before. But maybe something was beginning to turn.

Finally, they approached the old walled school, and Cass started checking the surrounding streets against the photograph in her lap. The aerial shot hadn't taken in much beyond the compound, but she could see a few homes on the periphery of the image. She tried to match those images to the homes in front of her. If she could be sure that this place and the one pictured from above were the same, they would alert Ava and back off to a safe distance.

Traffic was heavy this Monday, and Jordan slowed to a crawl near the school. Just ahead was the cow, painted pink with brown polka dots. "There it is!" Cass blurted. "But I still need to be certain. Let's see if this flat-looking little house in the photo is where it should be in real life. Take a right before you get to the school." She glanced at Jordan and noted the intensity in his face. "Please," she added.

He flashed only a marginal grin her way. As soon as he took the turn and cleared the corner, Cass spotted the small, flat house ahead on the right, across a narrow street from the brick wall surrounding the school property. She checked and double-checked the photograph against the house. Even the oddly angled front walk to the door was the same. "Okay, I'm calling Ava." She pulled the phone from her backpack. "But first, let's circle the block and give this place a good look. We'll need to tell her everything we can about it."

One thought loomed above all others. Hans might be inside. The man who was her father, her real father. It was a transforming thought, but one she'd have to probe later. Then another thought. Who else was in there?

"Cass, hide your face," Jordan warned as he pulled his hood over his head. "These people know us, remember? Good thing we're not in my car."

They were coming up on the opposite side of the school. An old two-story house rose above the wall, and a driveway ran from it through a side opening in the wall, now closed by a metal gate. "Go slow, Jordan. When you get even with the gate, stop. We need to see the grounds inside."

"Okay, but you need to call Ava. It'll take her team awhile to get here."

They were creeping along the wall when a car suddenly appeared at the gate ahead, and then it opened. A black BMW sedan turned out of the property and headed away from them. "Two guys in the front, but I can't see inside the back," Jordan said.

They had been so startled by the car, Jordan had stopped abruptly in the street, then inched closer. When they pulled even with the gate, they were surprised to see a man just closing it from inside. He looked up and stared hard at them.

"Jordan, keep going, but not too fast. I need a good look in there."

Jordan eased forward. As they cruised past the still-open gate, it was no longer the man attending it who held Cass's attention. It was the figure running away from the house behind him. In the opposite direction. A man bent over and loping awkwardly. A familiar shape.

"Hans!" Cass cried, then covered her mouth fearing the man at the gate had heard her even through the closed windows.

Startled, Jordan stomped on the brake and turned to her.

"Go! Go!" she cried. "It's Hans! Running to the other side!"

As Jordan gunned the car, Cass turned to the rear. The guy at the gate was no longer there. He was running fast behind them. "He's chasing us!"

Jordan was forced to stop at the cross street fronting the compound and wait for traffic to clear. He couldn't wait long, though. The man was almost on their bumper.

"Hang on!" he told Cass, and sped toward the far end of the wall. "You're sure it was Hans?"

"Positive."

"But there's no way out on the other side."

"He probably doesn't know that. He'll have to hide in one of the other buildings." She pointed ahead. "Stop when you get to the front entrance.

I'm getting out." She looked quickly behind them. The man was running back the way he'd come.

"You're *what*?"

She grabbed her backpack, pulled out the small handgun, and slid it into her coat pocket. "Right here!" she cried.

"Not without me." Jordan angled dangerously toward the right curb, jumped it, and brought the car to a precarious stop. He grabbed Cass's hand, and together they dashed across the street, dodging traffic like flags on a downhill course. At the main entrance, Cass was ready to scale the wrought-iron gate when Jordan stopped, steadied himself, then gave the rusted lock a mighty kick. The gate fell open, and Cass flashed a second of approval before they ran into the compound.

"There's Hans!" She pointed to the figure lumbering toward a small cottage near the back wall.

"And there's trouble," Jordan said, swinging the other way. Their pursuer was streaking from the house in full chase with a gun in his hand. "He's after Hans. I don't think he sees us. Get back!" He pulled her against what appeared to be a classroom building. Then he ran toward a pile of debris nearby and pulled out a wooden board about three feet long. "Use the gun if this doesn't work," Jordan said, then took a position near the corner of the building concealing them. As the pounding feet grew closer, he took a batter's stance and waited.

Seconds later, he stepped into the open and swung, bringing the full brunt of the board across the runner's midsection. When the man doubled onto the ground, Jordan landed another blow to the back of his head and grabbed the gun from his hand. Holding it on the unconscious man, Jordan looked behind him. "No one else coming?" he asked Cass.

"Don't see anybody. But we've got to tie him up." She released the braided belt from her waist and strapped it around the man's wrists, encountering no resistance. She noted the lump rising on his head, nothing she considered life threatening, then looked up at Jordan as if she'd never seen him before. "I didn't know shoe salesmen could do that," she said, tying off the last knot. She didn't wait for a response before dashing toward the cottage. "Hurry!" she called over her shoulder.

Approaching the spot where she'd last seen Hans, she studied the brick dwelling with the windows almost completely covered by wild growth. She and Jordan found one door on the opposite side. It was open. She turned to Jordan. "Would you wait out here?" she whispered, handing him her gun. "Give me just a minute." He nodded, comprehension clear on his face, and took a lookout position near the door.

Once inside, Cass saw that it was a studio with cobweb-laced easels stacked to one side and a few bare tables placed haphazardly about the room. The floor creaked beneath her next step, and she heard a stirring from behind a door.

"Hans, it's Cass. You can come out."

Something thudded to the floor behind the door as it opened slowly and a man stepped from what appeared to be a closet. "Cass?" His voice was pitched high in disbelief.

"It's okay, Hans. You're safe." Though she couldn't be sure of that. It was the shallow promise of one comforting another in an unpredictable storm.

"But how . . . how did you . . ." His pitiable face, his leaning body, the thick cording partially tied around his waist and restraining one limp arm—it was a sight too wrenching for Cass. She rushed to help him and untied most of his restraints. Then she embraced him gently, and he clung to her as if she were his last lifeline. He lowered his cheek to the top of her head and sobbed. All she could do was hold on.

Finally, he released her, and she led him to a dusty stool and made him sit while she untangled the rest of the cording. But now, he wouldn't look at her, and she could see the shame bead up on him like a vile secretion. "You don't know what I've done," he said, his voice rasping.

"Yes, I do. You left a trail. That's how we found you."

He stared at her, his face pinched with a painful processing going on inside.

"That's not all I know, Hans."

Now the eyes riveted on her.

"Mom told me." She searched his face. "Why couldn't you?"

His body tipped forward, but he caught himself and turned away from her, silent for too long. "It's best you ignore what you heard. Who would want me for a father?"

Cass made him look at her. "We all carry shame. Surely you know mine."

He reached for her hand and drew it to his chest, holding it as if it were a prize. "You have no idea how much I've loved you. And how I betrayed you and your mother with my reckless—"

"Cass! Ava's here!" Jordan announced from the door.

Hans dropped her hand.

"The FBI has been searching for this place," Cass said. "Jordan and I just found it first."

Hans stood and placed a hand on Cass's shoulder. She knew it was to steady himself more than her. "It's okay," he said. "This is the right thing."

He looked toward the door, then back at her. "I don't know how you found me, but there's no time for me to ask those questions. Right now, I've got to tell someone what's about to happen."

"What do you mean?"

She could feel the shaking in his body, and once more she hugged him to her. Then Mark Delaney and an army of agents rushed the small studio.

"Wait!" she called to them, but nothing was going to stop their rapid containment of this man even though he'd given no sign of escaping. They clamped handcuffs on him and led him out of the building.

"Listen to me!" Hans cried.

"Stop!" Delaney finally told his agents, then faced Hans. Ava came up beside them, followed by Cass and Jordan.

"In my right jacket pocket! Get the flash drive! It's names and locations of people about to blow this country up!"

Delaney thrust a hand into the pocket and retrieved the drive.

"They're all waiting for his signal. Find a laptop. Pull up the names. They're all over the country. A dam, a nuclear plant . . . you can't waste a second!"

Delaney sent one of his agents for a laptop in his car.

Hans swilled oxygen through his gaping mouth. "That's not all. A man named Cyrus Neale is going to blow up a tugboat near the Brooklyn Bridge!"

Delaney gripped Hans fiercely by both arms. "When?" he shouted.

"Now!"

Chapter 44

*E*vgeny hadn't left the camper all day. He'd risked a few moments now and then to stretch his cramped legs, but never walked more than a few feet away. It was now mid afternoon, and he was beginning to doubt the relevance of the handwritten date. In a near-reclining position behind the wheel, he'd just straightened in his seat and was about to get out for another stretch when he spotted an oncoming black BMW with its turn signal blinking toward the heliport. The car was about to cross directly in front of the camper.

Sliding even farther below the wheel, he noted two men in the front seat and two or three people in back, but couldn't see anyone clearly. He watched the car cruise slowly to the guard gate, stop for clearance, then proceed to a parking spot not far from the choppers. No one got out.

The longer they sat there, the more anxious Sonya became. "We shouldn't be here, Ivan. You know they're searching for us."

"All they have found is Cyrus's empty house and the bodies of Jeremy Rubin and his unfortunate brother-in-law. So relax, Sonya. We will be at sea shortly."

The BMW was parked facing the river, just a few steps from Ivan's private helicopter. From the back seat, where he sat with Sonya and an aide, Ivan leaned forward and spoke to his pilot, riding in the front passenger seat. "We will leave immediately afterward, Paul. You still anticipate no obstacles?"

"It is best that we depart before the skies fill with police and reporters."

"Understood," Ivan said, and clapped a friendly hand on his longtime compatriot's shoulder.

The other two men in the car also had faithfully served Ivan for many years, believing in what he envisioned for Russia's future.

"Sir, look there!" the driver alerted, pointing toward the river.

Ivan beamed with pleasure. "There goes a true hero. His memory will be exalted in the new Russia." Ivan opened the back door of the car and got out. All but the driver followed. They moved toward the seawall of the heliport and stood silently as a massive tugboat plied the choppy East River, heading northeast toward the Brooklyn Bridge. Massed beneath a black tarpaulin stretched across the bow was the mother lode of explosives Ivan had smuggled to the New York docks, where a team of his countrymen had received, off-loaded, and transported them to Cyrus.

As the fateful boat passed, Ivan drew himself up straight and raised a salute toward the wheelhouse, hoping to catch Cyrus's attention. As planned, the flag was rolled tightly on a staff near the helm. It wasn't the white-blue-red bars of the current Russian Federation, but the gold-on-red hammer and sickle of the USSR.

Ivan felt an exhilarating rush as the minutes to detonation passed. In the final moments, Cyrus would unfurl the flag and leave no doubt that Red Russia had returned.

Sonya's phone rang as planned. She confirmed the caller and handed the phone to Ivan, who answered jubilantly. "Cyrus, we see you! And we honor you!"

"And won't Hans Kluen and that nervous little fellow Jeremy be surprised when they find out this is no demonstration," Cyrus exclaimed. "No sirree! My boy deserves more than just a bunch of fireworks."

"You are right, Cyrus. Your mission is to bring down the bridge."

What are they doing? Evgeny wondered as he crept along the landside perimeter of the heliport. He could see four people assembled on the far side, gazing out at the river. He spotted the woman right away. Sonya Tretsky, he was sure. But there had been no vitals on the Architect, only a sketchy description from Jordan and the trawler captain. A couple of the men Evgeny now watched fit the stature, but all three men wore hats of some sort.

Evgeny inched as close as he could to the fence surrounding the heliport without drawing an inquiry from one of the guards. He could see only the hood of the BMW and the top half of the chopper. But those gathered at the seawall were in full view.

What was that? A salute? Evgeny thought he saw one of the men raise a hand to the brim of his hat as a tugboat passed by. Suddenly one small scrap of information Viktor had supplied about Cyrus Neale fell solidly into place, like the tumblers of a lock. A retired merchant marine. A man who knows boats. Certainly a tugboat. Was that Cyrus Neale passing in review this very instant? On his way to . . . what?

Evgeny looked upriver ahead of the tug. *The bridge!*

He felt the gun at his side. But the tug was too far away. There was no time. Only minutes before contact. Now the man in the wheelhouse stepped out and unfurled a flag, red with a gold—*the Soviet flag!*

"No!" Evgeny cried, but his voice sailed away with the wind. He lurched forward, about to race for the guardhouse, when he heard the wail of a siren. Then another. Evgeny looked far behind the tug to see two police boats screaming up the river. Two more came from the opposite direction, running head-on at the tug. Now a loudspeaker. "Stop your boat! This is NYPD. Stop your boat, or we'll shoot!"

The air began to convulse with something advancing from the south, and Evgeny looked up to see two NYPD choppers swoop down on the tug. In seconds, one hovered just off the boat's stern. The other flew past, banked into a U-turn perilously close to the bridge, then flew straight on at the bow of the boat. It hovered like a monstrous dragonfly directly in the boat's path.

A flurry of movement at the seawall caught Evgeny's attention, and he watched as the spectators dashed toward the BMW. Though he couldn't see clearly, he heard doors open and close. Then four bobbing heads, three men and the woman, moved quickly to the chopper and climbed in. In moments, the rotors began their preamble to flight.

Evgeny looked back at the boat, at the Soviet flag waving defiantly, at the man darting from the wheelhouse to the tarpaulin across the bow, gun in hand. Evgeny thought he heard the man squeeze off one round before his body arched violently and crumpled to the deck. It had taken only a couple of well-placed shots from the forward chopper to drop him.

But the boat remained on course, heading for one of the neo-Gothic towers of the Brooklyn Bridge. Evgeny watched two men drop from the aft helicopter onto the tug. One charged the wheelhouse while the other rushed for the tarpaulin. Even before the officer jerked away the cover, Evgeny knew what lay beneath and why those aboard the other chopper hadn't risked a hail of bullets to take down the tug captain.

About the time Evgeny heard the tug's engines reverse, another sound erupted. The piercing whine of the Bell 429 snatched his attention from the drama unfolding on the river. He watched the chopper slowly rise from the deck, then he reached into his pocket.

So you came to watch the show, Evgeny called silently, *and then fly off to gloat.*

The chopper lifted into the wind and pointed its glassy snout toward the harbor. It was well over the river and gaining distance when it exploded into an enormous fireball, spilling its remains to the deep.

Evgeny slipped the remote back into his pocket and returned to the camper. He was finished with it all.

He waited long enough to watch the BMW escape the heliport, tires squealing through the exit gate. There was no need to give chase. *Let the driver go,* Evgeny decided. *He just watched his boss and all the others die. And now we both must run to ground.*

Chapter 45

$\mathcal{M}$elanie Thompson was irritated that her husband wasn't answering his phone. She wanted him to start dinner before she got home. It was after five, and she still had to pick up Rudy from his music lesson at school.

She'd left the office a little early. A memo had crossed her desk that morning about the temporary closing of one of the gates to the power plant. A small inconvenience to most, a critical delay for her escape from the task that lay before her. She had spent the last hour cruising the facility, speaking to guards she knew well, eyeing the makeshift barriers that would facilitate construction of new guardhouses. *Progress*, she thought with only slight regret. Improvements to a doomed plant.

But when? She and Pete had been ready for some time and grew restless with each passing hour. They'd reviewed every orchestrated detail of their departure, even practicing evasive actions should that be necessary. They could vacate their rented house overnight and be on the next flight to Moscow. Then they finally would be home, though there was much work to be done there also, groundwork for the emergence of a new and indomitable Russia. She and her friends at the university had dreamed of such a revolution, ached to see their convalescing nation rise from its post-Soviet stupor and take its rightful place in the hierarchy of world power. At the top.

She pulled into the circular drive and parked in front of the school. Rudy's music teacher, Mr. Palmer, taught private lessons after school and had taken particular interest in her son's perfect pitch. Though Melanie had encouraged Rudy to choose a stringed instrument, which would afford greater access to a Russian orchestra one day, she supposed the French horn he'd chosen would suffice.

She was surprised to see no one milling about the front office, wrapping up the usual administrative duties of the day. A few familiar cars were still parked outside. She guessed there was a staff meeting going on somewhere.

The hallway to the music room was clad almost floor to ceiling with student art. She paused before a gregarious purple ape wearing a ball cap and holding a baseball bat. It was signed *Rudy Thompson*. Melanie was sorry her son would miss baseball season but confident he'd take to ice hockey with as much enthusiasm.

The music room was at the end of a long hall of classrooms. Melanie noticed that all the doors to those rooms, which usually remained open, were closed. She stopped in the hall and looked back toward the front desk. Still no one there. Just then, though, she heard a few notes from a French horn and continued on down the hall, her steps lighter now. Mr. Palmer always asked Rudy to perform for her, to play something he'd learned that day. She looked forward to that.

But when she entered the long room with the choir risers stretched across one wall, Rudy wasn't there. Mr. Palmer sat alone near the piano, the horn stilled in his hands. Something was wrong. He seemed uncertain what to do with his mouth. The pasted-on smile went flat too soon.

"Where's Rudy?" she asked, her mind beginning to hurtle toward full alert.

He didn't answer. Just then, his eyes shifted to a point behind her, and as soon as she turned, two uniformed officers stepped forward.

"Melanie Thompson?" one of them asked.

She knew. No one at the desk. The doors to the hall closed. A nervous music teacher. They'd been waiting for her. There was a scurry of hard-falling footsteps in the hall, and quickly her escape route filled with more uniforms.

How did this happen?

Chapter 46

"Travis, I'm sorry for what took place on the river yesterday." Shelton Myers stood before President Noland's desk. "That was a horrible death for them all. But if Hans Kluen hadn't alerted us, think how many on that bridge would have died. Still, I should offer condolences to you for the death of Ivan Volynski."

The president sat back in his chair and sighed. "For all I know, I'm the next of kin."

"Now there's a bit of intelligence worth keeping to yourself. That's my advice, Travis. The man's dead. You never knew him, not really. Let him lie." Shelton thought a moment. "It was fortunate closure that the heliport guard watched him board that chopper."

Shelton moved to a chair and sat down. "Odd, don't you think, that Volynski never exposed your kinship to the media?"

"Oh, it was coming," Noland said, getting up from his desk and taking a seat near his friend. "I always knew it was Ivan who smeared scandal all over my father. I suppose he was waiting for just the right moment to pick me off, too, probably in the aftermath of his attacks on us, when all the country was hollering for vengeance. At the right time, he would have claimed responsibility for the devastation and then dropped one more bomb—'And, oh yes, your president is my brother.'"

Noland shifted uneasily in his chair, unable to shake the needling thing inside him, growing louder, more insistent. A burning prompt. He must evade it for now and refocus. "Shelton, I wish everyone could have witnessed what local law enforcement all over this nation did last night. How they scrambled to find and arrest every terrorist listed on that flash drive, including our Secret Service traitor. I don't know how nick-of-time we were in each case. Only Ivan knew the signal hour. But his people were ready and waiting. Police apprehended one woman at her child's school. And the guy who would have blown a hole in the Lake Jenowak Dam was plucked right out of his chicken coop. The local cops who nabbed him said he'd always been a loner who preferred chickens to people. But he was a top-notch engineer. Unlike our Ellis Island bomber. They found him roaring drunk in a pub on City Island. When they started questioning him, he asked if they'd like to see his new coat. Turns out it was stuffed with C4 and a detonator."

"How many did you catch?" Shelton asked.

"Seven. The others were aiming for the New York Stock Exchange, Naval Station Norfolk, the Federal Reserve, a few more national monuments. I'm not sure what else."

"And Liesl Bower."

"Yes, Liesl." The president hung his head. "And then there's Ben Hafner." Noland sat still for a moment, then looked up. "Shelton, thank you for your advice and your loyalty."

"You're welcome, Travis. But one more question. Is the FBI any closer to an arrest for the Charleston attempt on Liesl?"

"The postman? No." He fastened on his friend's face. "Shelton, that flash drive was incomplete. There are others still out there."

Chapter 47

Pulling up at the hospital in midtown Manhattan, Mark Delaney avoided the crush of reporters near the entrance and parked in a restricted zone behind the hospital. Though accompanied by two uniformed officers, he had to present his badge when he and Liesl reached the NYPD security shield hurriedly installed around the hospital.

Ava met them inside and showed them to the elevators. She had just summoned Liesl to the hospital with little time for explanations.

Wasting not a second, Liesl reached past one of the officers inside the elevator and punched the floor number for ICU. When the doors opened, she darted out, leaving Ava, Delaney, and the two officers in her wake. "Liesl, wait!" Ava called. But Liesl slowed only to hit the wall button that activated the double stainless-steel doors. When they opened, ICU looked more like an NYPD precinct. Officers guarded the main entrance and lined the walls on either side of a glass-front room directly ahead.

She glanced back at Ava and the perennially irritated Delaney, who stiffly nodded approval for her to keep going. When she approached the two sentries at the ICU entrance, she expected them to question her, but what she heard was, "Go ahead, ma'am. They're expecting you."

A young nurse came alongside her. "This way, Miss Bower."

The door to the glassed-in room was open, but the curtains around the bed were drawn. Liesl heard an unfamiliar voice behind them. The nurse motioned for her to wait. Just when Liesl didn't think she could do that any longer, a white-coated doctor parted the curtains wide, and Ben Hafner's eyes fluttered open.

Liesl stood transfixed by his ashen face, by the ponderous bandaging across one side of his neck and over his chest. Too many emotions battled for dominance. Chief among them was an anger that wouldn't let go of her. She felt the sting of tears rise behind her eyes and a throbbing knot swell in her throat. She couldn't move forward, not until Ben lifted a limp hand and motioned her closer. That's when she stepped to the bed and bent over him. Her tears finally burst through and ran down her face. "You big idiot!" she sobbed. "Why did you do it?"

He reached for her hand and held it weakly. His words poured thin and ragged, as if strained through a sieve at the back of his throat. "Nobody messes with my girls." He swallowed with pained effort. "Not my family. Not you."

Liesl nudged a clump of brown hair off his forehead and kissed it lightly. This was the brother-friend she'd loved for so long. Now, he lay here gravely wounded. If not for the bulletproof vest he'd worn, the first rifle shot would have torn away most of his chest. But the vest only slowed the bullet's entrance into his body. The second shot had nicked an artery in his neck. He would have bled out if FBI agents hadn't been on him instantly and summoned the medevac on standby a short distance away.

"Ava just told me what you did, but not before I saw you at that house on City Island." She swiped at more tears. "Do you know what I thought?"

He nodded, his brows bunching with regret.

"But she understands now, Ben," Ava said, approaching the bed. "That you jeopardized your life and career to infiltrate Ivan Volynski's network."

"Why you, Ben?" Liesl persisted. "You're no secret agent."

"But they invited me," he teased, his words labored.

Ava filled in the rest for Liesl. "They tried to recruit him over a year ago, at the same time they were hunting you and the code. Ben reported it to Noland and the FBI, who asked him to accept should Ivan's people make any more overtures. The CIA had picked up too much chatter on a rogue Russian threat to the U.S., but nothing solid. They had to get inside."

Ben lifted a couple of fingers. "But it was the girl from Broadway and her stepfather who really stopped that tugboat . . . and the other attacks."

Liesl considered the young woman whose plight had entwined itself with hers. She hoped they would draw closer to each other, both survivors. Then she thought of something else. "Who killed Ivan Volynski?" she asked Ava.

"We can't be sure at this time," Ava said flatly.

"That sounds like official talk."

"That's exactly what that is," Ava said, then turned to Ben. "When do Anna and the kids arrive?"

"They're not coming," he whispered, trying to reposition himself in the bed, then giving up the struggle. "I won't let them. Anna's endured enough."

Ava looked at Liesl. "We had a wire on Ben. While he was still on the ground, he talked to Anna. He thought they were his last words. We thought so too, so we immediately transmitted them to her in Israel."

Liesl felt new tears spring to her eyes, imagining the moment Anna heard his dying voice. She looked up at Ben with pleading. "Let her come, Ben. She needs to see you."

Ava moved closer to Ben. "Do you think they're still in danger?"

"Don't you?" he asked with knowing eyes.

"It's possible," Ava answered. "You know that one of our saboteurs is talking. It seems we didn't get them all." She turned to Liesl. "And you may not be in the clear yet, either, Liesl. President Gorev, once again, is having to deal with subversives in his midst. We believe Pavel Andreyev and Vadim Fedorovsky are on a short list for execution now. Until they, like Volynski, are gone, you may not be entirely safe."

"Who is?" Liesl asked bitterly. "Certainly not all those people on the bridge yesterday. They were just going home from work, thinking about what to fix for dinner. They might have noticed the tugboat heading their way—like the postman coming down my sidewalk on a calm Saturday morning—but never suspected they might not make it off the bridge. So who among us is safe?" She paused. "I prefer to live like someone who's never been shot at."

Ben reached up and stroked Liesl's arm. She leaned over and laid her cheek on his head. "I'm so sorry about Jeremy."

Ben released her hand and picked up the call button. "Anna and I have known a very long time that Jeremy's days were numbered. I'm just sorry I ushered in the last one."

The nurse arrived with a syringeful of relief that she inserted into Ben's IV. It was potent enough to extinguish his words, slow his breathing, and lower his eyelids. Liesl and Ava moved quietly toward the door, where Liesl stopped and looked back at her sleeping friend. She returned to his side, laid a gentle hand on his head, and prayed, "Lord, please heal him. And make him know it was you."

Chapter 48

*T*he national address had been called for seven o'clock Wednesday evening. President Noland would speak from the Oval Office on a matter of national security, his press secretary had announced that morning. After the arrest of Hans Kluen, the aborted attack on the Brooklyn Bridge simultaneous with the mysterious explosion of a private helicopter over the river, the Inauguration Day attack, and the attempt to bring down the Supreme Court Building, the nation staggered under the weight of its own fear. Every news outlet in the country had stoked that fear until it was white hot. And they didn't even know about the contents of Sonya Tretsky's little flash drive. Not yet.

Cass and Jordan had just finished the dishes and moved into the living room of the Southampton house, its undraped windows overlooking the night sea. The following morning, they would accompany Jilly Kluen on her first visit to the prison where Hans awaited trial. It promised to be sensational, the media had drooled. Cass would liken it to an elaborate stage set where drama and pathos would play out to the end of the third act. Then the audience would go back to their normal lives, and a stagehand would turn off the lights. After the spectacle of Hans Kluen's trial, though, there would be no normal life for his wife and daughter to return to.

Even now, they had already lapsed into something like an altered state—like those *Titanic* survivors Cass had recalled after finding her apartment ravaged.

And so it was that Cass had come to pull two fleece throws from a cabinet, spreading one over her mother, who'd just come down from her bedroom and curled into a recliner near the television, with little more than a smile in greeting. Jilly Kluen had seldom spoken since her husband's arrest on Monday. For two days, she'd puttered silently about the house, cleaning out closets and drawers, rearranging accessories, polishing the silver service, and hauling withered houseplants to the garbage. One might consider such mindless chores mere distraction from the ruin, but Cass knew better. As Jilly had done her whole life, she was systematically shedding an outer layer of blighted skin. How many times could she do that before she discovered nothing new growing beneath? Had that time now come?

As Cass settled onto the sofa next to Jordan, she pulled the other throw over them both, warming to the soft spread of fleece and the symbolic bundling of two friends into one couple. When he stretched his arm around her and pulled her against his side, she fit. As if molded together in another time, predetermined by an unseen hand, they fit to each other. *Is that possible?* she wondered as she looked up at the contentment on his face. *Did God do this? If he did, will he now pull me and Jordan closer to him? And Mom, too?* Cass believed he would.

Jilly turned in her chair, her eyes lingering on Cass and Jordan, something fearful in her face.

"Mom, can I get you anything? A cup of coffee maybe?"

"No, dear. I just need to see you."

Cass got up and went to her mother. She knelt beside her and slipped an arm around her shoulders. "We'll get through this, Mom." Jilly stared into space. "And don't forget—it was Hans who warned the FBI about the bridge. It was Hans who dared to sneak that flash drive out of that woman's purse. Without the names of all those terrorists, imagine what might be happening all over the country right now. And it was . . . my father who positively identified the man responsible for all this." She searched her mother's stricken face. "We can be proud of him for that. Can't we?"

Jilly looked into her daughter's eyes, but only for an instant. It was long enough, though, for Cass to read her mother's dismissal of such a notion. "I will visit him every weekend, but there will be no pride."

She motioned for Cass to turn on the television. It was time.

Travis Noland watched the cameramen scurry around the Oval Office to connect their cords and test the lighting. His press secretary stood by with a copy of the speech in his hands and the pallor of doom on his face. The president had waited until just moments ago to issue the speech he'd written himself. There was no time to assuage the press secretary's misgivings or alter the message. Travis Noland had finally reckoned with that burning prompt inside him.

At the end of the 3-2-1 countdown, the president looked straight at the camera. "Good evening, my fellow Americans. I trust I have the ear of the nation at a time when everyone needs to listen and understand the truth about recent assaults on our country. Too much misinformation has compounded the harm. I hope to reverse that course tonight.

"Once again, our nation has withstood acts of terrorism within our borders. We suffer, yes, but we don't succumb. Terrorists interrupted our inaugural tradition. They didn't eliminate it. What they did was prove the necessity for it, lest we fall to their brand of tyranny.

"Whether to destroy the seat of this land's highest court or merely demonstrate that they could, the terrorists who bombed our Supreme Court Building only demonstrated their pathetic need for something they'll never have—power over the American people.

"Monday afternoon on the East River off Manhattan, a man charged the Brooklyn Bridge with a tugboat full of explosives, a man bent on revenge for his army son's death while serving our country in Afghanistan. You've seen the footage shown repeatedly on all the newscasts. While filming the FBI and NYPD's battle to stop the tug, one cameraman inadvertently captured the midair explosion of a helicopter just downriver. We believe the man responsible for all these acts of terror was on that helicopter. We are now certain his name was Ivan Volynski, a former Russian KGB officer who sought to intimidate us, to frighten us into submission, and to warn us away from interfering with his grab for power in Russia. It was his agenda to return that nation to its glory days as the USSR. But there is no glory in brutal tyranny or cowardly acts of hit-and-run violence.

"What hasn't been reported to you is the network of subversives this man left behind in our country, a sabotage network that would have brought widespread destruction upon us. Through the cooperation of two such saboteurs, others in that network have since been captured.

"Are we safe now? No more than we've ever been. Are there others out there who this moment are assembling their devices of destruction? Yes. Whether they act alone or within a terrorist cell such as we just uncovered, our greatest defense against these people is you, the private American citizen. When you practice situational awareness and report what rouses your suspicion, we're all safer. Terrorists must live somewhere. Maybe near you. Maybe they send their children to school with yours. They must gather materials for explosives and other devices and weapons, perhaps in your store or business. They must scout their targets. If they aren't lone wolves, they must gather with the rest of their cell. Be observant. No, don't spy on your neighbors or bring unfounded accusations. We won't tolerate McCarthyism again. But wherever you are, observe your surroundings and those who operate within them.

"Now, there is something else you should know. Ivan Volynski . . . was my brother. A half brother I didn't know I had until I was twenty-six. I haven't seen or heard from him in thirty-five years. Until this terrorist leader was recently identified, I had no idea this nation was under attack by one of my own kin. It grieves me to tell you this. I am not even entirely certain that my estranged relationship with him wasn't partial cause for his violence against us. I doubt I will ever know. But there's one thing of which I am certain. None of us can afford to ignore the peril around us. Whether it resides in our families or in foreign countries of strangers, we have to be alert and ready to respond.

"If this makes you fearful, then choose not to be. And listen to this.